Blackbeard

and the Sandstone Pillar

When Lightning Strikes

Audrey Penn

With illustrations by Philip Howard and Joshua Miller

Tanglewood • Terre Haute, IN

Also by Audrey Penn
Mystery at Blackbeard's Cove
The Kissing Hand
Pocket Full of Kisses

Published by Tanglewood Press, LLC, 2007.
Paperback edition published by Tanglewood Publishing, Inc., October 2009.

Text © Audrey Penn 2007.
Illustrations on pages 3, 13, 27, 39, 51, 61, 75, 89, 101,115, 127, 139, 155, 169, 191, 205, 221, 239, 247, 259, 273, 289, 301, 311, 335 © Philip Howard, 2007.
All other illustrations © Tanglewood Press, LLC 2004.

Cover illustration by Barbara L. Gibson
Cover and interior design by Amy Alick Perich

Tanglewood Publishing, Inc.
P. O. Box 3009
Terre Haute, IN 47803

Printed in the United States of America
Printed by Maple-Vail, York, PA, USA, in October 2009. First printing.
10 9 8 7 6 5 4 3 2 1

ISBN 978-1-933718-25-5

Library of Congress Cataloging-in-Publication Data

Penn, Audrey, 1947-
  Blackbeard and the sandstone pillar : when lightning strikes / by Audrey Penn.
    p. cm.
  ISBN 978-1-933718-08-8
  1. Teach, Edward, d. 1718--Juvenile fiction. 2. Stone of Scone--Juvenile fiction. [1. Blackbeard, d. 1718--Fiction. 2. Pirates--Fiction. 3. Stone of Scone--Fiction. 4. Buried treasure--Fiction. 5. Ocracoke Island (N.C.)--Fiction. 6. Mystery and detective stories.] I. Title.

PZ7.P38448Bla 2007
[Fic]--dc22
                                    2007002131

To Mom:

You were my friend and biggest fan.
I will miss your reviews and suggestions,
but most of all, your love and laughter.

To Amiel, who thinks like a pirate.

Peer into the future
and see how the past
leads you forward.

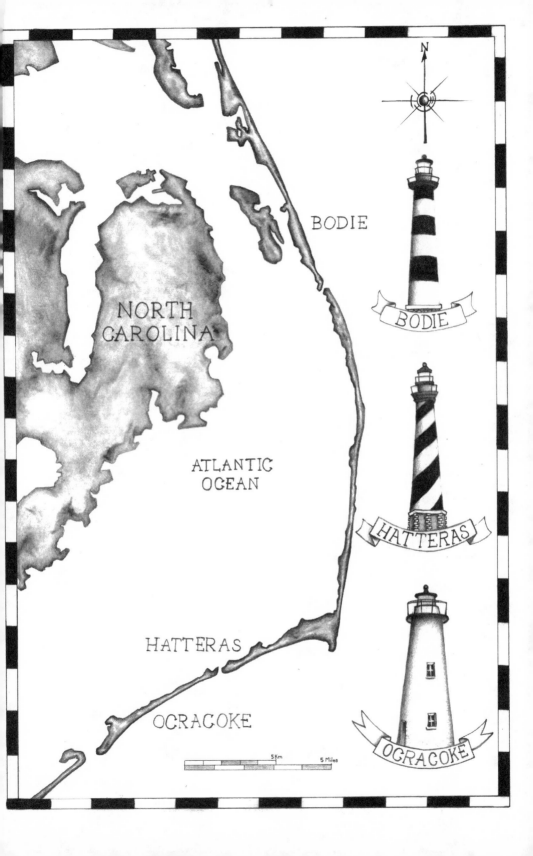

N

BODIE

NORTH CAROLINA

ATLANTIC OCEAN

HATTERAS

OCRACOKE

BODIE

HATTERAS

OCRACOKE

5 Km   5 Miles

And the pillow was to him

Like a mountain of blushing sand.

Water, fresh and cool,

Fell like crystal tears.

And psalms were born.

N

P R O L O G U E

The Knights Templar were the keepers of secrets, the lords of the mystic staff, and the couriers of the revered Pillar of Faith. The sign of the cross, embossed in thick, red thread flowed down the center of their long, white mantles. They were recognized by clergy and royalty as they traveled the world, possessing and protecting sacred and forbidden documents and artifacts privy to no one but the knights themselves.

It was the year 1296 a.d. in the town of Scone, Scotland. A massive and stately gray stone castle stood perched high atop a rocky hillside. King John Balliol's knights and sentries guarded the tall, thick fortress. Drawn across the hallways and partitions of the castle, large woolen tapestries picturing white knights on horseback, fair ladies with golden hair and flowing gowns, and hounds preparing for the hunt, covered the stone and mortar walls to help keep at bay the icy wind of winter and the blazing heat of summer. The castle walls divided friend from foe, royalty from commoner, the drawbridge lowered only when invitation to the walled boundaries was offered. But the king's heart was cold, his entire being as gray and unmoving as the stones that fortified his castle. After 1,600 years, Scotland had lost its most valuable prize to England— the precious Stone of Scone. No Irish or Scottish royalty had ever been crowned who had not sat upon the sacred block of sandstone.

Now, it was lost to England. Or was it? Only the ghosts of the Knights Templar and the fearsome Blackbeard know for sure.

Who are we to deny shared time?

Do we not embrace vivid memory as it

brings us to places long past?

Do we not slip into the familiar and pull

it about us like a warm cloak?

Do we not talk to those no longer with us

in our dreams?

And do we not tell them our hopes,

and wishes, and fears?

Who are we to deny shared time,

when all around us are the smells, and

trinkets, and sounds that bring such

loving ghosts into our

hearts and homes?

CHAPTER I

"A third trunk!" exclaimed Mrs. McNemmish in her high-pitched whistle of a voice. "There's a third trunk?"

"Aye, madam."

"I don't understand. How could there be a third trunk? I know every inch, crack, chip, hole, and puddle in that tunnel. I made the cement. I patched the walls! I never came across one hint of a third trunk." She observed the pirate coyly. "There's really a third trunk?"

Blackbeard, also known as Edward Drummand Teach, roared with laughter. He was both delighted and amused by this recently recruited ghost pirate, his great-grandniece. The glint in his coal black eyes made it

3

impossible for the now-young-again widow to tell whether her great uncle, more properly known as Edward Teach, was teasing her or really telling the truth. But it was obvious he was enjoying himself. He leaned in closer to his youthful mate and whispered, "Not only is there a third trunk, but it holds the promise of the most valuable treasure ever captured. 'Tis a prize of awesome magnitude and is hidden where no one but the devil himself could find it, and me doubts he'll be lookin'."

Theodora Teach McNemmish grinned. Now, as was her life-long dream, she stood beside the ghost of the greatest buccaneer ever to put fear into the blood of all who sailed the seas. She gazed up into his twinkling eyes and knew he was enjoying himself, for he was twisting the tip of his long, thick beard as he did when he played a trick on a crew member. "Tell me more," the widow encouraged him.

"Ah, there's the rub." Teach pointed to her with a wagging finger. "If I tell ye more, the more ye will want to know. And there will come a point when I can take me tale no further."

"Then take me where you can," begged the widow.

The captain withdrew his long pipe from his coat pocket, filled it with tobacco, and lit it. He took a long breath and let it out slowly. The pipe was one of his greatest pleasures. "Well, to begin me tale, ye must know that the prize I speak of is not the usual swag a pirate is accustomed to pillaging. In fact, it surpasses all worldly goods, and bears the legend of legends." He peered into the widow's eager, gray eyes. "'Tis a prize so mystifying, so splendid, the treasure must n'er be disturbed from its hiding place."

"My," sighed the widow. She could not even guess what this elusive treasure could be, or in which tunnel wall it was hidden. She pondered for a moment, then asked, "You and I are both ghosts. What is the harm in sharing your secret with me?"

"'Tis a fair query," admitted Blackbeard. He took another puff of his pipe, then turned and stared out at the darkening sea. His ghost ship, the *Queen Anne's Revenge*, was rocking gently and the brisk air smelled like salt. "Truth is, me lady, there are some secrets so grave and so dangerous they must remain untold, even after death. I will share this with ye, Theodora. 'Tis yer death that has me vexed. 'Tis yer death that could be the unveiling of me secret, and that would cause a great tragedy."

"My death?" gasped the widow. "How?"

"'Tis too soon to impart ye with such knowledge, for it may not be necessary. Yet, it frets me nonetheless." With that, he took another long puff and looked longingly out to sea.

"Tragedy," thought Mrs. McNemmish. How could her death have anything to do with such an elusive, tightly kept secret that, if discovered, would cause a tragedy?

Blackbeard recovered his good humor and detected a look of bewilderment on his niece's face. "Still contemplating me third trunk?"

"I am intrigued."

"Don't be. Truth is, the booty inside the third trunk is a red herring."

"A red herring? Then why hide it? And why would finding it be a problem?"

"All good queries, madam. Perhaps there'll come a day when I can answer ye and share me tale, but this is not the time."

Captain Teach turned and gave his attention to his spectral crew. A hundred mates were spread across the beams, furling sails for the night. Soft lantern light flooded the decks in a pale yellow glow and spilled like melted wax over the side of the ship into the blackening water. His eyes locked onto a ghost seated on a water barrel, whittling candles. The captain tipped his hat at the man, who acknowledged his captain with a fist to his forehead.

Teach invited Theodora to walk with him along the length of the ship. "Ye and I dwell in the spectral world, Theodora. We live in the company of ghosts and spirits. What modern treasure hunters don't understand is that we scabbards never intentionally left our loot to be found. Anything of true value was split with Governor Eden to keep me from the gibbet. The leftovers were divvied among the men or passed along to the colonists. We drank the liquid booty and procured armory and gunpowder for me ship. What trinkets were left were spent to please me gullet, gamble in an orderly or tavern, or buy gifts for the ladies. Oh, how I miss the company of a beautiful woman. . . ."

He winked at the widow, who was now young and fetching. "Though, I do have ye," he teased. Mrs. McNemmish blushed. Blackbeard chuckled, then stoked his clay pipe with a stick plucked from a coal pot brimming with red-hot embers. His pipe glowing, he closed his eyes and breathed in the aromatic tobacco, held his breath for a few seconds, then let out the cloud of gratification. Mrs. McNemmish turned quickly and gazed down at the ocean. Not 50 feet away, a family of dolphins leaped in and out of the water, dancing in the spilled candlelight and enjoying the play of the current. She wasn't sure if the dolphins were, like herself, ghostly apparitions from a time past, or whether they were alive and real, swimming along in the parallel world of today's saltwater and sea mist. She hadn't been dead long enough to reckon which things were ghostly and which things were present.

Suddenly, both she and Blackbeard looked sharp. The sound of hammered metal and the sight of bubbles rose from the water beneath the ghost ship. Blackbeard knew the sound well and smacked an angry fist on the railing. "Blast!" exploded the man.

"What is it, Edward?"

Blackbeard was very agitated. "'Tis a different kind of pirate," he said with disdain. "Think of it, McNemmish. Ye know yer ship so well that she is part of yer breath and soul. Ye know every knot in her ropes, every stitch in her sails, every crack in her floor planks. So much of yer own blood has spilled on the decks, ye and the ship are blood brother and sister, like in a child's game. Ye can hear her whistles, her drumbeats, ye know the timing of her cannons. Each member of her crew has become family and ye know every creak, every shiver of her hull. Every inch of yer ship is a personal part of yer very being. Then ye lose yer ship to a grounding and she sinks to the depths of the sea, where she stays forever, a monument. Then 300 years pass, and scavengers from the present, earthly world dive into the ocean and tear apart her mysteries. They pull apart the *Queen Anne's Revenge* with no reverence, no thought as to where she might have traveled, who may have entertained her bow, who fought hard for their lives, and what prizes were brought aboard her. They rip her apart like a chicken carcass, limb by limb, wrenching out her cannon tubes, tearing apart her inner wooden soul. Divers have been poking and prodding for years, reaping the goods we left behind."

Mrs. McNemmish laid a gentle hand over her great uncle's fist. "I'm sorry, Edward. But know this, sir. Those divers can collect all the artifacts they can, but they'll never know what you know, nor will they ever learn what I'm learning as a pirate under your command."

"I thank ye for that," said Teach. "Truth be known, pirating wasn't about the kill. 'Twas about the skill."

"How did the *Queen Anne's Revenge* come to end up here, in Beauford Inlet?"

"Beauford Inlet?" repeated Teach. "Oh! Ye mean Old Topsail." He chuckled. "Do ye know the name Stede Bonnet?"

"I do," prided the widow.

"Then ye will enjoy this yarn. I grew tired of piracy and me life on the waves, so I disguised meself and crept through the dark night streets of Bath to Governor Charles Eden's house. There, in the privacy of his home, he pardoned me and all me devilish deeds, but with a certain condition. He begged me to perform one last act of piracy before me retirement into society. Aye! He did! It seems piracy is disguised in the most pristine of homes."

"Now, me own wish," Blackbeard continued, "was to rid me life of piracy and live the life of a gentleman, someday becoming governor meself. 'Tis true! But, for the price of me freedom, I was to do what the governor required. I was sent to Spain, where I intercepted two galleons and captured both. I saw riches I had never seen before. There was so much gold, I feared me ship would sink from the weight. 'Twas on one of these ships that I happened upon a map. At first glance, it looked like nothing but a crude drawing of dashes and squares, and foreign writing. But I thought to keep it and study it. Months later, I became restless and desired to sail about, trying to figure out what secrets the map had to share. That, I did, Theodora. Eventually, the map led me to the treasure I have spoken about. Again, I did not understand the value of the plunder, but I took it for me own and kept it secretly stashed in me stow.

"Now comes the fun. It was a day in early June, 1718. I was carrying me prize when the *Queen Anne's Revenge* ran aground in Old Topsail Inlet, here, where we presently sit. There were three of us sailing together that day: I on the *Queen Anne's Revenge*, Stede Bonnet on the *Revenge*, and Israel Hands on the *Adventure*. Their two ships were temporarily grounded alongside the *Queen Anne's Revenge*, but it was me own hull that suffered the most. Me ship was lost, while the other two were spared. I had to work quickly. As there was a fishing boat in the vicinity, I had me men wave it down, then paid the captain in booty to take me friend Bonnet to the mainland. In a rather despicable act, I sent Bonnet (along with a handshake and letter) to Bath with the enticing prospect of being pardoned by Governor Eden. Stede Bonnet was most appreciative. 'Mr. Hands and I promise to keep watch over the *Revenge* whilst ye are away,' I told the gentleman. We waited until Bonnet was out of sight, then we quickly looted the good major's *Revenge* and stowed its goods on board the *Adventure*.

"Next, we undressed the *Queen Anne's Revenge*. It took a small crew to carry me secret prize, as it was great in size and weight, but afterward, I marooned the poor souls so they would never speak of what they had seen.

Then, when the tide rolled in, the *Adventure* was raised off the sandbar and Hands and I left. Stede Bonnet returned to find his ship floating near the sandbar, his entire cache gone." Blackbeard laughed at his own joke. "The good Major has never forgiven me for the dirty deed, yet thanks me often for the pardon.

"Mr. Hands and I then set sail to track down me friend, Captain David Harriot. I flagged Harriot down and had him bring his ship broadside. I took him in my confidence and traded Bonnet's treasure for a favor. Harriot was to spread the word that I had gone to Spain and would return one year hence. Hands and I then sailed to Ocracoke with the only treasure I have ever buried. I dared not bring it into the tunnel, for I wanted no one but the few I trusted to know the booty existed. Poor Harriot was run aground in Nags Head on June 25th and lost Bonnet's bounty to Spottswood." Blackbeard chuckled. "Come, Theodora. Retire to me quarters for a pint."

Think ye pirates large and loud

Plundering ships across the sea

Nostrils flaring, eyes on fire,

Brethren all! Their sacred creed.

But look ye further, you will find

A pirate's heart is carried wide,

Not on wings of masted sail

But places where young brethren hide.

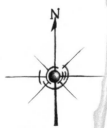

CHAPTER II

"If we get caught, they'll fillet us," 13-year-old Stefanie Austin warned her friends with teeth chattering from the cold.

Daniel blew into his hands. "Then why don't you shut up so the people next door don't hear you."

"Just hurry it up. I'm freezing." Dressed in her heaviest coat, thickest gloves, and a knit hat that covered her auburn ponytail, Stefanie jumped up and down in front of the widow's front door, desperately trying to get warm. It was a few minutes before midnight and the wind was blowing off the sound, making the temperature feel colder than it actually was.

Daniel's fingers fumbled for the key he had "borrowed" off his father's key chain. "Finally!" As soon as the door was unlocked, Stefanie pushed past the boys and hurried into the tiny shack of their now-dead friend, the widow Theodora Teach McNemmish. The old, familiar warmth was absent, but it was better than standing outdoors.

"Flashlights only," Billy O'Neal reminded everyone. He was a tall, blond, heavyset boy who, being the oldest of the group at 14, often took charge. "Mark, you stay close to me."

Eleven-year-old Mark Tillet's eye patch had finally been removed following his eye injury during the fire-in-the-tunnel incident, but his vision was naturally poor. Even with double-thick eyeglass lenses, he was practically blind in the widow's dark shack and willingly clung to his friend's arm. For a single moment, he allowed his memory to wander around the empty cottage. The shack wasn't the same without the widow. It lacked the comfort and warmth of invitation. The blanket of her affection had been folded up and put away forever.

"No way!" wailed Daniel. The small, lanky, 13-year-old stood beside the treasure chest that led to the secret tunnel where the kids had been recently trapped. Daniel aimed his flashlight at the front panel. "Teddy put on a new lock! There's no way we can get back into the trunk with a combination lock!" He turned toward Stefanie with desperation. "Can you pick it?"

"Not without a sledge hammer."

"Now what?" asked Billy.

"We go back to bed," Stefanie suggested with a yawn. "This was a stupid idea in the first place."

"You didn't think it was so stupid when we talked about someone sneaking into the tunnel and stealing our stuff," argued Daniel.

"If Zeek told his friends about our stuff, they might already have wiped us out," worried Billy.

"How would they have gotten down there? They would have had to break open the lock, yet the lock isn't broken," said Stefanie.

"They could have gone down before the new lock was put on," thought Daniel. "Maybe they took the stuff while we were in the hospital!"

"Or not. I say we stick to the plan and rescue the stuff tonight," Billy urged his friends. Mark agreed with an enthusiastic nod.

"How exactly are we supposed to do that? Wiggle our noses and zap into the tunnel?" asked Stefanie sarcastically.

"What do you think we should do?" Daniel challenged her.

"I think we should ask B.J. and Wade to go down and find out if our stuff is still there. They're firefighters. They could ask Teddy to open the lock."

"No one's allowed to go down there until those engineers come over from Wilmington to shore up the walls. Not even the firefighters," fretted Daniel.

"Then we must find a different way into the tunnel," insisted Billy.

"Oooh, I know!" spouted Stefanie, raising her hand and jumping up and down to be noticed. "We could close our eyes, click our heels together, and wish we were standing in the middle of a stinky puddle, with bats flying all around us, and the ceiling about to come crashing down on our heads, not to mention skeletons falling out of the walls and knocking us unconscious. And we'd say, 'I'm so glad I'm here. I'm so glad I'm here.'"

"What skeletons?" asked Daniel.

"There could be skeletons."

"Actually, I was thinking more like climbing down through the hole under the tree," uttered Billy.

"Are you insane?" freaked Stefanie. "We'll kill ourselves!"

"Besides, the tree's half burnt and boarded up," Daniel reminded him. "It's impossible."

Mark raised his hand and mimed climbing down a rope. He gave Billy the thumbs-up.

"See? Mark thinks it's a good idea."

"Mark also thinks Alaska and Hawaii are next to California because that's how jigsaw puzzles are made," Stefanie pointed out. "No offense, Mark."

Mark put his hands on his hips and scowled.

"Well, you used to think so," Stefanie explained in her own defense.

"I'm with Stefanie. It's too dangerous," said Daniel.

"Come on, y'all. We can do this," urged the ever-optimistic Billy. "We'll take the planks off the front of the tree where the lightning strike burned a hole in the ground, then tie a rope around the standing part of the tree and climb down. Once we get to the top of the mound of dirt and through the opening where we were rescued, it'll be a piece of cake." He waited for a response from Stefanie and Daniel, but neither of them said anything. "How hard can it be?" pleaded Billy. "We've already been down there, so we know the place. And we have these big, high-powered flashlights, and water bottles, and floral-scented dryer sheets to stick under our noses. Come on, y'all. It's our stuff! We have to make sure it's safe and bring it out of the tunnel before somebody else does!"

Stefanie rubbed her arms in an effort to get warm. "Well, one thing's for sure. I don't want anyone stealing our stuff, especially if Zeek Beacon has anything to do with it. I don't think the widow would have wanted that either." She looked at the boys. "I'll go if I can stand watch."

"No deal. If we're going to do this, we all do it," said Daniel, mustering up some of Billy's courage. "We're going to need all the pockets and backpacks we can fill."

Mark looked at his friends and blinked.

"He's right," considered Daniel. "What if somebody catches us going down there?"

"Who's going to catch us at midnight?" asked Billy.

"Teddy. He and his stupid dog do a last round-about on Howard Street before he goes off-duty."

Billy checked his watch. "It's already after 12:00. He's probably gone. Come on, y'all. Who's in?"

The three boys raised their hands. Mark walked over and raised Stefanie's. "I'm not doing this to help y'all out," Stefanie wanted the boys to understand. "I'm just doing it to protect our stuff."

"Whatever," muttered Daniel. "I'll have to stop at my house on the way and grab a rope from the boathouse."

"Did I mention I hate that tunnel?" announced Stefanie as they prepared to leave the shack. "I especially hate going back into the tunnel. And I hate you three for making me go back into the tunnel. It could collapse on us, you know. Do you know what my mother would do to me if I got killed down there?"

"We're not that lucky." Daniel looked at Stefanie and sighed. "Just do me a favor before we leave the shack."

"What?"

"Pee."

After a quick stop at the boathouse for rope, the kids rode their bikes toward the large Bobby Garrish tree located on historic Howard Street. They quickly hid their bikes in one of the bushier graveyards nearby. "I'm glad it's so dark out tonight," whispered Billy.

"Shh! Don't talk," hushed Daniel.

"I'm just saying that we probably won't get caught because it's so dark," whispered Billy.

"We will be if you don't stop yapping," Daniel told him. The two older boys stopped talking, and as noiselessly as possible pulled the wide, wooden planks off the bottom of the huge, 400-year-old tree and laid them on the ground.

Daniel tied one end of the rope around the most stable part of the tree's girth, then dropped the other end down the hole beneath the tree. He tossed Mark's and Stefanie's lit flashlights down the hole and onto the mound of sand in order for everyone to see where they were landing. "Billy, you go first."

Billy took hold of the rope, slid into the opening under the base of the tree, and began to lower himself through the hole. The smell of wet sand and burnt tree roots was overpowering. "It's hard to breathe down here!"

"The air will get better with the planks off," Daniel called down to him. "Drink some water."

Billy opened his water bottle and took a sip. It didn't help the air, but it washed away the taste of sand, smoke, and ash.

"Okay, Stefanie, you're next," said Daniel.

Stefanie stood with her arms folded, her feet tightly pulled together, and shivered from the cold and nerves. "I hate this. I hate you," she told Daniel.

"Hate me from down there. I don't feel like standing here all night waiting for you to make up your mind."

"We almost got killed the last time we were down there."

"Almost doesn't count. Just do it already."

"Fine!"

"Fine!" Daniel waited. "Well?"

Stefanie looked around. It was too dark to see much of Howard Street, but she could hear the creaking and swaying of branches above her. She listened to the sound of crisp, dead leaves tumbling in the four cemeteries closest to the Bobby Garrish tree. She took a deep breath. The air smelled like winter. She was admittedly scared to climb back down into the tunnel, but was a little excited at the same time.

With shaky hands, she grasped hold of the rope and slid into the opening below the tree. There was a lump in her throat and her heart was racing. "Here goes nothing," she told herself. She let out a yelp as her feet swung free. Her fingers gripped the rope so tightly, they nearly went numb in the first few seconds. She lowered herself slowly, one hand then the other, finally wrapping her feet around the rope that dangled below her. With the light from the high-powered flashlights, she could see the burnt, thick, twisted roots that wove in and out of the ground above her, and the upper part of the walls of the tunnel entrance. She screamed suddenly when a dream catcher made of silky spider webbing spread across her face and head. She coughed and rubbed her face on her coat sleeve. The air was thick and her mouth tasted like soot. She paused for a moment and closed her eyes.

"You're doing great!" Daniel called down to her. "It's just like climbing down the rope in gym class."

"Yeah. A gym class for mud wrestlers." Finally, the tips of her shoes touched the top of the sandy mound, and she froze. For a moment it felt like she had never been rescued. It was as if she were still living the nightmare, waiting to die. She wanted to scream and ask Daniel to pull her back up.

"Stefanie," called Billy. She turned her head quickly as her friend reached up and took hold of her hand. "Are you okay?"

"No."

Billy smiled. "Sure you are. Follow me." He led her down the mound and over toward the opening of the tunnel, where they had witnessed the fire, where Mark had been so badly hurt, and where the rest of them nearly lost their lives. "There's better air over here." Billy placed her in a safe spot and waited for her to calm down. "Stay here while I help Mark and Daniel." It was only a few minutes before all four adventurers were back together.

"Follow me," Billy told everyone. With flashlight in hand, he led the group through the small, dirt opening Todd and Teddy had dug during the rescue, and finally into the main tunnel. It was dark, dingy, and claustrophobic. The thick sand-and-seashell walls smelled of decay and stale smoke from the fire. Everyone reached for their dryer sheets and held them to their faces. "Come on," said Billy. He walked in the direction of the large, second trunk, which still embraced so much value and so much mystery. The tunnel was easier to maneuver this time, now that they were using bright light. The last time they were in the tunnel, when Zeek Beacon had locked them in, they only had a failing flashlight, a handful of candles, and the widow's ancient lanterns which were crushed during the cave-in. Even though tonight's lights were brighter, Mark still kept one hand clasped to the back of Billy's coat.

"Oh, shoot!" exclaimed Daniel.

"What?"

"Listen. I hear Teddy's car!"

"He'll never know we're down here," Billy assured him. "He won't notice the rope or the planks because it's too dark. And we're way out of sight, so he won't see our lights. Just forget about him."

"He might notice the planks," said Stefanie.

"Stop worrying. I know Teddy. If everything's quiet, he'll just want to go home and go to bed."

But Sheriff Teddy Jackson did notice. He noticed the planks lying on the ground and the rope tied around the tree trunk. "That's peculiar," he confided to Mustard. "I don't remember seeing the tree like this." He turned to his dog, which was yawning loudly. "We'll come back tomorrow and nail the planks back on. I'm too tired to deal with it now."

Billy grinned when he heard the car drive away. "See?"

"Oh, yuck," shrieked Stefanie. She aimed her flashlight at the puddle her right foot had splashed into. Swimming next to her shoe was the largest, greenest, hard-shell beetle she had ever seen. "Ugh! I think I liked this place better when I couldn't see it." Her eyes roamed up and around the walls and ceiling. Bats were hanging upside down from dozens of the wall's protruding seashells. "Don't anybody shine your light above the floor," she cautioned. But as soon as she said, "Don't," Billy did, and everyone ducked as several of the bats flew away from the light to other parts of the tunnel. "I said not to do that!"

"I know! I know!" Billy pulled his hat farther down over his ears. "I hate bats. And I hate short ceilings. I think every pirate except Blackbeard must have been under four feet tall." He walked stooped over in the barely six-foot-high tunnel as he continued to lead the way back through the labyrinth. Gratefully, it wasn't too long before they arrived at the large, second trunk. Since this was one of the widest and tallest places in the underground tunnel, Billy could stretch.

Stefanie grinned the moment she saw the chest. "Hello, nut shells! Quick! Let's open it!" She and Billy were rushing to push back the lid when Mark stopped them.

"What's wrong?" asked Daniel.

Mark swung a pointed finger over the entire area.

"You're right," said Daniel. He swept his flashlight over the entire floor. "When we were trapped down here, the trunk was open and there was junk everywhere. Now there's nothing here and the trunk is closed. Not even the seashell Snow Duck that had the key and tickets inside it is here."

"Maybe the firefighters put the stuff back into the trunk and closed it," suggested Billy.

"There's only one way to find out." After a slight hesitation, the foursome pushed open the heavy lid. Stefanie jumped back as a precaution. She couldn't face another dead body. But Billy and Daniel raced for their flashlights and flooded the inside of the trunk with light. When no one said anything, Stefanie rushed to their sides.

"Creep! Creep!" screamed the girl.

"It's gone! All of it. It's all gone!" moaned Billy.

"There's not even a seed left!" hollered Stefanie.

"Keep your voices down," shouted Daniel. "Someone will hear you."

Stefanie planted her face in front of Daniel's, aiming her flashlight at her seething expression, and hissed like a steaming teapot. "Do I look like I care? Is this the face of someone who cares for one second whether or not someone outside hears me? Hello! Hello out there! We've been robbed! They took everything but the dirt!"

Daniel grabbed the flashlight and smacked Stefanie on her shoulder. "Stop it! We have to figure this out!"

"Figure what out, you half-witted, caddywampus, dingbatter? Our stuff is gone. Someone came down here while we weren't looking and took all of our stuff!"

"You think it was Zeek's friends who did this?" asked Billy.

Stefanie rolled her eyes. "What difference does it make? It's not like we can ask them."

"Well, we can't tell anyone we know the stuff is gone, because then they'll know we were down here," fretted Daniel.

"Oh my gosh. They even took the lady!" freaked Billy.

"What lady?"

"The one we put in the box when her bones fell apart. Wait a minute! I know who did it! I know who took our stuff!"

"Who?"

"Birdie."

"Birdie?" asked Daniel. "Why would Birdie take our stuff?"

"Maybe he didn't understand it was our stuff. And

maybe when he visited Zeek in jail, Zeek told him to come down here and wipe us out."

Mark and Stefanie disagreed. "He wouldn't do that," said Stefanie. "He's dumber than bee spit, but he's honest."

"You're wrong," said Daniel. "Not about him being honest, but if Zeek told Birdie to come down here and take everything out of the tunnel, I think he would. He's scared to death of Zeek. Who isn't? Maybe we should ask Birdie about it before we go to Williamsburg. You know, just ask him if he's been down in the tunnel. He's not going to lie. I don't think Birdie knows how to lie."

Mark nodded in agreement.

"I'll talk to him before we go," volunteered Billy.

Everyone took one last, miserable look around before leaving the tunnel. On their way out, Billy's flashlight beam picked up something reflective in the wall. "Look at this, y'all." He waved his light back and forth to produce a tiny reflection. "That didn't happen the last time we were down here. Some more of the wall must have broken off." He pulled out his pocket knife and chipped away at the wall, exposing a small fraction of brass.

Daniel's heart pumped wildly as he stared at the sliver of brass peeking out from behind the sand-and-seashell cement. His anxious, green eyes widened and his breathing quickened. Mark and Stefanie huddled together, squeezing each other's hands.

"Keep chipping," urged Daniel.

A few moments passed, and Billy stood back and stared at the small, exposed hole in the wall. Daniel and Mark scrambled forward and touched it.

"No way!" gasped Stefanie. She covered her mouth and screamed quietly into her palm. "It's a third trunk!"

What holds more excitement
than not knowing?
Like Christmas morn beholding the
unwrapped package.
Do we quench our thirst for discovery,
Or stare and guess at what lies ahead?
For ahead could prove precious
or disappointing.
'Tis for ye to decide.

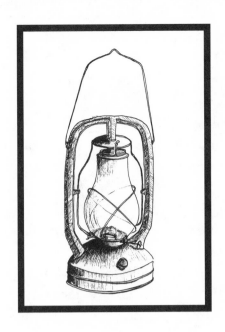

CHAPTER III

For the first time in her life, Stefanie was too stunned to speak. The boys were beside themselves.

"What do we do now?" exclaimed Daniel.

"Are you kidding?" laughed Billy. "We dig it out, that's what!" Mark grabbed his Boy Scout knife and began chipping away at the wall.

"Whoa! Wait a second!" shouted Daniel. "There's no way we can dig that trunk out of the wall. The whole tunnel would cave in. With us in it."

"Well, we have to do something," said Billy. "We can't just leave it in the wall. There might be some really good stuff in there."

Stefanie appealed to Daniel. "What do you think we should do?"

Daniel took a deep breath and let it out slowly. He rubbed his chin, then once again ran his hand over the tiny piece of brass peeking out from the failing cement. "Dig it out."

"What! You just said we can't dig it out. No way, y'all," objected Stefanie. "I don't care what's inside that trunk. It's not worth the whole place collapsing."

"How do you know it's not worth it? What if it's the greatest treasure ever found? What if it's Blackbeard's treasure of treasures? Come on," Billy urged everyone, "we have to find out what's in it."

"Step past it."

Stefanie turned toward Daniel. "Well, make up your mind!"

"About what?"

"The trunk. First you said, 'Don't dig it out,' then you said, 'Dig it out,' then you said, 'Step past it.'"

"I didn't say, 'Step past it.'"

"Yes, you did."

"No, I didn't."

"Yes, you did."

"No, I didn't!"

"Yes, you did."

"No, I . . . Great! She's hearing voices again."

"I am not hearing voices. You're just trying to confuse me."

"Stefanie, you were born confused, you don't need my help." Daniel waved his flashlight beam over the wall that surrounded the hidden treasure chest. Huge chunks of cement had already fallen to the floor, exposing rotted boat planks meant to shore up the wall. He aimed the light into one hole and a frightened bat flew out.

"Duck!" screamed Billy.

Everyone dropped to the ground and covered their heads with their hands. The bat swooped down and touched Stefanie's finger tips. "Get away from me!" she screamed. She smacked the frightened cave dweller until it flew out of sight, then she stood up.

"Why did you scream like that?" hissed Daniel.

"Because it touched me."

"You were loud enough to wake the corpses buried above us!"

Stefanie gazed up at the ceiling. "Oh, yuck."

Billy was busy thinking. "Y'all are right about one thing," he admitted. "If we dig the trunk out of the wall too quickly, the tunnel will collapse. We'll just have to do it a little at a time."

"You mean come back down here?" asked Stefanie.

Billy nodded.

"Ohhhh, maaaaan," whined Stefanie. Although, in fact, she was torn. She was definitely worried about the tunnel caving in, but what if Billy was right? What if this was Blackbeard's treasure of treasures?

"Who's in for digging it out slowly?" asked Billy.

All four raised their hands, Stefanie reluctantly.

"Wow! You're kidding?" Daniel remarked to Stefanie. "You're going to help us without an argument? No whining? How could that be?"

"Listen, prawn. Don't you have a dinner plate to crawl onto?"

Billy looked at his watch. "We'd better go. Help me patch up the wall." Everyone ran to the part of the pathway that had the dampest sand and returned with their hands full. Together they worked to hide the area they had chipped away. When they were satisfied, Daniel and Billy climbed back up the rope and out of the bottom of the tree. Stefanie tied the rope around Mark's waist, and the two older boys pulled him up to safety. Stefanie was the last to come out, but her temperament had improved. She brushed herself off and took a drink of water. "Don't forget to put the planks back on," she instructed the boys. She pushed her bike out of the graveyard, reported that no corpses had risen due to her "delicate" screaming, and rode home.

"Do you think she knows she's bossy?" laughed Billy as the two older boys walked Mark home.

"Are you kidding?" Daniel informed his friend. "She takes lessons every Monday, Wednesday, and Friday."

After school the following afternoon, the four children reluctantly showed up at their school library to work on their court-ordered community service project. Using the Internet, they were attempting to track down robberies, pirate lootings, and ship groundings that had taken place on June 25, 1718, as well as decipher what was written on Melanie Smyth's tickets, which were basically unreadable. No one had said anything to anyone for the first five minutes when Mark clapped his hands.

"What did you find?" asked Stefanie. She, Billy, and Daniel raced to Mark's desk and stared at his computer screen.

"You can't put a red queen on a black king," Billy showed him. "The red queen goes here." Everyone returned to their own desks.

"We're not getting anywhere," admitted Daniel.

"If y'all had listened to me, we wouldn't have found those stupid tickets, and we could be spending our time figuring out what to do about the third trunk."

"Stefanie, you bonehead. We wouldn't even know there was a third trunk if we hadn't found out about the tunnel, the tickets, and the first two trunks."

"That's beside the point. All I'm saying is that we wouldn't be sitting here staring at computers if we hadn't given Mrs. McNemmish her burial at sea."

"You know what gets me," said Billy. "After all the trouble we went to giving the widow her burial at sea, she didn't even stay in her coffin. She's like Houdini! She just disappeared. Then we buried a brand new, empty coffin in a graveyard with the rest of her family who aren't buried there either! It's like an entire family plot of evaporated dead people."

"We never should have put that gorgeous ruby ring into the coffin. I'm sure the widow would have let me keep it if she were alive."

"If she were alive, you knit-brained babbling brook, we wouldn't be in this situation!"

"Oh! And another thing," continued Stefanie.

"Here it comes," moaned Daniel.

"How come Theodora made us go into the tunnel to find the seeds and tickets? Why didn't she just leave them on her kitchen counter? And another thing. Why didn't she leave the Snow Duck with the key on the fireplace mantle since it really was a *key* key and not a *hint* key? You want to know why she made everything so difficult? I'll tell you why she made everything so difficult. Because she was nuts and squirrels. And how come we happened to be in the tunnel for the one and only time in history that the Bobby Garrish tree was struck by lightning? The tree is 400 years old, and that was the first and only time it was struck by lightning. What are the odds of that? And let's not forget we spent the whole day down there without a bathroom."

"We all know there's no bathroom in the tunnel," groaned Daniel. "The whole village knows there's no bathroom in the tunnel. You've told everyone on the island about a million times there's no bathroom in the tunnel. I swear, if you mention peeing again, I just may have to kill you."

"Well, I think Miss Theo should have left us a note telling us there were diamonds in the Snow Duck seeds. I mean, what if we had thrown our Snow Ducks away? Did she ever think of that? What if there are O'cockers who have thrown away their Snow Ducks? Oh, my gosh! I bet there are diamonds out there just sitting in a junk pile somewhere. Oh! And what's the story with the first trunk?" rambled Stefanie. "I mean, why did we have to sift through all that stuff crammed into the first chest just to get to the second chest, which had all the good stuff in it?

"Oh! And how come we had to deal with dead bodies, bats, and pirate skeletons when we had seeds in our own Snow Ducks all along? Ooh! Wait!" she said, flapping her hands like a bird. "Why did she leave all those nuts and seeds full of jewels down there when they could have been buried by the walls and disappeared for life? If she wanted someone to go down into the tunnel to get the rest of the stuff out of there, she should have said something. Then y'all could have gone down there on a nice day when there wasn't a storm with lightning, and Zeek wouldn't have known anything about it, and we wouldn't have been locked in, and I wouldn't have had to pee in a tin can, and we wouldn't have been robbed, and we could have brought up all the stuff ourselves AND found the third trunk."

"Shut up!" exploded Daniel. After a moment, he calmed down and faced Stefanie with a sly grin. "You know what? I just figured something out. It's actually your fault we're stuck here doing community service."

"My fault? What did I do?"

"You had a temper tantrum and kicked Miss Theo's trunk. That's how we found out about the fake bottom, the stairs, and the tunnel. So when you think about it, this whole mess is your fault."

"Good one," snickered Billy. Mark giggled, but made sure Stefanie didn't see him.

Stefanie gave Billy the evil eye, then turned back toward Daniel. "I don't have temper tantrums. I simply express myself. It's healthy."

"Then you must be the healthiest person on earth, because I have never heard anyone express herself as much as you do."

"All I know is that when my arteries get as hard as Miss Theo's were, I'm going to have somebody else do my thinking."

"Why wait?" Daniel looked over at Billy, who seemed to be staring through his computer screen instead of at it. "What's wrong with you?"

"Teddy stopped me on the way to school this morning."

"What did he want?" asked Stefanie.

"He wanted to know if I knew who took the planks off Bobby Garrish's tree and then put them back on."

Daniel gulped. "What did you tell him?"

"That I heard some of Zeek's friends talking about going back into the tunnel to see if there was anything left worth stealing."

"Brilliant!" applauded Stefanie. "And it's not even a lie, because it could have been Zeek's friends who wiped us out, they could have gone down through the tree, and no one can prove they didn't because no one saw them not doing it, and even though we saw them not doing it, it doesn't mean they didn't do it before we did, even though we know they didn't because the planks hadn't been taken off."

Daniel looked at Stefanie and shook his head. "I think I hear your arteries hardening." Out of boredom, he went back to work on his research. "How come none of the stories we've read in our families' journals are on the computer? There's hardly anything about Blackbeard visiting Williamsburg; just that his head was brought there after it was cut off."

"They sold it at auction!" emphasized Stefanie. "They made a cup out of it! You'd think they'd put that on the computer!"

"So what do you think Blackbeard's head would go for on eBay?" wondered Billy.

"That's disgusting," grumbled Stefanie. But Mark thought the question was interesting.

"I bet it would be worth millions," imagined Billy. "Can you imagine owning a sterling silver-and-glass mug made out of the skull of Blackbeard the pirate? It might still hold the essence of his brain! How cool would that be?"

"The essence of his brain?" repeated Daniel. "A brain can't have an essence if it's not in the skull."

Stefanie had a terrifying thought. "What if our ancestors lied?"

"About what?"

"About everything." Stefanie twisted her ponytail into a tight pretzel, as she often did when she was nervous. "What if the tickets we found are fake? What if the pirates who wrote on those tickets made the whole thing up and there really isn't anything in Williamsburg, and there never was a pirate looting, and we're doing all this research to return things that don't exist to people who don't exist because their ancestors didn't exist and the robberies never happened? We could be sitting here forever looking up all this stuff and never find any of it because it doesn't exist."

"You're hallucinating," Daniel told her.

"Those tickets are definitely real," Billy assured her. "Besides, we're going to find out for sure when we go to Williamsburg tomorrow. At least we're getting a trip out of it."

Suddenly Mark knocked on his computer screen excitedly. He had found a list of sterling silver items beginning with the letter *t* that were popular during the 18th century. Billy read the list out loud. "Teapots, teaspoons, tablespoons, thumbtacks, and toothpicks."

"Toothpicks?" laughed Daniel. "What kind of fruitcake would use a sterling silver toothpick?"

"A rich fruitcake." Stefanie sat back in her chair, pinched the diamond pendant that hung around her neck, and swung it back and forth on its chain. She wondered what it would be like to be really, really rich. She thought back to six weeks ago, when she cracked open her Snow Duck's belly button seed and discovered her very own diamond. It wasn't just the breaking-open part that thrilled her. It wasn't even just the fact that she finally had a diamond of her own. It was the wail of agony and the look of utter horror and disbelief on Zeek Beacon's face when he realized how many of those white seeds he had passed up before locking her and the boys in the tunnel. "Serves him right," she thought pleasantly. "Now, he's rotting away in jail, and we're jewelry and land owners."

She finished her two hours with a smile on her face. Eleven feet below her, among the stench of decay, flying mammals, and rotting boat beams was the allure of a treasure bigger and brighter than anything she could ever imagine. Now that was worth researching.

Mystery lies

In the depths of the sea

Where truth is found

To seek and read

Among fishes and anemones.

Davy Jones awaits his prey.

N

CHAPTER IV

Theodora walked with Teach to his private quarters. The door opened into a large room completely walled in deep-colored mahogany wood with windows that overlooked the sea. A pine bed and dresser took up one side of the room and smelled like Old Hammock Creek on the island, where the pine trees are thick and fragrant. Across the room was a large writing desk with drawers and mail slots. Scattered throughout the cabin were three enormous trunks. Theodora chose the rosewood rocking chair to sit in close to the private woodstove. She missed her cats and the company of children seated at her feet.

She looked up when there was a knock at the door. The ship's candle maker entered with two large steins frothing over with grog. The widow took a delicate sip from hers, pulled a hand-crocheted handkerchief out from beneath her long sleeve, and patted the foam off her upper lip. Sitting back, she watched with great curiosity as the candle maker whispered into his captain's ear. The captain became increasingly agitated by the man's words.

"Blast! Are ye sure?" asked Teach. The candle maker nodded, then saluted the captain, bowed his head to the widow, and left the room.

"Something wrong?" asked Theodora.

"'Tis too soon to tell, madam." Blackbeard took a great gulp of his drink and changed the subject. "Sitting here smelling the salt and sea whets me appetite fer a long sail, a fresh wind, and peace at me back, followed by a glorious battle."

He took another gulp and faced the widow with a gentle smile not often seen upon the face of this infamous pirate. "I married, ye know. Fourteen times! N'er bedded a woman until I married her. The last time 'twas a farmer's daughter in Bath on the mainland. Miss Mary Ormond was her name. A sprightly thing of 16 years, with a smile that could melt me heart. But before long, me restless blood put me back on the waves.

"And now I must settle for the ghostly haunts of Falmouth and Pirate Town. Of course, if a spirited lady should pass me by, perfumed with the fresh scent of vanilla soap and lilac oil in her hair, I shall not hesitate to take her as mine." He chuckled. "I do remember the ladies, Theodora. No offense to ye."

"No offense taken, sir. I've often admired a seaman's bronzed arms and chest."

"Still . . ." lamented the pirate, "there was nothing so uplifting as an ocean forested with ships' masts, carefully choosing yer prey—a Spanish galleon perhaps—capturing it, looting it, then celebrating with a bonfire party on the beaches of Ocracoke. Ah, McNemmish, ghosting is an improvement over Davy Jones's locker, but 'tis a tease for the business of true pirating."

Theodora rocked in her chair and soaked in her infamous relative. Blackbeard was as awesome and captivating in reality as history portrayed him. He was physically powerful and willfully intimidating. He stood over six feet five inches tall, had a muscular chest and thick torso, brawny arms, and Herculean legs. He had a wardrobe of thick, upholstered coats—having chosen the purple one on this occasion—large, wide-mouthed boots, and six guns and six knives across his chest. When thrust into battle, he wielded a gold-cuffed sword and razor-sharp cutlass. Before attacking a ship, he'd slice off a long piece of hemp cord, wind it around his head, and light it on fire beneath the rim of his wide-brimmed hat. Other times, he sported several long, lit fuses that hung down on either side of his face. In addition, smaller ribbons of smoldering hemp were woven throughout his long, impressive beard. He looked like the devil incarnate.

But Teach was a complex man if anything. Thoroughly at home on the seas with his band of pirates, carousing at beach parties and looting ships, he was equally at ease attired as a proper gentleman, dancing a waltz in a governor's mansion, or walking the lawn with a proper lady hooked onto his arm. Either way, Blackbeard was a giant among men.

"Sir?" asked the shy widow.

"Eh?" asked the buccaneer.

"I've been wondering if perhaps you might not share with me the tiniest hint about the third trunk. Especially where my death is concerned."

Blackbeard put down his stein and glanced at the pint-sized seaman. "Come, madam. What manner of freebooter would unfurl all his sails for the world to see? I will confess one thing. Though I admitted the prize be on Ocracoke, I never said the trunk was buried there. As I said, the trunk is a red herring."

Theodora accepted his answer good-naturedly.

Blackbeard said nothing for a moment, then sighed as if a great burden rested on his broad shoulders. He glanced over at his faithful companion. "At one time, the treasure was to be me bartering tool. It was to keep me neck from the hangman's noose and be the key to me freedom if ever I was captured. I did not have the chance to say so, as I was struck down in surprise."

He thought back to his last fight and to the bloody end of his own life. "We had been celebrating the evening prior and had fallen into an inebriated sleep. Howard, Hands, and many of me men were strewn around the island and had not made it back to the ship.

"Early the following morning, Robert Maynard and the crew of His Royal Majesty's Navy made a surprise attack on me sloop, *Adventure*, which I had obtained following the loss of the *Queen Anne's Revenge*. Still muddled in thought from the grog and lack of sleep, we fell for Maynard's ruse and were tricked into believing we had killed the lieutenant's crew. We had jumped aboard his ship to lay claim to it when his soldiers came out of hiding and lured us into a desperate fight. Most of me men were killed, as was I. I was beheaded and me body was thrown overboard." Teach lifted a hand to his neck. "I never expected to have me flame severed from me candle," he said with obvious detestation. "To have one's head lopped off and paraded in a public square is to be ripped of all dignity."

Blackbeard's mood had changed once more, and he suddenly felt uneasy. "Come, Theodora." He put down his stein and led the widow back up onto the top deck. There he stood silently for a moment, then pointed to the vast Graveyard of the Atlantic, where pirate and death frequently met in screaming, bloody battle. His eyes adjusted to the dark, and he glared out at the gibbets haunting the shore a short distance away from where the ghost ship now floated. Three pirate ghosts hung as a warning to other pirates. Later, their bodies would be cut down by a spectral guard and thrown into the sea. This tyrannical ritual played out every day in the ghost world, each day bringing new hangings and new warnings. He laughed suddenly, startling the widow. "Did ye know, I kept swimming after they cast me headless carcass overboard?"

"I heard the rumor. Some say you swam once around your ship, others say you swam around 21 times."

"'Twas no rumor, madam. Me arms kept thrashing and stroking, as if I were still swinging me cutlass and sword. I finally sank over at the hole where me outhouse hid me tunnel. I know not the number of death circles I swam, for the screaming of others made me lose count. I was shark bait after that. Still, caused quite a stir in the day," he chuckled. "Heard tales of me 'death swim' fer years. Souls and sailors alike swore that Satan had taken over me body. Ha! I could've told 'em that." He turned to the widow and brightened. "But Davy Jones never got his hands on me, nor me soul. Nay, mate. I was good to me women." His expression changed again and he looked at Theodora with disgust written across his face. "Me death had not been an option, madam. I am most disappointed in meself and in me crew!"

"You fought a good fight, sir. You were tricked by Maynard and his men." She smiled up at him. "You became the most notorious pirate ever to sail the seas. Why, piracy all but disappeared with your death. The name 'Blackbeard' still cries out of the mouths of children as they swing their swords and swear to take you down."

"Ye please me, madam, and ye have lifted me spirits. Therefore, I shall tease ye with a hint. Listen sharp. If the secret of the sleeping treasure is ever uncovered, kings and queens will know they sat upon a lie. There! I dare not say more. 'Tis time for a new topic. See that ship, yonder?" He offered Theodora his telescope. "'Tis the ghost ship, the *Treasure*. It once belonged to the rogue Charles Vane."

"Does Vane captain the ghost ship?"

"Nay, mate. Vane was rough with the ladies."

Mrs. McNemmish lowered the glass. "I don't understand. He was rough with the ladies?"

"Aye, miss. After Vane was killed, he went straight to Davy Jones's locker. He'll remain at the bottom of the ocean, cursed to be one of the walking dead, chained to the sands of time for all eternity. The code of the Brethren is sacred, madam. It is written in blood and honored by Davy Jones."

"The code?" asked McNemmish.

"It states that a pirate's behavior toward women is to be taken seriously. Women are to be treated with grace, respect, and honor. If a pirate breaks the code, he is condemned to spend eternity in Davy Jones's locker. Women pirates were treated equally as harsh."

"I see." Theodora stared into the depths of the ocean and imagined the plight of those pirates who betrayed the code. "What's it like—Davy Jones's locker?"

Blackbeard looked sharp for a moment. The question unnerved him. "That, Miss Theo, remains one of the greatest of all sea mysteries. First, a pirate's soul is ripped from his spirit, then he is pulled to the bottom of the ocean where he gets his first real glimpse of what eternity holds for him. As I am one of the few pirates who fell to the depths of the locker but was spit back up to the world of the living, I can tell ye what I know to be true." He reflected for a moment on the one image he retained from his few seconds on the ocean floor.

"When a pirate falls to his death, ships' bells toll from the deepest, darkest places beneath the sea. There, he is judged. If he has followed the code of the Brethren, he is privileged to be a ghost pirate fer all eternity. But if he has been cruel to the ladies or unmerciful to his crew, he does not return as a ghost pirate, but is sent to the gibbets for repeated hangins,' or is destined to live deep beneath the ocean where strange sea creatures live in near darkness. It is there that the dastardly scourge will take his place behind an anchor wheel, where he will walk in an endless circle fer all time, banished from the spirited world above."

Mrs. McNemmish closed her eyes and imagined one huge anchor turn that cut the earth in half, crowded with men pushing the turn poles slowly, painfully, and forever.

She emerged from her daydream and spied the *Treasure* approaching their own ship. "Who captains the *Treasure* now?" she inquired, pointing.

"A colorful man. Captain Calico Jack Rackham. He was Vane's quartermaster in the living world. Do you see the two ships rapidly approaching the *Treasure*?"

"Aye, sir. The two smaller ships."

"They are manned by pirates Anne Bonny and Mary Reed, two sisters of the Brethren who sail with Calico Jack. They're wicked, treacherous women, Theodora. Feisty squallers, those two. They can down a pint as well as any pistol-packing scurvy aboard me own ship. Ye will like them." Edward Teach suddenly laughed out loud. "See that ghost ship yonder, toward the southern horizon?"

"Aye, sir."

"That is the ghost ship *Revenge*." He grinned and shook his head. "That ship belongs to me good friend, Major Stede Bonnet."

"The man you left stranded in Topsail!"

"Aye, the very same. I'm afraid the good major defies explanation. He continues to captain his ghost ship, but only at the mercy and help of his crew." He chuckled as he turned to the widow. "I fear Major Bonnet lacks the finesse and quickness of sword it takes to be an adequate ghost pirate. If truth be known, the good man was only a fair sea pirate when he was alive."

Mrs. McNemmish appreciated the introductions and spent the next few pleasant hours listening to stories about each ghost pirate as they came into Teach's head or sailed into view. But it was the story about the third trunk that occupied her mind and her imagination, and she found herself slipping in and out of Blackbeard's monologue. A few times during his storytelling, she tried steering the conversation back to the alluring, hidden treasure, but Teach always guided her back to his topic of conversation.

"Curiosity has pushed many a pirate off the plank, madam. And there is something ye must know. Apparitions and spectral conversations can make their way into some mortals' dreams. If one of your young friends were to learn me secret just from our discourse, his or her life would be in peril from that day forward."

If I pass this way again,

I shall bring new lyric songs

Of sailing ships and treasure chests

And dance the dance of time long gone.

Tho' skin and bones be buried deep,

My soul still drinks the

sun-bleached clouds.

I celebrate the sight of gulls

And pray to hear the morning sounds.

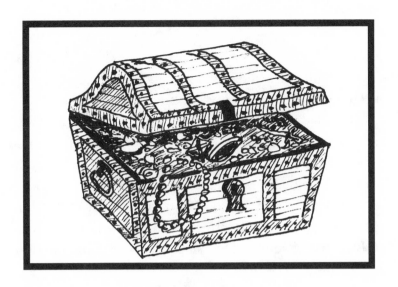

CHAPTER V

"I'll tell you what," bartered the widow. "Since we can't discuss the third trunk, pray tell me of the first two." Teach downed his drink, pulled a sleeve across his mouth, and erupted with a thunderous belch. "Let me see. We had just taken the *Queen Anne's Revenge* out of Barbados, where we had stopped to take advantage of me friend Stede Bonnet's hospitality, when in the distance, a Spanish merchant ship came across me starboard bow.

We doused our lanterns, and in the cloak of darkness approached the rig. As the morning paled, we blasted her decks, crushed her midmast, and disarmed her guns. Men and cannons were ripped from the ship. Smoke engulfed the top deck as bodies flew into the air and tumbled into the blood-stained pool. They fired back, taking six of me men and two of me guns, but we held steady and claimed the advantage. Next, me men and I rushed her decks. I pulled out me sword and knife and fought three sailors at a time, thrusting each in their hearts 'til they be dead. I slashed me way through the gun decks, neither taking nor giving quarters, and captured the ship and all its stash. After the transfer of goods, I burned the merchant ship 'til she sank. It was exhilarating, Theodora. 'Tis what I lived for." Blackbeard smiled. He could tell by his mate's expression that this part of piracy was not to her liking.

He continued with relish. "There were twelve trunks aboard the ship that night, filled with Spanish doubloons, silver wares, golden sculptures, and diamond and emerald trinkets. Also on board were Señor Santiago and his daughter, Señorita Rosa Santiago, along with the señorita's lady in waiting.

"Suddenly, the young and exquisitely beautiful Señorita approached me and demanded an explanation for taking her aboard the *Queen Anne's Revenge*. 'I don't think this is the right time to be pluck, me lady,' trembled her maid. 'I would have to agree with that, my dear,' said the Señor. 'We mustn't make him angry.'

"I was fascinated," Teach told the widow. "Never before had I witnessed such a purity, such an untouched soul as this vision that stood before me. Her skin was like polished teakwood and her eyes as black as the moonless sky. Her flowing hair was a lustrous ebony, and she faintly smelled of Persian rose oil. I was smitten, I tell ye. 'What are ye called?' I asked her. 'I am Señorita Rosa Maria Garcia Juego Romero Santiago,' she recited with a trained curtsy. 'And you are?'

"I was mesmerized, madam!" Teach recalled. "She knew not of me. I approached the young woman, took her small, gloved hand in mine, and bowed graciously. 'The name is Edward Teach,' I told her. I then looked at Señor Santiago and the lady in waiting and announced to them both, 'I admire pluck. The Señorita alone shall retain her personal belongings. You two, however, shall forfeit yer trunks.'

"I then lifted me right hand and removed a ruby-cluster ring set in gold from my smallest finger." There was a gasp from Mrs. McNemmish as she listened to this part of the story, for she knew the ring well. "I placed the ring on the Señorita's finger and said, 'If it pleases yer ladyship, I shall take yer hand in marriage and escort ye the rest of yer journey.'

"I then turned toward the helm and shouted for me quartermaster, 'Mr. Howard! Step lively!' I removed me hat and placed it in front of me chest and bowed to the beautiful, beguiling lady. She smiled back. 'Buenas noches,' she said to me pleasantly. 'I shall see you on the morrow.'

"The next day we were wed and set sail for the Carolinas. Two days later, we were attacked by a cutter, which we sank after only minutes of fighting, but the beautiful Señorita was hit by a fragment and died. I buried her, along with a bounty of riches, in her own trunk. 'Twas me own sailing master who added me personal effects to the trunk after me death. It was only a matter of time before somebody found that first treasure chest with me lady's remains and me personal effects. All that was needed was a sharp eye and a little luck."

"A little luck!" shrieked Mrs. McNemmish. "How about having to build a house over your outhouse opening without anyone suspecting anything, cutting a bigger hole in our floor, then hauling the trunk into our living room? I dare say, we were surprised to find a maiden inside. But the ruby-cluster ring was a beauty."

Blackbeard paused for a moment and aimlessly stared into space. "The Blood of Moritangia," the widow thought she heard him whisper.

"Excuse me?" asked the widow.

Blackbeard recovered. "Nothing, mate. Where is the ring now?"

"The children buried it in my coffin. Why?"

"'Tis not important. So, where were we? Ah! The second trunk. We had just sunk the schooner, *Susannah*, off the entrance to Old Topsail Inlet when 20 or so large trunks floated to the surface. Ye could have walked from trunk to trunk the way they lined up like stepping stones. I had me men bring the trunks on board the *Queen Anne's Revenge*, and I took interest in one in particular. It was made of a polished mahogany wood with brass trimming all around.

"When I looked inside the trunk, expecting to find coins and goblets, I found an assortment of nuts and large white seeds. Me men being hungry, they dove into the nuts with eager appetite. Hobbs, it was, broke a tooth on an emerald hidden inside a walnut shell. We opened a hundred or so nuts and found jewels in 'em all. Diamonds in the white seeds." Blackbeard whistled. "What a find that was."

"When we landed on Ocracoke later that month, I had me men break down the trunk and reassemble it deep in the wall of the tunnel to protect me loot. Seeing as how the booty was so extraordinary, and knowing I would need the prize later, I had two of me men shackled to the trunk, each with a pistol and orders to shoot any inquirers. That night, however, Ocracoke was raided by Lieutenant Robert Maynard. I sneaked off the island and back onto me ship where me crew and I disappeared into the night. I left the island with me cuff keys still hooked to me belt. By the time I returned to the island, the blokes were dead, but still keeping watch over me trunk." He looked at the widow and shrugged. "It happens. I can only imagine yer surprise when ye found me trunk with two men still fettered to it. But I would hardly call it treasure hunting. The winnings were there for the pickin'.."

"For the picking!" exclaimed Mrs. McNemmish. "You hid it in a wall, for heaven's sake! With two dead men practically petrified to its sides! And with a body in it!"

"Aye. Yolanda, me 13th wife. Met her in Cuba. Ah, what a beauty she was. Long legs, ample . . ."

The widow cleared her throat, and Blackbeard chuckled. He was about to continue when a disquieting blast of cannon fire exploded from a nearby ship. Mrs. McNemmish screamed and ducked. "We're being attacked, captain! Shall I ring the bell, or prepare a cannon?"

Blackbeard laughed merrily and offered the widow a hand up. "The blast was a greeting, madam. See how Major Bonnet's ship approaches. Mr. Howard! Send the major a welcoming blast. Have him come about and climb aboard!"

"Aye, sir!"

Blackbeard and Mrs. McNemmish stood beside the rope ladder as the *Revenge* sailed alongside the *Queen Anne's Revenge* and Major Stede Bonnet climbed aboard. In a rather comical, exaggerated action, he saluted

Captain Teach, then whirled around and twinkled at Mrs. McNemmish. "Enchanté, madame!"

"Delighted," squeaked Mrs. McNemmish. She bit her lip, trying not to giggle at the extraordinarily little man standing before her, dressed like a fancy, ripe blueberry. It was especially hard to peel her eyes off his foppish, blue velvet coat, his huge, blue velvet hat with a blue feather plume poking out of it, and his matching blue velvet shoes, each with a polished silver buckle adorning the top.

His frilly, white shirt collar overflowed from his waistcoat and shook with every movement of his white periwig. A pudgy, round face stood between two rolled-up curls above his ears, while the back of his head sported curly, white locks and a black-bowed ponytail. Bonnet wore white stockings that rose up and under his buckled knee britches, and he had such glowing, pink cheeks, the widow thought for certain he used "powdered blush number three." His short, stubby fingers were hidden beneath a pair of white cotton gloves and were bedecked with an assortment of large, mostly blue-jeweled rings perched on all ten digits. A fancy lace handkerchief floated out of his right coat sleeve, and a single eyeglass hung around his neck.

Blackbeard hid his grin under a bent forefinger. "This is my newest mate," he told Bonnet as way of an introduction.

"Brilliant!" cheered the gentleman, bowing low to an extended foot. "Bloody well done."

Theodora glanced up at Blackbeard and mouthed, "You've got to be kidding!" She returned to Bonnet and grinned. "How do you do, sir?"

The little man rose and smiled brightly. "I am Major Stede Bonnet, gentleman pirate. And ye are . . .?"

"Mrs. Theodora Teach McNemmish. Mate's apprentice to Edward Teach. Welcome aboard the *Queen Anne's Revenge*."

"Relative to Blackbeard! Oh! Bloody lucky you! So glad to make yer acquaintance. Bloody lucky of me, don't ye know."

"Bloody lucky," snickered McNemmish.

Stede Bonnet reached over and shook Blackbeard's hand. "Granddaughter?" inquired the man.

"Niece," answered Blackbeard. "Just joined the ranks of the Brethren."

"Good for you!" exclaimed Mr. Bonnet. "Well done!" He applauded the widow.

Mrs. McNemmish laughed out loud. "I really like him," she whispered into Teach's ear. "So," she asked Bonnet, "made any conquests lately?"

"Oh, dear me. Not a one. Bad luck and all that, you know. Joined the Brethren of the Coast, but can't seem to steal. Sad stories and all. Always see to the needs of the unfortunates I come across. Yer bloody good though," he told Blackbeard. "Took me fer a ride, eh, what? Old Topsail Inlet was a coup. Forgive and forget, I say. Old Harriot took me lot again. Twice in a fortnight, don't ye know. I could use a few pirating tips."

Teach rubbed his beard, then spread his large wing around his short, pudgy friend. "Quit while yer ahead. That would be me best advice. Though yer very welcome to sail with us. I'll just borrow yer schooner *Revenge* and hand it over to me mate Richards for a spell, and ye shall stay aboard me own fine ship."

"Oh, I see. Well, then. I shall be your guest. A guest of the Brethren. Well done! Bloody good advice." He removed a small, silver snuff box from his pocket, put a pinch of snuff in each nostril, then sneezed in a delicate, high pitch into his handkerchief.

"Now then," grinned Blackbeard as he led Stede Bonnet toward the captain's quarters. "What cache have ye got aboard yer sloop? Or did Harriot get it all?"

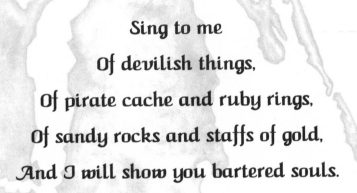

Sing to me
Of devilish things,
Of pirate cache and ruby rings,
Of sandy rocks and staffs of gold,
And I will show you bartered souls.

CHAPTER VI

"Harold! You'd better take a look at this." James Leonard, a tall dark-complected man who was gray-haired and old for his 55 years, walked briskly over to his partner's desk at the *Arlington Parade* magazine and plunked down an opened newspaper. He pointed a slightly tremulous, immaculately manicured finger at a column on page four.

Harold Owens peered over the rim of his dirty eyeglasses and blinked. "What's this?"

"Read it," James said, sounding urgent. "It's a story the Associated Press picked up off an Outer Banks newspaper."

Harold Owens checked his watch and scowled. He was pressed for time. The deadline for the magazine was only two hours away, and he hadn't finished proofing it so it could be put to bed. Reluctantly, he picked up the newspaper and sat back in his oversized chair.

He was an extremely large, nearly bald man who had the habit of combing what oily hair he had left from one side of his head to the other. While reading, he pulled out a handkerchief and blew his nose, neglecting to clean the orifice completely.

He readjusted his reading glasses and finished perusing the article. It read, "Armed with two ancient, barely legible tickets and a boatload of curiosity, 13-year-old Stefanie Austin, 13-year-old Daniel Garrish, 14-year-old Billy O'Neal, and 11-year-old Mark Tillet are headed for the county seat in Williamsburg, Virginia to reclaim pirated items. Students of the Ocracoke Island School, they are prepared to research the items listed on two tickets they discovered in an undisclosed place. Their ultimate goal is to return the articles to the descendants of those rightful owners who lost them to land pirates nearly 300 years ago. They will embark on their journey Friday when they arrive in Williamsburg to begin their research alongside the Minister of Antiquities."

Harold leaned forward and plunked down his glasses. He looked up at James and shrugged. "So?"

"What do you mean, 'So'? You don't find that remotely interesting? The fact that those kids have 300-year-old grounding tickets, they know the stuff is kept in Williamsburg, and they're from Ocracoke Island?" He tapped the article with his finger. "Admit it, Harold. This is more than a coincidence."

Harold pocketed his damp handkerchief, finished cleaning his nose with the side of his hand, then reread the article. He shook his head doubtfully. "I don't care what it says or where those kids are from, there's no way they have grounding tickets. In the first place, in all of our research we've never proven there really were such tickets. We haven't found any evidence confirming that land pirating even existed. Any one of those stories could have been fabricated and rumored. Besides, there were no land pirates on Ocracoke. Why would someone down there have tickets?"

"So, what are you saying? That a couple of disgruntled pirates claimed they lured in ships at Nags Head and stole their booty just so they'd look good? How do you know those tickets weren't left to someone who lived on Ocracoke? They might have been lying around in some family's attic for centuries, for all we know."

"If these kids have what they think are grounding tickets, they've been hoodwinked. The tickets are probably bogus and were discovered in some old trunk behind grandma's wardrobe. You know as well as I do that half the stuff written in pirate journals is a lie, and the other half is an exaggeration. Besides," added Harold, "if there really were such things as grounding tickets, they would have been destroyed the second the cache was taken off the ship. If a pirate was caught with proof of a planned looting, he and his captain were hanged." Convinced of his own opinion, he shook his head. "It doesn't wash."

"It couldn't wash any cleaner, if you ask me." James took the newspaper back to his own desk and sat down. He was a meticulous man, and his orderly desk exemplified the fact. He adjusted his silk tie, then unbuttoned and buttoned his suit jacket in an attempt to get comfortable. But he wasn't comfortable. The article upset him. He reread the paragraph for the third time. "You're wrong, Harold. These kids are on to something." He turned his chair and faced his partner. "If they have real grounding tickets, they could lead us straight to Spottswood's loot. No one has ever gotten into those crates. Those tickets are the ticket."

"If they exist, and if they're legit."

James took in a long breath of air and rapped his pencil on the table. His mind was spinning. He was obsessed with the article. He knew Harold was right about one thing: With all of their own research into pirate treasures and stolen booty, they found that the only real proof connecting land pirates and grounding tickets to impending plunderings rested in the very diaries and journals the descendants of the pirates refused to share. Both he and Harold had tried on several occasions to speak to descendants who lived in Bath and neighboring cities in North Carolina. Not to mention, pirates were known to speak in half-truths and exaggerations at best. But, something rang true about this article.

He narrowed his eyes at his partner of 25 years and interrupted him once again. "Why would kids from Ocracoke Island, the home and site of Blackbeard's beheading, go to Williamsburg, Virginia to retrieve pirated goods if they didn't really have grounding tickets? They'd have to know the stuff was being stored in Williamsburg, which gives veracity to their story. Obviously the children knew Williamsburg was the seat of government back then, and it's where Maynard's men brought Teach's head to present it to the sitting judge. That's in schoolbooks. But how would they know that confiscated booty was being stored there? Nobody knows that except the people who work there, and they're hush-hush."

Harold sneezed into his used, damp handkerchief and sniffed. "You're making a big deal out of nothing," he said while clearing his throat. "Whatever those tickets are, they're a dead end."

James rubbed his forehead nervously. "I'm sorry, but we've been researching land pirating for 25 years. I've read entire library shelves filled with books and articles going back to the 18th century, and now four kids come along and waltz into the minister's office with what might be actual grounding tickets? And what about the letter? You've had the letter authenticated. What if they found the loot referred to in that letter? Excuse me," James spat, his anger rising, "but I have no intention of letting four snot-nosed ankle-biters butt in line! If they have legitimate tickets, I want them, and I don't care how I get them. I've worked too hard and waited too long for a break like this to let someone else walk away with the prize."

Harold drew a red line through a sentence at the bottom of the last page of the magazine, called for his secretary, and threw down his glasses. Turning his chair toward James, he rocked back so far he nearly tipped over. His partner was right. There was the letter to consider. He went to the file cabinet and pulled out a copy of the original letter he acquired at an auction ten years earlier. The original letter was being safely guarded in a nearby bank vault. He reread it to himself.

"From Stede Bonnet to my niece Priscilla Farnsworth of Bath, North Carolina, in America, whom I keep in my most sacred confidence," the letter read. "I have sent this birthday token to you by way of my personal assistant so I am confident of its arrival. I pray this gift will meet with my sister's approval, knowing your age may be shy for such a splendid golden trinket. Since she would not approve of the way said gift was obtained, I ask you not to share this letter, as is usual. I am confident you will be amused by the tale. It unfolded thus. While on route to Cuba, I overtook a schooner. On board the schooner, I met a pirate who was carrying a most brilliant prize. A few months earlier, a different pirate had managed to unburden the Abbey of some of its multitude of abundance, leaving the Abbey in considerably more likeness to the poverty the church and its royal highnesses speak of. The treasure had changed hands a multitude of times prior to the pirate aboard the schooner, who had recently obtained it, though I did not ask how. However, I truly believe he had done all involved a favorable deed. Such wealth should be distributed to such caring souls as myself, who would bring a more lucrative life to an abundance of others, such as friends and family, and would make use of these gifts for much more auspicious good. The adventure of winning a fight and looting was indeed stimulating."

The letter continued, "I later met up with several Brethren on the island of Ocracoke, where we celebrated a fortnight and where I heard rumor that my friend Teach had obtained and hastened off with a precious prize unlike any have absconded with in the history of piracy. Blackbeard, himself, would not speak of the treasure, except to say that he believed it to be of greatest importance. In Topsail, Teach and a fellow pirate, Hands, helped themselves to my ship full of loot, leaving my boat floating while I went to Bath for a pardon. Bloody bad luck for me, eh? Before I left for Bath I had pocketed the trinket I have now sent to you. I shall meet with Teach in three months' time and will hopefully look upon his mysterious cache and hear its tale. I have n'er seen the man as secretive or guarded. Your aunt wishes you well, as do I. Take great care. Your loving uncle, Stede Bonnet."

Harold glanced across the desks at James. "Let's just say, for a lark, that the tickets are real. Exactly how do you plan to get them? Steal them?"

"If I have to."

"Right."

James snapped his fingers and rushed to his computer. "Maybe some other papers have picked up the story. One of the North Carolina papers might have written a more complete article." While he searched for other articles he told Harold, "If those kids have real tickets, that means they had access to some kind of cache. We'll have to find out what else they discovered. If even one item can be traced back to one of the English robberies, we can probably find out which ship it came off of. My God, Harold! This could lead us to Blackbeard's treasure that Bonnet wrote about."

"Now you're really dreaming," said Harold. He handed the magazine to his secretary and sent her to put it to bed for the next day's release. He returned to James. "First of all," he said in a calculating voice, "there are a whole lot of 'ifs' to get through. We don't even know what the treasure is, or if there really is a treasure. Secondly, if the tickets are real and if the kids get in to see the minister, we're still no closer to the truth. Not without the booty itself. Look, whatever you decide to do, just make sure you do it on your own time and not on the magazine's."

James took out a mirror, checked his perfectly coiffed hair, then returned to his computer screen. He logged on to the website for Ocracoke Island. It was a picturesque tour of a small village surrounding Silver Lake harbor. Just outside the mouth of the lake was the Pamlico Sound, which led to Teach's Hole where Blackbeard was beheaded. Beyond the hole, the narrow inlet led to the Atlantic Ocean.

One area of the website looked promising: "Pirates of the 18th century." James read that it wasn't just Blackbeard who frequented the island. Apparently, pirates who sailed with Teach but were not captured and killed came back to live on the island where their descendants still resided. William Howard, Blackbeard's quartermaster, had returned and purchased the island, and it was his descendants who owned and ran many of the stores and motels. James was somewhat versed in the connection between Blackbeard and Ocracoke Island because of other dealings he had had with a piece of scum named Zeek Beacon. But he was unaware that so many other families were related to the pirates that sailed with the infamous buccaneer. Five hundred families, to be precise. If the four children were descended from pirates, they may not only have tickets in their possession, but some of the pirated loot as well!

James logged off the computer, dusted the keyboard, then closed it up for the night. "I've got to meet those kids and get a look at those tickets. I'm not going to let 25 years of research go down the drain while some young upstarts waltz in and take the loot. Not when I've got buyers on five continents." He checked his calendar. It was already Thursday afternoon, and the children were expected to arrive in Williamsburg the next day. "I'll go to the minister's office and sit there all day waiting for those kids to arrive if I have to."

"And then what?" Harold, too, was hastily straightening his desk as he prepared to leave for the day. His idea of straightening was to make sure nothing that had fallen on the floor stayed there long enough to be swept away by the night clean-up crew. Ruminating on what James had said, he let out a loud grunt, swung his legs upward, and stretched his feet across the top of his desk. The bottom of his right shoe had the remains of dog dung that he had stepped in on the way to work that morning. Oblivious, he reached into his top drawer, withdrew a cigar, bit off the end, and lit up. He puffed several times and sighed satisfactorily.

"Give me the paper," Harold relented. He took it from James and reread the article while combing his long stretch of hair from one side to the other. He then wiped his comb clean of oil on his rolled-up, long-sleeved shirt, and tucked it back into his pants pocket.

"Give the Associated Press a call and find out what newspaper had the original story. Then get in touch with someone at that paper and see if you can trace the reporter. Bribe him for the story if you have to.

"Next, call down to Ocracoke Island and get someone to talk to you. See if Beacon's on the island. He's always coming to me looking for a cash cow. Tell him we're doing a story on the Outer Banks' history, or something numbing like that. If Beacon finds out what we're really doing, he'll glom on.

"Oh! And find out who the elders are down there. They tell the best stories. See if they have their own island rag. It might be carrying the story of the kids coming up to Williamsburg. Maybe someone on the island clips articles and can come up with something more than the press wrote. And for heaven's sake, find out where those tickets came from. That'll tell us whether or not it's the real deal."

Tom smiled coyly, "I figured you'd come around."

"I'm not saying I have. What I am suggesting is that you track down as much information as possible. We can't do anything until we know more of the story. If those tickets are legit, I want to know exactly where they came from and what's written on them."

"I've waited a long time for a break like this," exclaimed James.

"Then don't blow it. You can't just hang around the minister's office without a plan. Besides, he'd recognize you and know you were up to something. You'll have to wait until the kids meet with him and see if they're taken to the storeroom. We'll let the kids do the groundwork for us, then find a way to get those tickets. The Colonial Williamsburg Foundation is not about to hand over any of its precious collection, I'm fairly certain of that."

James sat back and closed his eyes. "What if we had papers? What if we could show proof that we could find the descendants of the owners and return the items to England or wherever they came from? The minister might turn the loot over to us."

"Where exactly are you going to get the paperwork?" asked Harold.

James smiled. "From the printer."

Harold chuckled. "Forgery. How original. Listen to me. You'll need to meet with the children while they're in Williamsburg. Find out where they're staying, where they're going to eat, and so on. And take a camera with you. Tell them you want a picture of them for our magazine. Be sure to get some shots of the tickets."

James nodded. "I'm about to become indispensable to them. After all, I'm the only one who can possibly connect the items to a particular robbery. It might be the loot from the Abbey robbery the letter talks about. Those kids need me. Let's just make sure they know that."

James could taste his first inkling of success. All those years of research, metal-detecting, begging the Minister of Antiquities to let him go through the crates of rumored pirated loot . . . . He sharpened the six pencils standing at attention in his pencil holder as he stared out of the seventh-floor window. He could see the cleaning crew in the office across the causeway. He wasn't happy with his cleaning crew. They weren't thorough. He looked at Harold, who was retrieving his coat and scarf from the hook on the wall.

"There is one problem," ventured James. "Once those kids get in to see the minister, everyone in Williamsburg will know about them and their tickets. There might even be a reporter traveling with them."

Harold shook his head and sniffed. "I doubt it. Those people haven't got a clue as to what they might have." He suddenly looked up sharply. "Go home and pack. Drive down to Ocracoke first and find someone who will talk to you. Money opens a lot of mouths. Use bribes if you have to, especially with kids. I'm sure those youngsters have friends who are more than willing to share a story for a price. Try and make the last ferry. Otherwise, sleep over on Hatteras and go on over to the village in the morning. Find out what you can about the kids' itinerary, then go straight to Williamsburg. I want answers."

James said nothing. He grabbed his coat and ran from the room. Harold puffed on his cigar as he locked the door to the office. His heart was pounding unusually fast. For a moment, he allowed himself to daydream. "The 'prize' alluded to in Bonnet's letter." He whistled. "Now that would be a coup no matter what the prize turned out to be."

Let me share with you my past,

For I have grown in wisdom so,

And learned of stranger things by far,

Than I believed I'd ever know.

I have listened well and learned

Of foreign things and pirate lore.

I am ever changed in mind

And dream and sing the songs of yore.

CHAPTER VII

Billy left his house early Friday morning and rode his bike over to the Community Store. Clinton Gaskill was seated in his rocking chair whittling a pelican out of cedar. Next to him his beloved cat Ollie slept on the porch, shaded by the seat. Billy leaned his bike up against the store wall, then waved to Birdie who was in the parking lot sweeping sand and pebbles back into the sound. "Hey, Billy!" called Birdie.

"Hey, Birdie! Hey, Clinton." Billy climbed the steps of the front porch, read the local news on the blackboard, then sat in the rocker next to Clinton, being careful not to rock over Ollie's tail.

"You goin' to Williamsburg?" called Birdie.

"Yep. We're leaving in an hour."

"You're real lucky," said Birdie, walking over to the porch. "I like Williamsburg. It's a nice place. I had my first caramel apple in Williamsburg. Granny had one too, but her upper plate fell out when it got stuck in the caramel, so we had to get her to a dentist to glue it back in. She has no top teeth when she ain't wearin' her plate. Took almost three years for all of us to collect enough money so granny could have a plate. But the caramel apple took it right out of granny's mouth, one-two-three. Daniel told me that Williamsburg is where they took Blackbeard's head after it was cut off and they threw the rest of him in the sound. Did you know that's where they took Blackbeard's head after they threw the rest of him in the sound? Daniel told me that's where they took

Blackbeard's head. I've only been there twice. I've never been to Jamestown or Yorktown, but I've seen the boat they keep there. Looks just like the boat that attacked me and Zeek, only that one disappeared and the one in Jamestown didn't. Have you ever seen the ship? The one in Virginia, not the one that attacked me and Zeek. You should go to Jamestown and see the ship. Are Mark and Daniel and Stefanie going with you, or are they going in their own cars?" He asked all of this with his eyes glued to the pavement so he wouldn't make a mistake and look either Billy or Clinton straight on.

Billy grinned. It was hard to keep a straight face when Birdie went on one of his ramblings. "My dad and I are going with the Tillets. Everyone else is going in their own cars." Billy glanced over at Clinton, who was still chuckling at the conversation.

"Hey, Birdie, do you ever go visit Zeek in jail?"

Birdie looked up at Billy, his chameleon-like eyes facing in various directions. "Sure I do," he said excitedly. "Oh, sorry." Birdie knew he was allowed to look at Billy when he spoke and Billy wouldn't smack him like Zeek did, but he thought it was better to practice staring down at the floorboards.

"Tell me about visiting Zeek," asked Billy.

"Well, I visit Zeek on all the visiting days so he doesn't get mad at me and smack me for ignoring him. I bring him Miss May Belle's cooking. The cooking at the jail ain't very good 'cause they cook it for a lot of people. My granny used to cook stew for a lot of people and she would lose track of what she put into it, so we'd try it out on the hounds first before we ate it. If it were okay for the hounds, then we ate it. But we don't have to do that with Miss May Belle's cookin' 'cause she uses store-bought ingredients from the Community Store instead of the stuff the dogs drag in. Sometimes, when we had no money and the hounds didn't do their job, she'd cook the roadkill."

"Yuck! She really cooked roadkill?"

"Sure. Granny didn't waste nothin'. Sometimes she'd go out to the highway and wait for something to get run over, then run and pick it up and add it to the stew. She never let nothin' go to waste, like I said. We ate possum, rabbit, squirrel, groundhog, snake, birds, deer, but not my parrot except that one time when she shot it after the dog got this nervous condition cause of the 'sit, go ahead' thing."

Billy put up a hand. It was a trick the islanders used to clue Birdie that he should be quiet long enough for someone else to speak. "Uh, Birdie. Did Zeek say anything to you about the stuff we left in the tunnel? The seeds and stuff?"

Birdie lit up. "He sure did! He told me lots of stuff. And he was boiling mad when he told me. He said the treasure that was left in the tunnel belonged to him because he's Israel Hands' great-grandson and Israel Hands was Blackbeard's best friend. He said that makes the stuff more his than anyone else's because Hands would have been on Blackbeard's ship during the last fight with Robert Maynard if Blackbeard hadn't blown his kneecap out, and William Howard wasn't on the ship because he complained of his bad back, which was just plain wimpy. So none of you 'upstarts'—that's what he calls you kids— should have any of the stuff because it really doesn't belong to you. Then he said that you kids are goin' to get what's comin' to you when he gets out of prison, which I guess means he's gonna share the stuff with y'all, and that he was gonna take the stuff that was left over and pawn it and get himself off this island forever. That's when he said he was goin' to get my headlights fixed." He grinned as if he were sharing a secret. "I think he means my eyes."

"He said all that?" asked Clinton.

"Yep. He says it every time I visit him."

"Did he ask you to get the stuff out of the tunnel for him?" asked Billy.

"He sure did! He said, 'Birdie,' that's me, 'I want you to go down into that tunnel and bring out as much stuff as those mitts of yours can carry and stow it in the *Lucky Beacon*. If you don't, I'm gonna rip your throat out and use the rest of you as shark bait.' Then he told me that he'd make sure I was gettin' what was comin' to me, too. But I don't need nothin' since I got my parrot and my white seeds. Miss May Belle says I'm as rich as Midas. Midas was Greek, and he was really rich. Everything he touched turned to gold. I wouldn't want to be that rich. Just a little rich."

"So did you?" asked Billy.

"Did I what?" asked Birdie.

"Did you go down into the tunnel and take the stuff out and stow it in the *Lucky Beacon*?"

Birdie looked surprised by the question. "I couldn't do that," he told the boy. "Teddy and Todd and Miss May Belle told me I couldn't go down into the tunnel, not even to help out with the cement, until it was shored up by them people from Wilmington. But don't tell Zeek. He'll smack me if he finds out I ain't been down there yet. So, I just tell him what he wants to hear. I figure I'd go down and take the stuff out before he gets out of jail, because he'd never know the difference."

Clinton stopped whittling and narrowed his eyes at Billy. "What's going on?" he asked the youngster.

"I was just curious," he told the elder. "I thought Zeek might try and steal our stuff before the tunnel was shored up. I guess I was wrong."

"The stuff in that tunnel doesn't belong to Zeek," Clinton told Birdie. "It belongs to everyone on the island. You remember that, Birdie, or you'll have to answer to me."

"Okay, Clinton."

Billy shook his head. Talking to Birdie was like taking a ride on an out-of-control merry-go-round. "So you didn't go down into the tunnel? Not at all?"

"Nope. Not yet," said Birdie. "But don't tell Zeek."

Clinton pursed his lips and addressed Billy. "Are you sure there's nothing you want to tell me?"

"No, sir. Please don't ask."

Clinton nodded. "Okay. Just don't do anything you'll be sorry for."

"I won't." Billy was actually disappointed that Birdie

hadn't cleaned them out. Now they may never find out who did. He was sure Zeek was behind it, though. At least if Birdie had gone down and taken the stuff, they'd know where to begin. "Thanks, Birdie. I'll see you when I get back. Bye, Clinton." Billy bounced up, jumped onto his bike and returned home just as his father started breakfast. Clinton watched him until he rounded the corner and rode out of sight. "I think he's up to something," he told Ollie. "What do you think?"

The Austins were the first to load up their car and leave the house. They drove to the Tillets' house where Billy and Drum O'Neal met up with them. When the Garrishes arrived, the four families headed for the 9:00 ferry.

Stefanie put on her headset, punched up her blue, puffy pillow, scooted farther over to her side of the car, and rested her head against the back door. Taking the hint, Matt, Stefanie's brother, curled up on his side of the car with his crumpled backpack doubling as a headrest.

The ride to the Hatteras free ferry took 20 minutes. The morning had started out sunny, but clouds soon moved in and, with them, brisk air and a steady wind. Stefanie let the rocking of the ferry lure her into a light sleep as she listened to country music on her CD player. By the time they drove off the ferry and were halfway up the road toward the Hatteras Lighthouse, Stefanie was sound asleep.

She had only been asleep for a few minutes when someone kicked her awake. She figured it was Matt and kicked back. "Let me sleep," she told him.

"Arise, ye lazy landlubber! Ye have guns ta clean, swords ta sharpen, and ships ta loot. Do ye think y'are on a pleasure trip, mate, or do ye wish to see yer captain's wrath?"

Stefanie stretched and blinked her eyes until they reluctantly opened. "Captain? What captain?" She reached up to remove her headphones and discovered she wasn't wearing any. She searched for her CD player and discovered that was missing as well. "Matt?" She sat up and looked around for her brother, but he was nowhere to be seen. She suddenly realized she was freezing. Wait a minute. She distinctly remembered going to sleep in the back seat of her car. Yes. She was on her way to Williamsburg. Why wasn't she in her car on the way to Williamsburg now? Where was her car? Why was she seated on the cold, damp sand just a few feet away from the ocean?

She looked around. A folded, red cape had been supporting her head, not her blue, puffy pillow. She picked up the cape, shook off the sand, and wrapped it around her shoulders. She didn't remember owning a red cape, nor the blue dress she was wearing, nor the bonnet that covered her waist-long hair. And when had the weather turned so foul? Stefanie scooted farther back onto the beach as seafoam washed ashore just inches from where she was seated. She finally stood up and stepped back to avoid getting her lace-up shoes wet. Lace-up shoes? There was something very strange about that.

She turned her back to the sea and faced the sound side of the island. She recognized the huge mountain of sand opposite where she was standing. It was Jockey's Ridge in Nags Head. She strained her eyes, looking for sand skiers and wind surfers, but there were none. The dune was bare. Maybe it was too early. Wait. There was something else very strange. Where were the streets? Where were the cars? What happened to all of the houses, motels, and strip malls? And why were all the tourists wearing clothes like hers?

She jumped when a man tapped her on the shoulder. Stepping away, she stared at the stranger. He was dressed in torn pants, a ballooned shirt, a bandana that covered his bald head, and a braided beard. He had two pistols tucked into his belt and a sword swinging by his side. She stared at the man's hands. He was whittling candles!

Stefanie frowned and folded her arms in front of her. These were not the sort of people she was used to being around. "Who are you?" she asked the stranger. "What am I doing here? Where's my family?"

The man laughed so hard, that he coughed up phlegm and spit it out, revealing two missing teeth in the front of his mouth. "Who am I?" he asked in a cockney English accent. "What are ye doin' here?" The man clucked his tongue and slapped her on the back, propelling her forward. "Yer feelin' the drink, ye are, Mary. But what do ye expect? Ye had three pints afore breakfast."

"Mary? Who's Mary?" asked Stefanie. "And pints of what?"

The man scratched his head in bewilderment. "'Tis ale, me lady! Ye drank yerself a barrelful. Don't ye remember?"

"I don't think so!" snapped the girl. While glaring at the despicable man, she became aware of other similarly dressed men bustling around her. Some were whistling. Others were imitating her figure with their hands and winking at her. Stefanie became increasingly uncomfortable. "What . . .am . . .I . . .doing . . .here?" she enunciated slowly and loudly.

"Yer . . .job," the candle man enunciated right back. "Are ye not Jack Rackem's mate, here to help Edward Teach?"

"What? No. I'm Stefanie Austin and I'm on my way to Williamsburg to get stuff."

"Stefanie Austin? Ye be Mary Reed," exclaimed the man. He shook his head and clucked his tongue. "Ye be makin' no sense, miss. Ye had better stay away from Williamsburg if ye want to keep yer head from the noose. Don't matter none. Ye are here to do yer job, jest the same."

"What job?" asked Stefanie.

"Do ye not see that ship yonder out toward the horizon?" Stefanie looked. "So?"

"Y'are to board a boat and sail up alongside her, climb aboard, and loot her hold."

"Excuse me? Loot her hold? I don't think so!" spouted the girl. "I'm not looting anything. I'm in enough trouble. Do you have any idea what 200 hours of community service is? Boring and a waste of time, that's what it is. I have no intention of adding more hours, especially if the boys don't have to. So you can tell Jack

Rackham and Edward Teach they can loot without me."

"Don't matter how ye feels about it, miss. Ye'll be in a lot more trouble if ye don't do yer job." He turned and pointed toward Jockey's Ridge dune. "See the man draggin' his nag up yonder?"

Stefanie looked. It was true. A man was leading his horse up to the top of the dune. "So?"

"He'll be puttin' a lantern round that nag's head and bracin' 'is fetlock so he'll limp. Then the captain of that ship out there where the fog be rollin' in will think it's a ship in safe waters and aim his ship toward the light.

When the ship runs aground, ye will hop into a boat, row out to her, climb aboard, and loot her hold. Just like I said."

"No, I won't."

"Ye will, I say."

"You can say 'ye will' all you want, but I'm not doing it!" argued the girl.

"Yes, miss, ye will. For if ye don't climb aboard one of them boats, mate, ye'll be swingin' from the gallows by sunset. And that's such a pretty neck. I'd hate to see it stretched." He rubbed his hands together. "We're gonna strip 'er clean, Miss Reed."

"I'm not Mary Reed. Mary Reed died 300 years ago!" shrieked Stefanie.

"Three hundred years ago?" howled Simple. "Ye have truly scrambled yer brain."

Stefanie scrunched up her face and stepped away from the pirate. "Who are you?" she asked the appalling man.

"Don't ye remember?" laughed the pirate. "I be Simple." He bowed clumsily. "And when that ship out thar becomes me captain's ship, and after we've delved into her treasures, the ship will go to Mr. Richards, and I'll be a mate, same as ye." He looked around and spoke to Stefanie confidentially. "I heard say it's the *Adventure*. The *Adventure* is Captain Harriot's ship." Simple leaned in closer to Stefanie and whispered with breath that reeked of alcohol and raw fish. "Ye would think Blackbeard would leave his friends alone, but not he."

"First of all, you need a breath refresher," grimaced the girl, "and secondly, I just want to know where my family is." She looked around. "Where's my car?"

"Yer what, mate?"

"My car, you ditz brain! Where's my car? You know. Our van. Where is it?"

Simple looked honestly puzzled. "What be a car, mate?"

"A car! The thing you drive when you want to go someplace!"

Simple looked at Stefanie sympathetically. "Ah, don't ye worry, little lady. Perhaps 'tis the bump on yer head from the last raid makin' ye think ye sees things."

Stefanie growled. "I didn't bump my head and I didn't drink anything, and I don't think I'm seeing things. I'm not Mary Reed, and I sure as heck didn't go on any raid!" As she turned to walk away, she stumbled over something. She looked down and saw it was one of her own shoelaces that went to her high-buttoned shoes. "Excuse me, but where are my clothes?"

"They be on yer bones, miss."

"No, you fruitcake. My clothes. Not these clothes!"

"They be yer clothes," laughed a large, imposing man walking toward her. The man had a long, black beard, large hat, long coat, and thigh boots. Six guns and six knives were strapped across his chest. Simple saluted him with a fist to his forehead. "Are ye prepared?" he asked her.

"Prepared for what?"

"To do yer job." Blackbeard stood tall and commanding as he stared down at the young girl. His large features were made even larger and scarier by the shadows on his face caused by the lighted hemp cord knotted throughout his beard. When he chuckled, it was deep, cold, and ominous. His coal black eyes bore into hers while his body blocked the sun, causing a chill to run up her spine and out her neck. "Well, are ye?" rumbled the infamous pirate.

"Oh, yeah. Loot the ship. I'd rather not."

Blackbeard grinned, but evilly. "There be time fer the looting," he told her. He reached into his wide pocket and pulled out a fistful of handmade paper tickets with the date "June 25, 1718" hand scripted on one side. He thrust them at Stefanie. "Take Simple here into town and sell yer tickets to the next grounding. Tell the villagers we're bringing in the ship *Adventure* and will be looting her by midday."

Stefanie looked at the tickets. They looked like the ones she and the boys had found in the tunnel and were taking to Williamsburg. She looked up at Blackbeard and raised her eyebrows. "You're joking, right? I mean, you're not serious."

"Aye. 'Tis a good job fer a new buccaneer as yerself. Do yer job or lose yer head. Take yer pick."

Stefanie gulped. "I'll take the job. But I'm no pirate. I'm Stefanie Austin and I'm 13 years old. I'm supposed to be going on vacation. But do I get to go on vacation? Of course not. I get to go pirating with Blackbeard and Simple here, while everyone else gets to go on vacation. This is the weirdest thing that's ever happened to me. I thought finding skeletons was weird, but that doesn't even compare to this weirdness."

"What skeletons, miss?" asked Blackbeard.

"The ones you left in your tunnel."

"What tunnel might that be, miss?"

"The one on Ocracoke." Stefanie placed her hands on her hips and sneered at the towering pirate. "I'll sell your tickets, but after that I'm going to find my father's car and go to Virginia. So if you think you have another job for me, you have another thing coming."

"Silence!" thundered the man. He was shaken by the mention of his secret tunnel. "Ye will sell me tickets, then loot!"

In the darkness secrets hide,

Beyond the reach of sand and tide.

Curious fingers wander through,

But riches hide from curious view.

What was once a pirate's cache,

Now becomes a child's task.

Beware of bold and curious dreams,

Some riches should remain unseen.

CHAPTER VIII

Stefanie's eyes flew open like Venetian blinds, and she fell backward into Simple's chest. Blackbeard had suddenly become the fearsome, dreaded giant she had always heard about. His black, bulging eyes pierced her confidence. His tight, muscular chest raised and lowered with his wrath, thrusting forward the pistols and knives that crisscrossed his upper body. He lifted a hand that was big enough to squash her face with one squeeze and placed his forefinger on the tip of her nose. "Do ye hear me?"

"Y-yes, sir," she acquiesced. She reached out and took the tickets. "Bully," she mumbled under her breath. She looked at Simple and sighed. Suddenly the

odd candle man with missing teeth, no hair, and a silly grin
was the closest thing she had to a friend. "Lead on," she
told him.

"I'll take good care of 'er, captain." Simple waved a
hand and told Stefanie to follow him west toward Jockey's
Ridge. As they approached the large mountain of sand,
Stefanie noticed a few houses built on the north and south
sides of the dune. Farther on, a small town comprised of
tiny houses and a church emerged from behind the dune
on the sound side.

When they arrived at the first house, Stefanie appealed
to Simple for help. "What do I do?"

"Go ye to the door, knock, and tell 'em yer sellin' tickets to a plunderin.' Let 'em know she's a three-mast. That
means jewels and gold."

Stefanie licked her lips. Maybe this wouldn't be too
hard. She had sold Girl Scout cookies one year. No one
attacked her for that. And she had sold raffle tickets to the
church bazaar. Oh! And she had sold chances for the pick-
le jar at Tuesday night bingo. How different could this be?
"Okay, Stefanie. You can do this," she said out loud. She
looked at Simple for one last smidgeon of courage, then
walked to the door. She knocked timidly. When no one
answered, she knocked louder. A small boy answered. "Is
your mother or father home?" she asked the child.

The youngster ran and got his father. "Hello, sir. My
name is Stefanie Austin and I'm selling tickets to a plundering. We're going to loot the ship *Adventure*, and if you
buy a ticket, you can have a prize. It'll be great fun. The
horse with the lantern around its neck is walking back and
forth across the top of Jockey's Ridge to fool the captain
of the ship out in the ocean so the pirates can lure it onto

the sand to be grounded. Then y'all can loot it. When the captain and the pirates are done taking the stuff they want, you can get something with your ticket. How many would you like?"

The man looked at Stefanie for a moment, told her to get lost, then slammed the door in her face.

"That went well."

"Don't ye fret yerself none," Simple told her. He pointed to the next house. "Perhaps 'twould help if ye were a bit firmer with the folk."

"Hmmm," thought Stefanie. When she got to the second house, she tried a new tactic. She knocked on the door and waited for the lady of the house to answer. She held out two tickets. "These are tickets to a looting that is about to happen at Jockey's Ridge dune. Blackbeard is the pirate who is doing the plundering. Buy a ticket, or I'll send him over to burn your house down." The woman took both tickets.

"Ye are a fast learner," laughed Simple. Using her Blackbeard bit for the rest of the houses, Stefanie sold almost all of her tickets, casting threats of pilfering and burning. Before returning to the beach, she pocketed the last two tickets for herself.

When she returned to Blackbeard's post with money in hand, she saw a great commotion coming from the sea. Stefanie peered through the thick fog as Blackbeard's crew climbed into skiffs and headed out for the grounded ship. She jumped as a sudden blast echoed from the ship and cannon fire bit through the morning. Several bursts of flaming smoke accompanied the explosion, splintering some of the small boats that were on their way to the ship. Stefanie covered her ears to block out the screams of men falling to their death. She was appalled at the paying villagers who sat on the edge of the beach cheering and applauding the cannon fire and swordplay.

Soon the looting commenced. Someone handed Stefanie a telescope. She put it to her eye and watched land pirates leap out of their dingies and climb aboard the grounded ship. Some of Blackbeard's pirates and their captives boarded rowboats and returned to the shore. Others stayed and fought on. Stefanie watched in horror as swords were driven deep into men's guts. She cringed at the sound of pistol and rifle fire. She felt sick as she watched men fall into the Graveyard of the Atlantic.

Just then, the first boats filled with looted goods and prisoners arrived on the beach. Fights broke out as prizes were divvied up. More swordplay ensued. Pirates drew their pistols at their own comrades in competition for booty, and men began dropping like flies. Villagers quickly huddled together and moved to safety behind a dune. Simple turned to Stefanie and slapped a pistol into her hand. "Shoot!"

Stefanie stood with the pistol in her hand, her face tense with fear. "What?"

"Shoot the pistol!" cried Simple.

"Are you nuts? I'm not shooting this thing."

"Why not?" shouted Simple.

"I don't know how!" said Stefanie.

"What do ye mean? Mary Reed is a crack shot!"

"I'm not Mary Reed! I'm Stefanie Austin!"

"As ye wish, mate. But ye had better shoot. Thar's a pirate headed straight fer ye who thinks ye be stealin' his plunder!"

Stefanie froze. Simple was right. There was a pirate running straight toward her, his cutlass aimed at her throat, his eyes burning deep into hers.

Her hands shook so hard she could barely hold the gun. She lifted it and held it in front of her. BANG! The gun went off, the bullet went straight into a sand dune, and Stefanie flew backward and landed on her butt. Simple turned just in time to shoot the pirate as he came just yards away from her. Stefanie could barely breathe.

"Come on!" shouted Simple. He took her by the hand and pulled her toward a sand dune, where villagers were hiding out and watching the beach battles. "Stay here," he told her. "Blend in."

"Blend in? You've got to be kidding!" To view all the commotion that was going on around them, the people from the village who had bought tickets to the grounding had seated themselves a safe distance from the gunplay and sword fights, eating out of picnic baskets and speaking freely. The screaming had ceased. No one seemed the slightest bit concerned. The villagers watched the looting and fighting the way she watched television and movies.

Stefanie reached into her skirt pocket to see if she was carrying a pistol or knife and felt an apple she didn't know was there. She observed those around her and ate the apple while applauding the pirates who returned from the grounded ship. She wouldn't have applauded at all if the man next to her hadn't given her the evil eye.

Eventually, all of the sword fighting and gunplay ceased. Blackbeard's pirates had overtaken the ship and all its cargo. Teach let his crew of higher ranking officers board the ship and roam the decks, selecting the booty they desired. First, however, they had loaded the captain's personal dingy with his choices, and without a single objection. The lower class of officers were next to choose the cache they yearned for.

Finally, the villagers who had paid for a ticket, which purchased the right to watch the pirating, got their turn to walk the decks of the tall-masted ship. With object in hand, they handed Israel Hands their ticket. He wrote the name of the item first on the ticket and then in a ledger. He returned the ticket to the villager as a receipt and instructed them to hide it immediately. Food, clothing, chickens, and galley items were the favorite choices of the villagers. Now they wouldn't have to pay English prices for the items or be forced to pay the English tax.

One woman threw a bolt of linen over her shoulder, but the pirate in the boat wanted it for his wife. Blackbeard settled the argument. "Fetch us a pint," he ordered his man. He then turned to the lady and bowed. "Enjoy yer cloth, madam."

"I thank ye," curtsied the lady.

Stefanie felt someone grab her elbow. The next thing she knew she was being escorted to a rowboat. She was taken to the grounded ship. "Climb aboard, miss," Blackbeard invited her.

Stefanie climbed aboard the *Adventure* and was led downstairs into the bowels of the ship. Blackbeard pointed to the remaining treasure. "Because ye are not me own ship's mate, ye didn't have first pick. But there be plenty of swag left." He winked at her and slipped a couple of precious items hidden in his large pockets onto the table. Stefanie reached down and touched a delicate, gold bracelet with alternating diamonds and emeralds. She allowed her eyes to roam the galley table where the prizes were laid out. She noticed a pair of silver candlesticks. Her mother would like those. She could hide them until Christmas and then present them as a gift.

As she reached for the pair of candlesticks, a delicate hand gloved in white lace reached for the same pair. Stefanie's eyes met hers. There was something remarkably familiar about the young woman, who smiled back at Stefanie with obvious shyness. Stefanie noticed the lady had two tickets in her hand. When she saw the two tickets, she withdrew her own hand from the candlesticks and indicated that the young woman should take them. The woman curtsied to Stefanie and in a lilting, soft Southern voice said, "Thank ye, miss."

Stefanie watched the woman as she scanned the rest of the table. She was reaching for something, but Stefanie couldn't quite make out what it was. It was a silver . . .a silver . . . "Hmm. What is that?" she asked herself. "I think I've seen one before, and it begins with the letter *t*. I can't quite make it out. I just need to move a little closer. I can almost see it. It begins with the letter *t*. It begins with the letter *t*."

Stefanie was being shaken. "What begins with the letter *t*?" asked Matt. "Stefanie, what begins with the letter *t*?"

Stefanie's arm was outstretched in front of her. She was reaching for something on the back of the front car seat. She sat up suddenly. "I almost had it!" she screamed.

"Had what, dear?" asked her mother.

"The *t* thing. I could almost see it!" Stefanie groaned as she glanced out the car window. They were already at Kill Devil Hills and she could see the sand dune where the Wright brothers took their first flight. Across the street were hotels, strip malls, and houses on stilts. Stefanie closed her eyes and recalled her dream. "It was so real," she thought to herself. "He thought I was Mary Reed? Well, why not? She was a great pirate. As good as any man."

"Want to play cow poker?" Matt asked her out of boredom.

Stefanie didn't respond.

"Hey!" shouted Matt.

Stefanie faced her brother as if she were seeing him for the first time. "What?"

"Do you want to play cow poker?" repeated Matt. "It's simple."

Stefanie's eyes widened. "What did you say?"

"I said it's simple. What's the matter with you?"

"Nothing. I want to go back to sleep."

"And dream about *t* things?" teased Matt.

Stefanie threw the pillow at him. "Are we going straight to the Minister of Antiquities' office when we get to Williamsburg?"

"Todd said our meeting is later in the day," the charter captain told his daughter. "Personally, I'd like to know about those tickets as soon as we get there."

Todd Garrish, in his car, felt the same way. But the minister had asked to meet the children after three. He put a hand over his coat pocket, where the tickets were safely tucked in a plastic bag.

"I expect the four of you to be on your best behavior," Daniel's mom, Elizabeth, told him. "I don't want any surprises. I don't think I could take any more surprises."

"We're not planning to break into the minister's office, if that's what you mean," remarked Daniel.

"Please. Don't even joke about that."

Billy and his father, Drum, were traveling with Margery and Jeffrey Tillet and their children Mark and Jennifer.

"I'm hungry," announced Billy.

"You just ate!" said Drum.

"I'm a growing boy."

Mark giggled. He turned toward Billy, puffed out his cheeks, and poked Billy's stomach.

"I do not look like the Pillsbury dough boy. I'm just wide for my height."

"And getting wider," laughed Jenny.

Three more hours passed, and the four families arrived in Williamsburg, Virginia. The town was surrounded by forests, and the buildings were all in the colonial style of the mid-1700s, with outside paddocks containing sheep, horses, and goats. It was just after Thanksgiving and the Christmas decorations were already up. The streets were donned with garland and white lights. As they drove parallel to Duke of Gloucester Street, Stefanie jumped in her seat when reenactors dressed as soldiers fired rifles into the air during a pretend skirmish. "How cool was that!" exclaimed Matt.

When they arrived at the Visitor's Center, the four older children ran inside and purchased their weekend passes. First on the list was a movie about Williamsburg and the birth of democracy.

"What did Birdie say?" Daniel whispered to Billy once inside the dark theater.

"He said a whole lot of crazy stuff, but he hasn't gone into the tunnel. Zeek told him to go, but Teddy and your dad told him not to, so he didn't."

"There goes our theory."

"Maybe not. Zeek could have sent someone else."

"What if the minister lets us see the stuff, but wants the descendants to come to Williamsburg to get it?" whispered Stefanie.

"Not possible," said Daniel. "If the descendants live in England, Ireland, France, or Spain, they're not going to hop on a boat or plane and come all the way to America for a pair of candlesticks and a sterling silver toothpick."

"We don't know it's a toothpick," said Billy.

"The point is, no one's going to come all the way to America just to get some old antiques lost by their ancestors."

Mark suddenly brightened and pointed to himself, Daniel, Billy, and Stefanie.

"Forget it," said Daniel. "It took a cave-in, a hurricane, and near-death to get them to let us come here. They'd never let us go to Europe. Besides, where would we get the money to go?"

"We could have a fundraiser," whispered Stefanie. "We could have a car wash. Dingbatters are always getting their cars stuck on the beach."

"There are no tourists on the beach in the winter," Daniel reminded her.

"We'll think of something," said Billy. "We'll hit up each parent separately. Divide and conquer! They'd have to let us go to Europe if we have the stuff and come up with the money."

"A trip to Europe," daydreamed Stefanie. "That would be worth peeing in a tin can!"

Soft satin beneath my feet,

The rising and falling of gentle waves,

Secrets clutched in my heart and soul,

Tell not the visitor who asks to stay.

Songs and tales are island gifts,

A sky that smells of ocean spray,

An island rich in history,

Tell not the visitor who asks to stay.

N

CHAPTER IX

James Leonard missed the last evening ferry to Ocracoke Island and chose to sleep in his car rather than take a room at the Hatteras Motel. He stretched awake at 8:00 the next morning, changed into a freshly ironed shirt, tied his tie, reached for his neatly laid-out suit jacket and caught the 9:00 ferry after downing a cup of coffee at a nearby shop. Halfway across the small sound inlet, his ferry passed another ferry going in the opposite direction, toward Hatteras. He glanced over to where some of the passengers stood outside of their cars, enjoying the crisp, clear morning and the slightly choppy seas. James didn't know that three of the cars on board that particular ferry were headed for Williamsburg, Virginia.

When he arrived at the tiny village of Ocracoke, he pulled over and asked a bicyclist for a good place to eat breakfast. He was given directions to the Pony Island Restaurant. When he walked into the restaurant, he was immediately taken by its casual warmth. It was a homey, inviting place with wood-lined walls and rustic sea decorations that made it appear more like a private ship's galley than a restaurant. The walls of the dining room were decorated with art depicting the famous Ocracoke Lighthouse, painted on driftwood and pieces of boat piling. Carved gulls and pelicans sat on shelving that dotted each wall, and photographs of the last Boy Scout troop hung on the wall beside James's table. In front of him was a placemat that laid out a map of the village, along with a drawing of the island's famous wild ponies. A stickler for cleanliness, he was pleased. He sipped coffee and ordered breakfast, then pulled out a notebook and pencil. In a quiet moment, he called over the waitress who had served him.

"Excuse me. My name is James Leonard," he started pleasantly. "I'm with the *Arlington Parade* magazine in Virginia. I've come down here to do a story on the four children who found pirate tickets. I was wondering if you knew anything about that?"

His waitress gave a quick, sly glance at the waitress cleaning the table beside her. She pursed her lips, thought for a moment, and shook her head. "No. Can't say as I have heard anything about that. Sounds exciting, though," she admitted in her thick, Ocracoke brogue. "I did hear something about tickets, but no one told me they were pirate tickets. Did anyone say anything to you, Ruth?"

The waitress continued to gather up used plates and cups. "I do remember someone saying the tickets weren't worth anything. They can't be used for a movie, or a video, or anything. Seems they're too old." Her mouth crinkled upward into a cunning smile and she took her tray of dishes away.

"You know, I believe she's right," his waitress told him as she poured fresh coffee into the reporter's cup. "I do remember one of them saying that they had found some tickets of some kind, but they were too old to be any good. Guess they were thrown away."

James cleared his throat and took a sip of coffee. He was smart enough to know when he was getting the run-around. These two women were obviously teasing him. They knew more than they were saying, he was sure. He smiled and thanked his waitress. He had the oddest sensation that everyone in the restaurant was watching him. He waited until she put his bill on the table before he spoke to her again.

"You're positive the children didn't say anything about the tickets being part of a pirate booty? I would have thought that would be big news around here. I'd be willing to pay for the right answer."

His waitress glared at him as she put another basket of hushpuppies on the table. "No one said anything about pirate booty," she told him. "Of course, we're pretty private down here. They might have kept the information to themselves. Maybe Mickey and George over at Teach's Hole can help you. They're the pirate experts." She walked away, soon to return with his change. "You might want to lose the tie," she suggested. "By the way, nice hands. If you want to touch up your manicure, I get off at two."

"Thanks for the tip and the offer." James finished his breakfast, then followed her directions to Teach's Hole pirate museum and store. A huge sign reading "Grand Opening" welcomed him into the parking lot. He parked facing a life-sized cutout of a pirate with a place to stick your head and have your picture taken. A little girl with pigtails had her face pressed into the sign as her father stood back and took her photograph. James never understood why tourists were amused by such things. He certainly wasn't. Maybe it was just his mood. Alongside the cutout, Blackbeard's flag hung proudly from a 20-foot flagpole. James got out of his car and took a picture of both for reference. He paused a moment, removed his tie, straightened out his suit jacket, then walked up the long ramp to the entrance of the new store.

He was greeted by a young woman dressed in pirate garb who offered him a ticket to the museum in the back room. "Maybe later," he told her, and continued inside. Pirate flags measuring from one to five feet long hung along one side of the room, representing more than a dozen different pirates. Pirate books, license plates, shirts, patches, lunch pails, mugs, and statues filled the shelves around him. As he walked farther into the store, he found everything from objects of booty such as pirate coins and fake jewels, to maps, posters, and amazingly beautiful prints. Behind the glass-enclosed shelves were pistols, swords, and fancy pirate pipes. He purchased some novelties and a pipe before introducing himself.

"Are you Mickey?" he asked the proprietor.

The owner nodded. "Can I help you?"

"I hope so. My name is James Leonard," he said, extending his hand. "I came down from Virginia to do an article for the *Arlington Parade* magazine about the four children who found the pirate tickets. I was wondering if you could tell me anything about the kids or the tickets. Someone at the Pony Island Restaurant thought you might know something."

"Tickets," hummed Mickey. "Yes, I did hear about that. I think they were tickets to a plundering, but I never saw them. There's a new museum on Hatteras near the free ferry that has some of the artifacts brought up from the *Queen Anne's Revenge*. I imagine the tickets are there. Would you like to take a tour of our museum? I can start the show for you."

"I would like that. Thank you."

James paid, then walked into the entrance where he was immediately greeted by a large woodblock print of Blackbeard. The original woodblock hung on the opposite wall. Around the corner stood a life-sized statue of the pirate. The walls were covered with information about the pirate Edward Teach, including stories, legends, and newspaper articles dating back to 1719, months after he was killed in Teach's Hole off the sound side of the island. After reading the articles and looking at the various artifacts encased in glass, James sat down and watched a short video of the actor Ben Cherry dressed as Blackbeard. It was an impressive museum and show. When it was over, James returned to the counter. "How well do you know the children?" he asked Mickey.

"Very well. Mark is kin. That means *relative* to you Yankees."

James grinned. "Yes, I know what kin is. Did Mark say anything to you about the tickets?"

Mickey laughed. "Mark doesn't say much about anything."

"How about any of the other kids? Did they mention

the tickets?" He unfolded the Associated Press article and showed it to Mickey. "It says here that the tickets are 300 years old."

Mickey read the article. "That's very exciting. But I don't know any more than what's here in the newspaper. Just that the kids found some tickets that were really old. Like I said, they probably donated them to the new museum."

James shook his head. This was getting him nowhere. "Well, thanks anyway," he told Mickey.

"You might try asking around the Community Store," suggested Mickey. "Ask for Clinton Gaskill. He may know something."

"Thank you. I'll do that."

James was frustrated. He got directions to the Community Store, then drove down Route 12 and parked at the dock next to Silver Lake. Two pelicans came to the car and greeted him. James sidestepped them and walked up the front steps of the Community Store.

An elderly gentleman seated in a rocking chair was whittling a wooden duck while greeting people as they walked in and out of the grocery store. Next to the rocking chair, barely escaping a squashed tail, was the largest orange cat James had ever seen. A wooden cut out of the cat with the name Ollie written on it was nailed to the wall next to the rocker.

James opened the screen door and walked inside the dated grocery store. He was about to ask a woman at the checkout counter if she had seen Clinton Gaskill, when he spied Birdie stocking a shelf. James looked around for a moment, then stealthily approached the large, pudgy seaman.

"Birdie!" hissed James.

"Hey, Mr. Leonard!"

"Shh!" Again, James looked around. "Where's Zeek?"

"In jail."

"In jail!" exclaimed James. "What for? And talk quietly."

"Okay, Mr. Leonard. Zeek went to jail because when Theodora died we went to sea with a map Zeek found and we was going to get the booty left at the Diamond Shoals, but Blackbeard's ghost ship came by and it was awesome. It fired cannonballs at us and splintered up the *Lucky Beacon* something awful, and then Zeek got hit in the head with a belaying pin, which I took to be a baseball bat 'cause I could hardly see 'cause of the storm and all.

"Then we got grounded in the storm and I got pretty quamish, and Blackbeard's ghost ship kept blasting us while we was grounded, and we got captured by Rudy, and the kids came up missing, only I thought they were blowfish, and the widow's things were in the hold.

"A wooden cut out of the cat with the name *Ollie* written on it was nailed to the wall next to the rocker. But the kids are fine now, thank you for askin'. And the *Lucky Beacon* is fine, only it ain't bein' used 'til Zeek gets out. You want me to tell Zeek you came by? I can tell Zeek that you came by."

James Leonard had heard enough. "Who's this Clinton Gaskill I'm supposed to talk to?"

"You going to talk to Clinton? That's great! He's full of stories about the island and the history and pirates. He's right outside on the porch, whittling ducks."

James turned to leave, then turned back toward Birdie. "What do you know about grounding tickets some kids found on the island?"

The question was barely out of his mouth when May Belle tapped him on the shoulder. "I believe Birdie has work to do," stated the woman with a harsh stare.

James narrowed his eyes. "Fine," he told her. He leaned over and whispered into Birdie's ear. "Don't tell anyone I was here. Especially Zeek."

"Okay, Mr. Leonard."

James waited a moment, then walked outside and approached the old man. "Mr. Gaskill?"

Clinton never looked up from his whittling, but indicated the chair next to him. "Who wants to know?"

James sat down. "My name is James Leonard. I write for the *Arlington Parade* magazine."

Clinton continued his whittling. "Do you like ducks?"

"Excuse me?"

"I asked you if you liked ducks," said Clinton, continuing to whittle.

"I never really thought about it. I suppose so."

"I think ducks are amazing," offered Clinton. His ancient hands worked the knife with the delicacy of a surgeon as he whittled a tail feather. "Some ducks are plain, others look like they were a canvas that the Lord painted. Take the wood duck. It comes in the most amazing colors."

James was about to interject something when Clinton said, "So you want to know about the kids."

James sat up, surprised. "How did you know that?"

Clinton chuckled then reached over, grabbed his pipe, took a draw, and blew out a sweet-smelling smoke. He returned the pipe to the ashtray beside his rocker. "It's a small island, Mr. Leonard, and you're a stranger. It doesn't take long for word to get around. I knew about you two seconds after you woke up this morning."

James was uncomfortable. There was something about the man that unnerved him. It was as if Clinton Gaskill could see deep down into his soul without ever looking up and seeing his face. In some odd, distant memory, Mr. Clinton reminded James of his grandfather, who unnerved him equally. The reporter continued, "Look, I know that four kids found pirate looting tickets. What I really want to know is whether or not they told anyone what was written on them. Did the kids say what the tickets were for? I'd like to do a story about the kids and their find for my magazine. This could be really important, historic information. I understand from the article that was written, the children are up in Williamsburg for the weekend."

"You seem to know quite a bit," said Clinton. He glanced down to make sure Ollie's tail was nowhere near the rocker, then reached down and gave the cat's backside a shove, putting the tail a few inches farther away for safekeeping.

James waited. "I can't seem to find out anything else about either the kids or the tickets," he admitted. "Mickey at Teach's Hole thought you might be able to help me."

"Is that so?"

"Yes, sir. So if you could tell me how the kids found the tickets, or who the tickets belonged to originally, I'd be most indebted. Anything you can tell me would be helpful."

Clinton finished his whittling and showed the duck to James. "It's yours for six bucks," he offered the gentleman.

James reached into his pocket and pulled out a five-dollar bill and a single. Clinton smiled and made the exchange. He then put down his whittling knife, sat back in his rocking chair, and shut his eyes.

"We never had a lot of visitors on the island until a few decades ago," Clinton explained to the reporter. "After the Bonner Bridge collapsed and made the news, people started hearing about our beautiful beaches and our little village, and suddenly we were swamped with tourists and off-islanders. That new hotel over there ruined my view of the creek. Could be worse, I suppose. I've met some remarkable people." He opened his eyes and looked at the reporter quizzically. "Do you have a car?"

"Yes, sir. I'm parked right over there. Why?"

"Let's go." Clinton struggled as he pushed himself up and out of the rocker, then slowly straightened. He told Ollie to stay put, then shuffled behind James as they walked toward the stranger's car. When they got to the car, James helped Clinton into the passenger seat, then jogged over to the driver's side. The pelicans had left their calling cards on the hood of James's immaculately polished car. Clinton knew his kind and chuckled when he saw Mr. Leonard's disgusted expression.

When the reporter was settled in the driver's seat, Clinton pointed to the right side of the road, which led to the center of the small village. "This here is Cockle Creek," he told the reporter. "We call the entrance to it 'the ditch.' Most tourists call the creek Silver Lake, but to us it's just the creek. On the sound side of the ditch and down a ways is Teach's Hole, where Blackbeard was beheaded. Sold the head at auction, you know.

Today it would go for a couple of million. Think of that prize hangin' on your wall." Clinton laughed at his own joke.

"Half the families on the island are either related to Blackbeard or his quartermaster, William Howard, or one of his mates. Of course, most of the older relatives are gone now, but Blackbeard's spirit still lives here. Some people say you can see Edward Teach walking along Try Yard Bridge, leading his horse and looking for his head. Bobby

Garrish saw him once. And one of the youngsters at school saw him by the cove."

He waited a moment, then added, "I've seen the ghost lights from the *Queen Anne's Revenge*. Theodora saw them, too. The two of us were just kids when we first saw the lights while swimming off Springer's Point. Theodora's on his ghost ship right now."

"Theodora?" asked James.

"Theodora Teach McNemmish. Blackbeard's kin. They were her tickets. She was Blackbeard's great-grand-niece times three. Tickets were passed down to her. Now they belong to the kids."

"Are any of the kids related to Blackbeard?"

Clinton nodded. "Stefanie is. Can't say how, though. Generations have gotten all mishmoshed together. That's how it is on the island."

He left the subject of the tickets and continued the tour. "Now, that white building over there is The Island Inn. It's in the 'down point' side of the island. Most of the village houses are 'round creek.' Anyway, before the building was an inn, it served as one of the island's schools. Before that, the 'down point' kids boated out to Portsmouth Island. That whole island of Portsmouth is a ghost town now. Come to think of it, so's Ocracoke. That is, if you believe in ghosts." He chuckled to himself, then told James to pull over.

James pulled into a small, gravel parking lot and looked up. There, looming in front of him, was the Ocracoke lighthouse. "That white stucco building is the oldest lighthouse still in use in the state of North Carolina. It was built in 1823. It was the beacon of hope that saved many a sailor and fisherman from losing their lives during a storm."

Clinton took a moment to savor the building, then continued. "Okay. Let's go." Clinton directed James to turn around and go back to the main village. They drove through the village and up toward the northern tip of the island.

"Why are there statues of horses with wings on so many store roofs?" asked James. "I saw them on Nags Head and Hatteras as well."

"Oh, that. It was to celebrate the Wright brother's centennial. The horses represent the wild ponies that roamed the Outer Banks, and the wings represent flight." Clinton directed James to the pony pen. "These are some of the banker ponies that are possibly direct descendants of the horses that came over with Sir Richard Grenville, the leader of Walter Raleigh's second expedition. It's our pleasure to have them here. They used to run wild 'til the island got too crowded with visitors." Clinton and James paused there for a moment, then Clinton instructed James to drive north until they finally arrived at the free ferry. "And that, Mr. Leonard, is your way back off the island."

"Excuse me?"

"Leave the children to do their work and have their privacy, Mr. Leonard. You have your story. Don't go looking for another one."

Clinton got out of the car and walked over to the small coast guard station, where several ferry workers were finishing up their scheduled shift. "Can I catch a ride back to town, Wilson?"

Wilson looked up at Clinton and grinned. "Hop in." As Clinton climbed into the passenger seat, Wilson slipped into the driver's seat and leaned out the front window, calling, "Good day, Mr. Leonard. Have a nice trip home."

Is beyond, beyond?

Or is beyond here and now

In fetching dreams

And wishful minds?

Who is to say what is beyond?

Not I. For I hear the sounds

and see the sights of yesteryear.

CHAPTER X

After the movie, the families took a short tour around the colonial village. Their first stop was the courthouse. They entered the building quietly and sat in the back two rows. A man dressed in a long, brown coat with a white vest, brown pants that buckled below the knees, and a gray ponytailed wig was continuing his prepared speech. "This is the building where commoners and slaves were tried. Free people and aristocrats were tried at the Capitol. In the 18th century, if you were found guilty of perjury, you were put in the stocks outside and your ears were nailed to the back of it. When you were released, your ears were then ripped away from the nails. That way, wherever you went for the rest of your life, people would see your torn ears and know you had once been convicted of perjury."

Mark, Stefanie, and the younger kids slapped their hands over their ears.

"That's just plain nasty," squirmed Billy.

When the speech was over and everyone was back outside, Daniel ran up to the stocks and stuck his head and arms through the holes. "Billy, Mark, take my picture."

"We'll go on ahead," Elizabeth said of everyone else. "Meet us at Josiah Chowning's Tavern in half an hour."

The boys said goodbye, then Billy reached into his pocket and pulled out his camera. When he looked through the lens and zoomed in, he saw something he hadn't noticed at first. He lowered the camera and whispered something into Mark's ear. He then took his time putting the camera back up to his face. He took several pictures from different angles, encouraging Daniel to stay still. In the meantime, Mark found two sticks on the side lawn and slipped them into the hole on each side of the stocks, preventing the top from reopening. "Okay, your turn," Daniel told Billy. But when Daniel tried to stand up and get out of the stocks, he couldn't. Billy and Mark shrieked with laughter.

"Hey! Very funny!" hollered Daniel. He tried to break free, but the stocks remained locked. "Mark, let me out of here! Billy! Tell him to get me out of here."

Mark jumped up and down excitedly as Billy took more pictures. "I give ye two hours in the stocks as your punishment for being a dingbatter," joked the boy. "If ye lie, I'll nail yer ears to the stocks."

"That's not funny, Billy. Let me out of this thing!" Daniel squirmed and wiggled, but it was no use. The stocks held steadfastly. "My back hurts from standing like this!"

"That was the point," said a deep voice from behind Billy and Mark. The man in colonial costume who had been speaking inside the courthouse was enjoying the antics of the two boys. He chuckled and walked away.

"Whew," sighed Billy. "I thought we were toast."

"You've had your fun, now let me out," seethed Daniel.

Mark and Billy both turned suddenly when they heard the fife-and-drum corps marching up Market Square. "Come on, Mark. Let's go watch. We'll see you at the tavern, Daniel. Don't do anything we wouldn't do." Billy grabbed Mark's arm and ran after the musicians dressed in red coats. "We better hurry before someone lets him out," laughed Billy.

Daniel screamed at their backs. "Hey! Where are you going? Come back here and get me out of this. Hey, y'all! Let me out of here!"

Neither Mark nor Billy looked back. They simply laughed as they blended in with the crowd on Duke of Gloucester Street. Abruptly Daniel stopped screaming. Billy looked over his shoulder. A sympathetic tourist had taken pity on Daniel and unlocked the stocks. "Oh, shoot! Mark! Run!"

"Oh, no you don't!" screamed Daniel. He tore after the two boys with the intent of inflicting harsh pain on both.

Billy and Mark darted in and out of tourists, revolutionary war reenactors, and horses and buggies, with Daniel charging after them. Suddenly an arm came up and grabbed Billy and Mark from behind. Daniel caught up with the two villains and lunged for Billy, but the statesman dressed in colonial attire stopped him. "Let's take it down a few notches, shall we?" he asked the kids.

"Thanks a lot for leaving me in the stocks," heaved Daniel.

"Just calm down, all of you." The statesman addressed all three boys. "I know you're here to have fun, but you have to stop running around like that. There are too many people and too much commotion going on. It's okay to enjoy the place, but you're in a park where horses can get spooked easily. They're used to gunfire and crowds, but not people running in and out of the street. Where are you from?"

"Ocracoke Island," said Billy.

"Well, then, this is quite different from your home. Have fun while you're here, but take it easy."

By the time Daniel started explaining, the statesman was gone. "Thanks a lot," he told Billy. "You too, Mark." Billy threw his arm around Daniel's shoulders and aimed him toward the cobbler's bench across the street. But Daniel shook loose and headed elsewhere.

"Where are you going?"

"To talk those soldiers into using you as target practice."

Mark and Billy finally coaxed Daniel's good humor to return and the three of them walked to Josiah Chowning's.

"So? What did y'all see?" asked Elizabeth.

"Mark and Billy locked me in the stocks."

Stefanie laughed. "Wish I'd been there."

"Wish you'd been the one locked in the stocks."

A waitress dressed in a long skirt, puffy blouse and round cap, and a man dressed in a long coat, knee-length pants and round cap came outside and invited the fourteen visitors to follow them inside. "Welcome to Josiah Chowning's Tavern. It's spelled 'Chowning,' but pronounced 'Chooning,'" she explained. "This tavern was built over its original foundation dating back to 1774. We've joined two tables so you can sit together. Help yourselves to the peanuts, and your server will be with you soon."

Inside the white clapboard building were wide-planked floors, high ceilings, and a staircase leading up to the second floor. There were two dining rooms. The four families were led to the right dining room, where they sat at wooden tables with bench seats.

Mark pointed to the unusual window glass. "It looks like that because of the way glass windows were made back then," Jeffrey explained to his son. "Glass is actually a liquid that moves really slowly. That's what makes old glass sag in the center."

When everyone was seated, they passed around the baskets of peanuts. A moment later, two violinists dressed in colonial apparel strolled into their dining room. One musician had a regular-sized violin. The other musician had an instrument called a pouchette, or a pocket-sized violin. They played music from the 18th century and encouraged the families to sing along if they knew the tune. No one sang, but Billy took pictures.

When their snacks arrived, Todd rose to his feet. He held up his thick, blue-and-gray mug filled with root beer. "I'd like to offer a toast to Mrs. McNemmish. Thank you for passing your history onto our children. If you're watching from above, Miss Theo, I hope the kids prove you right in entrusting them with the tickets. To Mrs. McNemmish."

"To Mrs. McNemmish," cheered everyone.

Stefanie finished her second root beer, then called a costumed waiter to her side. "Where's the restroom?" she whispered discreetly.

"It's outside," Daniel told her. "They didn't have indoor plumbing back then."

The waiter smiled. "We've redecorated since then. You'll find the ladies' room through that door, at the top of the stairs." He winked at Stefanie, then told the boys, "Only the men's room is outside."

Stefanie left the table. She was halfway up the staircase when a gentleman dressed in a powder-blue velvet suit blocked her way. Stefanie guessed him to be either one of the waiters or one of the musicians. In addition to the blue suit, the man wore a white frilly shirt that puffed out from his neck and coat sleeves, high white stockings that met his pants at his calves, and high-heeled, silver-buckled, square-toed shoes. He was carrying a handkerchief in one hand, which he kept waving in the air as if he were striking at invisible insects. He held an elaborately decorated ale stein in the other. A large, blue wide-brimmed hat flaunting a long, blue-feather plume donned his round, rather pudgy head, which was outlined in white curls. He was a short, stout man and had a pleasant grin and a twinkle in his eye. He bowed to Stefanie by extending one foot and bending over. Stefanie nodded her head, then excused herself and tried to move around him, but the gentleman continued to stand in her way.

"Excuse me," said Stefanie. "May I get past?"

The gentleman didn't seem to hear. "May I be of service to ye, miss?" He asked in a lilting accent.

"What's with the 'ye' stuff again?" she asked herself. She answered, "I need to go upstairs to the bathroom."

The gentleman looked honestly confused. "The bathroom. The bathroom. Ah! Yes. Ye wish to use the necessary. 'Tis out back, miss."

"Excuse me?"

"Ye wish to use the necessary."

"The necessary?" queried Stefanie. "No. I don't need a necessary, whatever that is. I just want to go upstairs to the ladies' room."

"I understand ye, miss," said the gentleman. "But the necessary is out of doors. 'Tis located just behind the garden wall for privacy. Would ye like me to escort ye?"

Stefanie wrinkled her eyebrows, then narrowed her eyes and glared at the man. "First of all, what's with all this 'ye' stuff? I had enough of that selling tickets. Second, I don't go anywhere with strangers and—I don't mean to be rude—but you're about as strange as it gets. And third, it's not 'necessary' to go outside when the bathroom is right upstairs. But!" she exclaimed to the foppish-looking gentleman, "I can't go upstairs because you're standing in my way. So if you wouldn't mind moving over, I really have to pee." She tried to sidestep the man, but again, he purposefully blocked her way.

"Look, mister. I have to pee *really, really* badly. I drank two root beers."

The man waved his handkerchief in the air, took a drink from his ale stein, then put up a gloved finger to speak. Stefanie couldn't help but notice the enormous, blue ring that sat perched at the base of his forefinger. The man perused her up and down with curiosity. "Of what manner of form and fashion do ye wear? I do not recognize this strange dress ye have adorned yerself in. Are ye foreign?"

"Say what?" asked Stefanie.

"Why are ye dressed in this odd manner of costume?"

"Whoa. Why am *I* dressed in an odd costume? *You're*

the one standing here dressed in historical stuff. Are you a waiter or a musician?"

"Madame, you have affronted me to the very core." He pulled out his lacy handkerchief and foppishly dabbed his forehead. "I am neither a server nor a minstrel. I am a guest of Mr. Chowning's, who resides in this ordinary. I am accustomed to dressing for dinner. I see that ye are not."

"Hey! There's nothing wrong with the way I'm dressed. You're the one dressed like a blueberry. Besides, Chowning's is casual. Are you from England? You talk like you're from England. Are all English actors rude, or just you?"

"Actor? I am no thespian, madame. I am a businessman and farmer. I am English, however. Bloody clever of ye to notice. I reside in Barbados. I have a large plantation. I grow and trade sugar. And ye are from . . .?"

"Ocracoke."

"Ocracoke! Bloody lucky you. Nice place, Ocracoke! I have frequented the island many times. Many times. Do ye know Teach?"

"Teach who?" asked Stefanie.

"Edward Teach," exclaimed the man. "He often resides on Ocracoke."

Stefanie snickered. This guy's wig was on too tight. "No, can't say I've met the man. Well, actually I think I might have. But that was in a dream and dreams don't count. Except this one might have counted because I could almost see the 't' thing. And in case you were wondering, I'm not Mary Reed," she added. "Can I go upstairs now?"

"What make of shoes are ye wearing? Are they for comfort or fashion?"

"They're sneakers. That's what people wear in this era."

"And what era might that be?"

"What era do you think it is?"

"The year of our Lord 1774."

"1774! What planet are you from? If this were 1774, everyone in the restaurant would be dressed like you. But since they're all dressed like me, I guess it's not 1774."

"Everybody who?"

"Everybody, everybody," said Stefanie, pointing to the room filled with patrons.

The fop looked around curiously, then looked at Stefanie, totally bewildered. "Perhaps ye should return to yer dinner seat. I will let Master Chowning know ye called."

And with that, he turned and ascended the staircase, still blocking her way. "That's it!" bleeped Stefanie. She rushed up the stairs, squeezed past him, and disappeared down the hall. Fuming, she returned to her seat 15 minutes after leaving it. "Fruitcake."

Arise, me child.

'Tis not a dream that thou has had,

But some mystic manner ye behold.

Fear not the images that

play upon your mind.

'Tis such visions that make ye bold.

N

CHAPTER XI

"Who's a fruitcake? And what took you so long?" Stefanie's mom, Marylee, asked her. "Some man dressed in a costume wouldn't let me get past him on the staircase." Stefanie wiggled her finger and called her server over to the table. "I think you should tell your waiters that when somebody has to go to the bathroom, they shouldn't block the staircase. Who was that man, anyway?"

The waiter looked puzzled. "I apologize if someone wouldn't let you go upstairs, miss, but I'm not sure which man you're referring to. Was he in a waiter's or musician's costume?"

"Not exactly either of them. He was dressed in a blue velvet suit."

The waiter stood up straight, nearly toppling the water glass he was refilling. "He was wearing a blue velvet suit, miss?" The waiter looked around the corner at the staircase, then back at Stefanie. He suddenly paled a bit and became quite uncomfortable with the subject. Finding his voice he asked, "What else was he wearing, miss?"

Stefanie reflected for a moment. "He had on a big, blue, floppy hat with a big, blue feather sticking out of it. I remember that. And he had big, silver buckles on his shoes. And he had this lacy handkerchief he kept waving around. And he wore makeup! Talk about weird."

"Well, whoever he was, I don't like the fact that he stopped and talked to my daughter," objected Marylee.

The waiter apologized to Mrs. Austin, placed his water pitcher down on the table, and stared at Stefanie incredulously. "Let me get this straight," he said with piercing, narrowed eyes. "You say you saw a guy dressed in a blue, velvet suit with a big, blue hat with a feather in it and buckles on his shoes, and he had a lacy handkerchief he kept waving around, and he was standing on the staircase."

"Yeah. Standing on the staircase."

"Did he say anything?" asked the server.

"He said the necessary was outside."

"I told you."

"That's enough, Daniel," admonished his father.

The waiter was flabbergasted. "Wow. That is so amazing. He's never stopped anyone from going upstairs before." He mentioned this more to himself than to the families, causing great curiosity all around. "Did he say anything else?"

"Yeah. He didn't like my clothes. He said I wasn't properly dressed for dinner. Although I think he liked my sneakers. He was very rude. He said he was a guest of Mr.

Chowning's and that he'd let the man know I was here. Oh, yeah. He asked me if I knew Edward Teach."

"You're lying," Daniel accused her.

"I am not. The guy stopped me on the staircase, told me I couldn't go up to the bathroom, and then asked me if I knew Blackbeard. He said he'd been to Ocracoke."

"Maybe we should have a talk with this man," said Drum.

The server scratched his head, took a deep breath, and forced a smile. "Uh . . .you can't actually talk with him, sir. At least most people can't. Actually, I've never met anyone who could, until now, although I've heard stories about people talking to him. He's never stopped anyone from going to the bathroom before."

"Well, why can't we talk to him?" asked Marylee. "He has obviously upset my daughter."

"He didn't upset me," said Stefanie. "He just wouldn't let me pee."

"How come everything happens to you whenever you have to pee?" asked Daniel.

"That's enough, Daniel. Drum's right," said Elizabeth. "We didn't come here to have one of our kids upset. I really think we should speak with him."

The waiter grimaced. "You can't."

"Why not?"

"He's dead."

"He's what?" erupted the group.

"He's dead," repeated the waiter.

"What do you mean, he's dead?" asked Drum. "Dead, dead?"

The waiter nodded. "He's an apparition. Says his name is Major Stede Bonnet. He was a pirate. He's been dead for nearly 300 years. According to himself, he was hanged in 1718 but visits here in 1774. It's like he knows he's a ghost."

Daniel looked at Stefanie, wiggled his fingers at her and made a spooky *woooo* sound.

"I said that's enough, Daniel." Todd closed his eyes and shook his head. Everyone else just stared at Stefanie.

"That man was not an apparition or a ghost," insisted Stefanie. "Apparitions don't appear on a staircase, keep you from peeing, and compliment you on your sneakers! Besides, you can see through ghosts. I just talked to him five minutes ago. He's probably still in the tavern. Someone in that room probably saw us standing on the stairs. Go ask someone in there."

"They wouldn't have seen anything, miss, except for you talking to yourself. That's all they ever see. Only about a dozen people over the past 50 years have admitted to seeing and talking with the gentleman. And they've all described him exactly the same way you have: blue velvet suit, big hat with a feather. And he's always standing on the staircase, but as far as I know, no one has ever complained that he wouldn't let them go to the ladies' room. He does tell everyone that he's a guest of Mr. Chowning's. But I've never heard anyone say that he commented on their attire." The waiter suddenly looked at Stefanie and gasped. "Oh, my gosh!"

"What's the matter?" asked Marylee.

The waiter looked as if he were about to burst with news. "You're a hyraphyte!"

"A what?" shouted everyone.

"A hyraphyte!" exclaimed the waiter. "I've never met a real one, but that would explain everything! Oh, my gosh. An actual hyraphyte right here in Chowning's Tavern!"

"What the dickens is a hyraphyte?" asked Stefanie's father, Jackson.

The waiter was beside himself with excitement. He reached for an empty chair and joined the families at the two tables. "I've been studying about this in my parapsychology class at William and Mary. A hyraphyte is a living person who can bridge two worlds: the world of the living and the world of the dead. You see, a ghost can't be seen in the flesh or do physical things in the present-day world unless there's a hyraphyte enabling him by connecting the two worlds! So if a ghost wanted to do something in the present world, he wouldn't be able to do it without the presence of a hyraphyte. Wow! I'm so honored to meet you," gushed the young man.

"Then you'd be the first," teased Matt.

"I still don't get what a hyraphyte is," said Billy.

The waiter thought for a moment. "A magnet is just a magnet if you're holding it, right?"

"So?"

"But if you have a metal door, the magnet has something it can grab on to," said the waiter. "She's like a metal door," he said, pointing to Stefanie, "and the ghost is the magnet that finally has a place where it can stick and show itself off. Without the metal door, the magnet's just a piece of metal that can't be seen for what it is."

"So, you're saying, Stefanie is like a refrigerator door?" laughed Daniel.

Everyone at the table laughed, so the waiter tried a different tactic. "You know how when you go into a dark room, you can't see the color of anything?"

"Okay, yeah," agreed everyone.

"Well, you can see the color once you shine a light on it."

"What's that got to do with refrigerator doors?" asked Matt.

"A hyraphyte acts like a light. When there's a hyraphyte present, a ghost can be seen for who he or she is and can physically do things they couldn't otherwise do in the present world."

"So if you put the two things together, you have Stefanie as a refrigerator door who always keeps her mouth open in order to shine her light!" Daniel concluded proudly.

All four families looked at Stefanie and burst out laughing hysterically. Stefanie wasn't at all amused and kicked Daniel in the shin.

"Hey! What are you kicking me for? Everybody else is laughing, too."

Todd quickly apologized to Stefanie, then asked the waiter to please remove his chair and leave the table. "But thank you for your insight," he said, sounding somewhat baffled.

The young man caught Todd's drift and left the room. Poking his head back in he told Stefanie, "I'm really glad to meet you."

"I haven't been around that much manure since the last time I cleaned out a stable," chuckled Drum.

"This is ridiculous," said Jackson. "My daughter is not a ghost magnet. This must be their version of a tourist joke."

"No, sir," piped up the waiter who had listened in on the continuing conversation. He walked back to the table. "Ask anyone who works here, and they'll tell you that they've heard stories about this fop ghost who claims the year is 1774 and he's here as a guest of Mr. Chowning. He also says he hung out with Blackbeard in 1718 before he was killed, and that he was a pirate himself, although not a very successful one. Now he hangs out at the tavern and talks to people. Not very often, though. There aren't a whole lot of hyraphytes in the world."

Stefanie scrunched up her face. "Well, if he is a ghost, he's a rude one," she said firmly.

"Well, I'd love to have him apologize to you, miss. But since I nor any of the staff have ever seen him, that would be impossible. Let me apologize on his behalf."

Mark looked at Stefanie and shrugged.

"No way," she told him.

"No way, what?" asked Margery Tillet.

"He wants me to go back on the stairs and see if the ghost comes back."

"Hey, give it a try," Billy urged her.

"No. I am so done with dead people."

"Hey, Stefanie," laughed Daniel. "You're more popular with dead people than you are with the living."

"Wanna find out?"

"No really," Daniel told her seriously. "What about all those voices you heard in the tunnel?"

"You heard voices in the tunnel?" Matt asked his sister.

"You know what?" said Billy. "I'll bet you have an extra brainwave or something that taps you into dead people's brains."

"If I have an extra brainwave, it's because y'all are missing some of yours."

Conversation became pretty animated after the waiter left. Waiters and waitresses throughout the tavern stopped by and poked their heads into the room, trying to get a peek at their special guest, the hyraphyte. When the families were ready to leave Chowning's, the costumed manager approached their table and spoke to Todd. "Excuse me, sir. A gentleman from the *Arlington Parade* magazine wishes to speak to you."

"The *Arlington Parade* magazine? Did he say what he wanted?"

"He says he wants to meet the kids from Ocracoke."

Todd look dubious. Why would someone from a magazine wish to speak to the kids? More importantly, how did he know they were eating at Chowning's?

"I don't like this," said Elizabeth.

"Neither do I," agreed Todd.

"Maybe you'd better go talk with him," suggested Jeffrey Tillet.

Todd paused for a moment, then got up and followed the manager to the front foyer. The gentleman waiting to see the kids led Todd outside.

"My name is James Leonard," he said, extending his hand to Todd. "I'm with the *Arlington Parade* magazine. I understand that you and your families are here in Williamsburg with the intent of collecting pirated goods. The magazine feels this would make a fascinating story. Is there any chance I could interview the kids while you're here in town? I'd love to take a photo of the tickets. We can make it worth your while," he said, fingering a wad of cash in his pocket.

Todd shook James's hand quickly. He didn't trust the man. "Look, Mr. Leonard. I don't know how you found out about the kids, or how you heard we were eating here, but publicity is out of the question."

"Actually, we picked up the story from the Associated Press," explained Mr. Leonard. "We think the public would be fascinated with the story of the children returning plundered goods to the descendants of those who lost them. We wouldn't get in the way of their research."

Todd held his temper and tried to appear civil. "Like I said, I'm not sure how you found out we were at the tavern, but I don't want these kids followed or interviewed by anyone. They don't need publicity, and they don't need a bunch of people keeping track of their whereabouts. I don't know how the Associated Press got the story, but it's not going any further. Now if you'll excuse me, I have to get back to my family." He turned abruptly and walked back into the tavern.

"Who was that?" Margery asked him.

"Are we going to be famous?" asked Jennifer Tillet.

Todd sighed. He wished the story had never been released to the press after coming out in the Hatteras paper. "It was a magazine reporter. He wanted to do a story on the kids. I don't like the fact that he knew where we were eating. He either followed us here, or asked questions before we got here. We're going to have to be careful. I don't want press coming out of the woodwork and making more of this than it is."

"What's wrong with the magazine finding out?" asked Billy.

"Yeah," agreed Daniel. "We can use some publicity. Then the minister would have to help us."

"We're here to do a job, not get our pictures in the paper," Todd said firmly.

"I think it would be cool getting our picturth in the paper," lisped Lena, Daniel's sister.

Matt agreed. "Billy, Daniel, Stefanie, and Mark got all the attention when they got stuck in the tunnel. I think it's our turn to get some attention."

"And the Minister of Antiquities can't turn us down if everyone reads about us in the magazine," argued Daniel. "He'd look like a real jerk if he didn't give us the stuff after we made the trip up here."

"There will be no interviews. Now let's go," said Elizabeth.

When the bill came, the manager informed the party that their snack had been paid for.

"What do you mean, it's been paid for? By whom?" asked Marylee.

"By the gentleman who came looking for you. He said to tell you that his magazine picked up the check, and for you and the kids to have a great vacation. Then he left."

"We don't need anyone paying our way," insisted Drum.

"I'm sorry, sir. But the bill's been paid. Have a nice stay in Williamsburg." With that, the manager left the table.

"How do you like that?" asked Marylee.

Todd frowned. "I don't."

Young souls ache to touch the past,

Breaching time and holding fast.

Taking in the sights and sounds,

As things of ages past abound.

What of things thus buried deep

Beneath the earth, beneath the sea?

Do they prove that time has passed,

If we hide those things that last?

CHAPTER XII

Todd made a quick phone call, and then joined everyone outside. "The minister said he's ready for us, so I'll take Mark, Daniel, Billy, and Stefanie over to his office. Why don't the rest of you sightsee, then meet us back at the hotel before we go to dinner."

"I have an idea," said Drum. He gave a loud, shrill whistle through his fingers, then waved over a horse and carriage. "Can you take this fine group of people on a walkabout?" he asked the driver.

The horseman tipped his hat and smiled. "My pleasure." He waited for everyone to climb aboard, passed out blankets, then started up slowly. The sound of the horse's *clip clop* against the distant sound of a train

brought the new millennium and the colonial past together. "See the large clothes trunk in the back of the carriage?" the driver pointed out. "That's where people back
in the colonial days stored their belongings when they
traveled by horse and buggy. That's why the back of your
car is called a trunk." The driver continued to fill the trav-
elers with historic trivia as he steered his horses around the
colonial village.

Meanwhile, Todd escorted the four older children to
the Minister of Antiquities' office. "Listen to me," Todd
warned them. "It's very important we follow protocol.
We'll go inside and meet with the minister and show him
the tickets. Then tomorrow, when there's more time, you
can start your research. I'll be glad to help you get around
Williamsburg, but the rest is up to y'all. Understood?" The
children nodded.

The main office of the Minister of Antiquities was a
red brick colonial building with winter gardens in the front
and on both sides. A maze of boxwood led to the backyard
and storehouse behind the office. Todd and the children
entered the building and were greeted by Dr. Paul
Hardison, a tall slender man with dark wavy hair, an inviting smile, and a confident air. His manner of speaking
reminded Stefanie of a foreign movie actor as he said
"How do you do" with a British accent.

"Welcome to Williamsburg," Dr. Hardison told the
group. He greeted Todd with a handshake, who in turn
introduced the minister to the children.

"This is my son, Daniel. This is Billy. This is Stefanie.
And this young man here is Mark."

Each child stepped forward—Mark hesitantly—to
shake Dr. Hardison's hand. After their initial greetings, the

children's eyes wandered around the minister's office, taking in the colonial artwork of various Williamsburg buildings, a glass-enclosed display of the reconstructed buildings, and a framed copy of The Declaration of Independence. There were also several oil paintings of tall-masted ships, and a glass-enclosed shelf displaying antiques as well as artifacts dug up by archaeologists while searching for original building sights. A portrait of John D. Rockefeller, who funded the reconstruction, hung over the minister's large, polished mahogany desk.

Dr. Hardison clapped his hands. "Well! What's all this about pirate tickets? Sounds very exciting. We had pirates in England, you know. Always enjoyed reading about Blackbeard and Calico Jack, and all that."

Daniel retrieved the tickets from his father as he explained, "We found these on Ocracoke Island. They're tickets to a plundering."

"How do you know that?" asked the minister.

"They have the date, June 25th, 1718, written on them and some lettering on the back. When Miss Theo's Last Will and Testament was read, we found out about her ancestor, Melanie Smyth, who went to the plundering on that day. She kept the tickets, then later passed them on to her nephew or grandson or somebody. Anyway, they ended up with the widow and then with us. We think the tickets were used as some kind of receipt."

"It seems you know quite a lot. I'm very impressed. I didn't know Ocracoke Island was so full of history and antiquities. May I see the tickets?"

Dr. Hardison took the tickets and laid them out on the top of one of the glass counters. "Wow. I'd heard about land pirating while researching Governor Spottswood, but never knew about grounding tickets until a Mr. Springer spoke with me and sent me a copy of the newspaper article. He seems right on top of things. If these tickets prove to be the real thing, you've got yourselves quite a story."

Dr. Hardison went to his desk and returned with a large notepad and magnifying glass. He perused the thick, handmade tickets for several moments, then glanced at his notepad. "Mr. Springer mentioned Mrs. McNemmish was a direct descendant of Edward Teach's sister from Bath, North Carolina." He looked up and saw the children nodding. "I've never met anyone related to a pirate, to my knowledge, but I am curious about one thing. When I spoke with Mr. Springer, he explained that the four of you found the tickets after a long search. Why didn't Mrs. McNemmish just will them to you?"

"That's the six-million-dollar question," Todd answered. "We haven't been able to figure out why she sent these kids on a scavenger hunt."

"Interesting. Well, according to Mr. Springer, the paper company that produced the tickets went out of business in 1790, so we know they're at least that old. Come over here, children. Look at the writing on the tickets. This particular kind of script can only be made by a quill pen and inkpot. And the style of writing, what would now be called font, goes along with that era. Now, on one side of both tickets is the date, June 25, 1718.

That's not proof they were penned that day, but it is most probable. Look at this first ticket. The word *sticks* is written at the end of the line with *cr l* and *st r g silv* before it. I'm guessing that this ticket is for crystal-and-sterling-silver candlesticks, which were very popular during that time in history."

"That's what we thought," said Daniel. "All but the crystal part. But what's all this writing that looks like chicken scratch?"

"Those are the tradesman's marks. Those same marks are probably somewhere on the items. Manufacturers at that time took great pride in their workmanship. The marks are like an artist's signature."

"Now, this second ticket is less obvious," he continued. "I can make out the letter *t*, but the rest of the writing is too faint to see."

"We think it's for a sterling silver toothpick," said Stefanie.

"Well, that would certainly be interesting," admitted Dr. Hardison.

"So there's no way to find out what was written on that ticket?" asked Todd.

"There might be. Look closely at the paper. There's an imprint where the ink was printed before it rubbed off. So . . ." Dr. Hardison reached over and picked up his large powerful magnifying glass. He placed it over the ticket and had the children take another look. "See how the scratching takes form? It's easy to see that it was once script. Now watch this." The minister placed a piece of onionskin tracing paper over the ticket. He then reached into his desk drawer and withdrew a block of black chalk. Working in a tiny circular motion, he delicately rubbed the chalk over the tracing paper with his finger and watched as the scratch marks began to surface. He then turned on a blue light and stood away from the magnifying glass. "Want to take a look?"

He guided each child to the glass one at a time to let them see what the tracing paper had revealed. Todd was the last to take a turn.

Stefanie took her turn and frowned disappointedly. "We thought the ticket was for a toothpick, or a teapot, or a toothbrush. What's a trowel?"

"A trowel is a masonry tool," explained Dr. Hardison. "Back in history, when a building of importance was being erected, the stonemason would be given a sterling silver trowel to lay the cornerstone. It was very prestigious for an artist to have his silver trowel used, so the silversmith would put his initials or markings on the back after he designed and decorated it. The trowel listed on this ticket must be very special to have come from one of the plunderings."

"This is great!" shouted Billy. "Now we know we're looking for a set of crystal-and-silver candlesticks and a silver trowel. All that's left is to find the families they belong to and return the stuff to them."

"This could be easier than we thought," admitted Daniel. "If we trace the markings on the silver, maybe we can find out who manufactured the stuff, who they sold it to, and who had it before it went on the pirate ship. Then we wouldn't have to know what ship it was on when it was robbed."

"Piece of cake," agreed Billy.

"Thank goodness," exclaimed Stefanie, "because I sure as heck didn't want to spend the rest of my 200 hours of community service looking for people who may or may not exist, because their things may or may not exist, because their ancestors may or may not exist.

As a matter of fact," she told Dr. Hardison, "I don't understand why y'all haven't located the families that own the stuff and returned it yourselves. Even without the tickets, you could have tried to return the stuff. Don't you have a list of who lost the stuff? People made lists back then. I read about it on the Internet. Ships' logs had lots of lists. Maybe you do have a list. Do you? I mean, y'all have had the stuff right here all along. You should have just returned it when you found it.

For that matter, Governor Spottswood should have returned it when he took it away from the pirates. Come to think of it, that makes the governor as much of a pirate as the pirates, doesn't it? I mean, he took possession of the stuff and never bothered to return it to the people who lost it. Of course, you didn't either, which is why we're up here, because if you had returned it, we wouldn't have had to come. Now we're stuck doing the governor's job and your job. How's that for the worm eating the fish?"

Stefanie shook her head and narrowed her eyes as she glared up at the minister. "All I know is, I just want to collect the stuff and return it to the families who lost it. Then I can finish doing my community service by doing stuff I like doing, like fencing in the turtles or hairspraying sand art. So, if you'll just go and get the candlesticks and the trowel-thing, we can take them back to the island, find out who they belong to, and mail them off. Could you go get the stuff now? We have a dinner appointment and everyone else is sightseeing."

"So much for being subtle," coughed Todd.

Dr. Hardison's jaw dropped. He couldn't quite find his tongue. Gawking at the exuberant teenager, he uttered, "I'm not sure I understand."

Stefanie knit her eyebrows. She didn't understand what he didn't understand. She explained it slowly. "You need to go get the candlesticks and the trowel-thing from the storeroom so we can return them to the descendants after we find out who they are. Dinner's at seven and I want to go sightseeing."

The minister looked at Todd, then at the boys, then at Stefanie, and spoke apologetically. "I'm afraid what you're asking is impossible. There's no way I can get the trowel and candlesticks. I'm sorry."

"Why not?" asked Billy. "They're here, aren't they?"

"Don't you know where they keep the stuff?" asked Stefanie. "Maybe you should ask someone where they keep the stuff."

The Minister of Antiquities took a long, deep breath. "I'm afraid it's a bit more complicated than that. Even if I knew where the items were being kept, there's no way they could be taken out of storage. They're the property of the governor of Virginia. I didn't realize you wanted to take the items with you. I would have saved you the trip up here. I thought you just wanted to know what items were listed on the tickets. I'm afraid I can't let you have the candlesticks or the trowel. I'm sorry, but my hands are tied."

"Who can untie them?" asked Todd.

"To be honest, I don't know," answered Dr. Hardison. "My advice would be to use the markings on the tickets themselves to find out who manufactured the items, and go from there. Maybe, if you actually find the descendants of the people who once owned the items, something could be worked out. That's the best I can do."

"That's so unfair!" objected Daniel.

"Can we at least see the stuff?" asked Stefanie.

"Well . . . that gets a little sticky," said Dr. Hardison.

"What do you mean?" asked Billy.

"I'm not really sure where they are and I can't allow you into the storeroom. Besides, I'm not allowed to remove anything from any of the crates. There are hundreds, if not thousands of valuable artifacts stored back there, and not just items taken from pirate ships. There are relics that have come from local digs, donations from colonial families, things that were discovered during reconstruction, and most of the valuables are very fragile. No one is allowed to see them. Not even the curators of the museums."

"Well, that's the stupidest thing I've ever heard," spouted Stefanie. "This whole place is a museum. What's the use of having stuff if no one can see it?"

Todd put a gentle hand on her shoulder. "That's enough, Stefanie."

"You have to let us see the stuff, Dr. Hardison. We came all the way from Ocracoke Island to see it," pleaded Billy.

"We made a promise to Mrs. McNemmish," Stefanie explained, trying to control her anger, "and now she's with Blackbeard on his ghost ship so she can't be here with us to help out. We have to get the stuff back to the descendants because she might be with the actual people who lost the stuff and is counting on us to make sure the stuff gets back to where it belongs."

"I sympathize with you, really I do. And I'm sorry, little lady, but I can't let you back there."

"Little lady, huh?" Stefanie thought to herself. "He'll find out who's a little lady." Stefanie narrowed her eyes and leaned her elbows on the glass countertop. "Let me tell you something."

"Stand back," warned Daniel. "She's gonna blow."

"First of all!" expounded Stefanie as she leaned over the counter and closer to the minister. "Those pirate tickets meant a lot to Mrs. McNemmish, and she wouldn't have put us in charge of them and put us in her will if she didn't think we could get the stuff and return it to the descendants. Do you know what it took to get those tickets? No, of course you don't!

"First we had to steal our daddies' boats in the middle of the night, then walk through the cove in pitch black rain, which is really scary, not to mention getting stuck in the ivy. Then we had to break into the church, which was really hard because Mark is ticklish, but he can't tell you that because he doesn't talk. Then Daniel got stuck up in the steeple window with his butt asleep while Mustard barked at him, and then he fell and knocked over the stack of chairs and the candlestick holder fell over, then the candle rolled down the aisle and caught the whole church on fire including the coffin cover which the church ladies worked really hard to make, and then the church got covered in foam when Billy put out the fire, then when we left the church with the coffin and gurney I tripped on the step, and the coffin slid and knocked me into the bell, which rang and woke up the minister, which was really gross because we could hear the widow rolling around inside the coffin, and then the gurney got stuck in the sand and the coffin flew off the end of it and the cover broke, and Mrs. McNemmish fell out and we had to put her back in, which was really disgusting since we're Southern and don't touch dead bodies, then we buried her in the ocean like she asked us to but she ended up missing anyway, then I got trapped in that horrible tunnel with these three dingbat dimwitters, and because of Zeek Beacon I nearly died of pneumonia and a collapsed lung and ran into skeletons that were playing cards and had their finger stuck in the wall, which is why I don't eat chicken anymore, then Daniel killed Mrs. McNemmish's pet bat because we didn't know it was her pet bat and the stupid flappy animal kept squeaking and was hurting Billy who practically caught on fire when the tunnel collapsed, and Mark had a piece of glass in his eye so he almost died which was sort of my fault—I'm sorry, Mark—and I had to pee in a tin can, all so I could come here and be told that I can't even see the items, never mind take them to the people who belong to them like Miss Theo wants us to, because you say 'it's sticky!' and I bet you don't even know what you have in the storeroom and that's why you won't let us back there.

"Well I'm going to tell the magazine man who paid for our snack at the tavern after I met the guy in the blue suit on the stairs if we ever see him again that we came all the way to Williamsburg from Ocracoke because of our community service hours and you said NO! Do you know how hard it was to get all the families together so we could come here and get those things so we could finish our community service hours? NO. Do you even care? NO. Well, you know what I think? I think it's really dumb that you have all that stuff in storage where no one can see it since this is a place you come to see things!" She stopped, coughed, got dizzy for a second, then stared at the man like she was ready to begin all over again.

Dr. Hardison held his breath during the entire tirade. His eyes blew up like tiny balloons and his eyebrows shot straight up into his forehead as he stepped back from the countertop and gulped. "Wow!" He stopped cold for a moment. "You actually stole the coffin with Mrs. McNemmish in it?"

"Of course we stole the coffin! Miss Theo wanted to be buried at sea so she could be a ghost on Blackbeard's ghost ship. If we did that for her we would be rewarded, and we were because we already had our Snow Ducks with the belly button seed and found the tickets that were stuffed in her really big Snow Duck. In her Last Will and Testament she told us to bring the tickets here and collect the items." Stefanie ended her speech in a hoarse voice and coughing spell.

The minister cleared his throat and rubbed his forehead. "Look, kids. I'd really like to help. I'm intrigued, to say the least. But the truth is, my hands are tied. The governor is the only person who can make a decision like that. I have nothing to do with it."

Todd Garrish was both annoyed and tired. He'd have to figure out what to do tomorrow when they had the whole day to deal with the situation. "Come on, kids. Let's go back to the hotel. You can swim or watch a movie before we go to dinner." He looked at the Minister of Antiquities. "Thank you for your time and help with the tickets, Dr. Hardison. I'm sure the children have learned a lot." Todd picked up the tickets, put them back into their plastic bag, and pocketed them. He walked to the door and addressed the children. "If we have to go to the governor, then maybe that's what we'll do." He led the children outside and began walking toward the bus back to the Visitor's Center.

Daniel caught up to his father and took him by the arm. "That's it? You're not even going to argue with the man?"

"I think Stefanie took care of the arguing. Besides, it wouldn't do any good. Dr. Hardison is what's called a bureaucrat. That means it's his job to get in the way of people doing the right thing. Let's go to the hotel and we'll figure out what to do next."

Stefanie's mind was racing with ideas. She knew what she needed to do, just not how to do it. She'd have to improvise. She knew she'd have to act quickly if her 'sort-of plan' would work. She got Daniel's attention and put her finger to her lips for him to keep quiet. "Todd?" she asked sweetly. "Is it okay if the boys and I stay here and look around on our own? We promise to do other stuff with y'all later. It's kind of boring hanging around the hotel while everyone else is sightseeing. We could meet you at the restaurant."

The boys glanced over at Stefanie with total bewilderment, but said nothing. "You told me you wanted to go to the hotel to swim," said Todd.

"I don't think I'm well enough yet. *Cough. Cough.* See?" She winked at the boys.

Daniel figured she was up to something and jumped in. "Uh, I don't feel like going back either," he told his father. He looked at Billy and Mark, urging them to follow suit. "We'd like to hang around here and take in the atmosphere. Isn't that right?" he asked the boys.

"Sure, I guess so," Billy answered dubiously.

Mark cocked his head to the side, then nodded in agreement.

Todd looked suspiciously at all four kids. "Take in the atmosphere, huh? What exactly do you want to 'take in'?"

"Lots of stuff!" Stefanie said exuberantly. "I didn't get to see all the stuff the boys saw today because I was with y'all. I want to see the locks."

"Stocks," whispered Billy.

"Stocks," repeated Stefanie.

"We're not going anywhere near the stocks," announced Daniel.

"That's okay. There's plenty of other stuff to see," said Stefanie.

"Sure. We'll show Stefanie all the stuff we saw earlier," volunteered Billy.

Todd chuckled to himself. He knew better than to give in. The kids were definitely up to something, but he couldn't figure out what. Perhaps they were planning to go back to the Minister of Antiquities and ask more questions. Well, why not let them? Maybe they'll have better luck without a grown-up along. "How much trouble could these kids get into?" he thought to himself. "That's a dangerous question." He pursed his lips. It was in his better judgment to say no and make them go back to the hotel. But the minister had dealt them a harsh blow. Letting them go back to the office may help to soften their disappointment.

"All right," he told them hesitantly. "But stay out of trouble. I mean it." He glanced at his watch. "It's five to five. Meet us at the King's Arms Tavern at a quarter to seven. And no funny business. We're trying to keep a little decorum."

"What's decorum?" asked Billy.

"We're supposed to make a good impression," Daniel told him.

"Oh, not to worry," Billy told Todd. "We'll be on our best behavior."

Todd cleared his throat. "I wasn't aware y'all had one."

Fear not the mysteries that lie in wait.

Fear not the steps in darkness take.

Forge ahead. Don't abate.

Embrace the consequence of your fate.

CHAPTER XIII

D aniel waited for his father to walk away, then turned to Stefanie. "Since when do you want to sightsee instead of swim in a hotel pool? Besides, it's already dark."

Stefanie broke into a wide and cunning grin. "I have an idea."

Daniel grimaced. "Why doesn't that cheer me up?"

"No, it's great, really!" Stefanie waved the boys over to a secluded tree where she was sure no one would overhear her. "Mark, do you think you can find your way to the King's Arms alone?"

Mark nodded.

"Good. But first I need you to go back into the minister's office and get him to talk about the pirate tickets.

155

Get him to log on to his computer and search for some of the markings on the back of one of the tickets. The trowel has the most markings, so that's the best place to begin."

"It's 5:00. He's probably already left," said Billy.

"I've been watching the door. He's still in there, but we have to hurry."

"Hurry and do what?" worried Daniel.

"Shh! I'll tell you in a minute." She turned back to Mark. "Spend ten minutes with Dr. Hardison, then tell him thanks and leave. Then go over to the King's Arms and wait for everyone."

Mark frowned and held up two fingers.

"I know dinner's not for two hours."

Mark folded his arms.

"I know you want to stay with us," sympathized Stefanie. "But we really need a decoy, and we need the minister to think everyone else is out of the building. We really need your help."

"Doing what?" Billy asked with dubious concern.

"Is it going to land us in military school?" fretted Daniel.

"No! Look, y'all. Do you want to get the candlesticks and trowel or not?"

"If the minister doesn't know where they are, what makes you think we can find them?" asked Daniel.

Mark pointed to the sky and smiled, then looked at each of his friends and nodded confidently.

"You can't argue with that," said Stefanie. "I bet she had something to do with us finding the third trunk. Come on, y'all. We'll just sneak into the warehouse, look inside a couple of crates, find the candlesticks and trowel and sneak back out. It can't be any worse than digging around in an old pirate chest, stuck in some stuffy, old tunnel that could collapse on our heads at any minute. Compared to skeletons and stinky air, this should be a piece of cake."

"We're supposed to be at the King's Arms at a quarter to seven," Billy reminded her. "I don't want to miss dinner."

"It'll only take a few minutes to find the stuff. Then we can go to the restaurant. Come on, y'all. They'll never know the stuff is missing, and we can go home and find out who the stuff belongs to and send it to them and we'll be done! Don't you want to be done?"

Daniel made a face. He had a gut feeling that whatever scheme Stefanie cooked up would land them in hot water. "I don't know, Stefanie."

"Pleeeeease?" implored the girl. "If we find the stuff and return it to the descendants, y'all can spend the rest of your time finding out what's in the third trunk."

"We leave by 6:30, no argument," insisted Daniel.

"I don't want to miss dinner," repeated Billy.

"You'll have time for two dinners." Stefanie put her hands together as if she were praying. "So can we do it?"

"I know I'm going to regret this . . ." sighed Daniel. He looked at Billy and Mark, then turned back to her. "What do you want us to do?"

"Yes! Follow me." Stefanie led the three boys to the side of the minister's building. "We'll wait here while Mark goes inside." She reached inside her coat pocket and removed the plastic bag containing the two tickets. "Here, Mark. You'll need these."

"Hey! How did you get those away from my father?" asked Daniel.

"I hugged him and took the plastic bag out of his pocket."

"Criminee, Stefanie. First you pick a lock with your barrette, then you pick my dad's pocket!"

"Not bad, huh?" She looked at Mark, who frowned back at her. He wanted to stick around and find out how the rest of the plan was going to turn out. "We'll fill you in after dinner, I promise. This is the best way for you to help." Mark nodded his head, took a deep breath, and walked into the minister's office. No one was at the front desk, so he rang the small bell on the glass counter. A moment later, the minister strolled out of the back room.

"Hello, Mark. Did you forget something?"

Mark shook his head.

"Is there something I can do for you?"

Mark nodded.

Dr. Hardison checked his watch. "It's past five. The office is actually closed. Can you tell me quickly what you want?"

Mark shook his head, then put the plastic bag with the tickets on the countertop. He shrugged as if to say he didn't know what to do with them, then pointed to Dr. Hardison's computer.

The minister paused. "I'll tell you what. Come back tomorrow morning and we'll try to find out about the markings. There might be a list of markings at the learning center or over at the College of William and Mary. It's too late to start researching now."

Mark stuck out his bottom lip and appeared disappointed. He then raised his forefinger in hopes that the minister might check out just one of the markings. Since that didn't seem to work, he put his hands together as Stefanie had in order to ask 'please.'

Once again, Dr. Hardison checked his watch. "How about I give it one try? If none of the markings match the lists that are available, we'll wait until tomorrow to research the rest."

Mark gave a thumbs-up and followed Dr. Hardison to his computer. While the minister sat down and began typing, Mark became distracted by the front door silently opening, seemingly on its own. Curious, he looked past one of the counters near the door, but still didn't see anyone enter or leave. He scratched his head. Then he felt a presence, as if someone were staring down the back of his neck. He turned and jumped when he saw Stefanie, Billy, and Daniel crawling single file, like a string of summer ants, across the carpet to the other side of the room. He watched out of the corner of his eye as they stealthily scooted behind the glass counters and over to the storeroom door. He gasped and Dr. Hardison looked up. Mark quickly brought the minister's attention back to the computer by pointing to the screen. When the minister went back to work, Mark turned his head and watched the storeroom door open, stay open for a few brief seconds, then shut silently.

Mark bit his lip. "Don't smile," he admonished himself. He forced himself not to giggle, then turned and faced the minister to make sure the man hadn't seen or heard anything. He hadn't. Stefanie, Billy, and Daniel were safely inside the storeroom. He wished he could join them for whatever it was they were going to do.

"Mark?" asked the minister.

Mark's heart jumped and he turned abruptly.

"Sorry, didn't mean to scare you. I just wanted to say that it's really wonderful to see young people so interested in history. You have such a rich history in the colonies. Have you been to Jamestown and Yorktown yet? No? Well, you'll find them very interesting. And I really am sorry about the candlesticks and trowel. I wish I could have been more help. Well, as I suspected, we're going to have to do a lot more research on those markings."

Mark started suddenly and looked at his watch. He quickly grabbed the tickets and put them back into the plastic bag. He shook hands with Dr. Hardison, then waved and ran from the office.

Dr. Hardison stood up and watched the youngster leave. "I'm sorry I couldn't find anything!" he called after Mark. "We'll try again tomorrow!"

In the meantime, Billy, Daniel, and Stefanie crawled into the storeroom, scooted up against the inside wall and sat silently on the floor to get their bearings. The room was pitch black, except for the red exit sign over the door. Daniel pulled out his key chain flashlight and aimed it around the room, looking for a light switch. He found one just to the right of the doorway. He turned on the light and a small portion of the storeroom lit up.

"Criminee!" exclaimed Billy. "It's *Raiders of the Lost Ark!*"

The warehouse was half as large as an airplane hangar. It contained row after row of wooden crates stacked on shelves that rose from the floor nearly all the way up to the ceiling, some 20 feet high. The children stayed seated and quietly gaped in awe at the immensity of the building. "Jackpot," whispered Stefanie.

"This is no jackpot," whispered Daniel, "this is impossible."

Billy took in a deep breath and blew out his cheeks. "Well," he said in his slow Southern drawl. "We could get lucky."

"Right," said Daniel. "And how exactly do we get lucky? Pretend it's Christmas, toss a coin, and open the crate it lands on?"

"That could work!"

"I was joking, Billy."

"Let's wait for Dr. Hardison to leave the building," suggested Stefanie, "then each of us can take a row and look in each of the crates. There might even be a list in his office of what's in the crates."

"If he had a list, why didn't he tell us this afternoon? Or why didn't he tell Mark about a list when he was at the computer? I heard him. He said he didn't have a clue what was in the crates. And what if he comes back here and finds us looking inside the crates? You don't think that will get 'a little sticky'?" asked Daniel, imitating Dr. Hardison's English accent. "He's never going to understand why we're doing this. I don't think he cares whether we made a promise or not."

"Well I care," said Billy. "Stefanie's right. We're just doing what the widow asked us to do. Besides, even if he does come back here, there are plenty of places for us to hide."

"Are the two of you cursed with the need to get into trouble?" asked Daniel. "Because you both excel at it."

"I'm not the one who started all this," said Stefanie. "Y'all started it with, 'Let's give the widow her burial at sea.' All I want to do is finish it."

"Hey guys. I really think we should turn off the light until the minister leaves," Billy whispered urgently.

"And another thing," argued Daniel. "What if Dr. Hardison works late? What do we do if he doesn't leave the building before 7:00? We're supposed to be at the King's Arms Tavern at ten of seven, which means we have to leave here by 6:30. Look around. Do you really think we're going to find two candlesticks and a trowel in one hour?"

"Shut up and cut the light!" whispered Billy urgently. He put his finger to his lips and quieted everyone. Daniel quickly reached up and turned off the light seconds before Dr. Hardison popped his head into the storeroom. The minister reached over and flicked on the switch. Stefanie, Billy, and Daniel plastered themselves up against the inside wall and ceased breathing. Stefanie could feel the hairs on the back of her arms stand up. She closed her eyes and crossed her fingers.

"Don't look down. Don't look down. Don't look down," she thought over and over again.

"We're going to die. We're going to die. We're going to die," Billy silently wailed.

"Please don't see us," prayed Daniel. Suddenly his eyes widened and he clenched his fist. He could feel a burp welling up inside of him. "Please don't let me burp," pleaded Daniel. The situation reminded him of those horrible moments in school, when his teacher would ask a question and he wouldn't know the answer. He'd be so intent on his teacher not calling on him that she would call on him. It's like he was sending out some kind of radar that shouted, "Pick me so I can look like an idiot."

Luckily, Dr. Hardison didn't possess the same kind of radar receiver. He never did look down. He scanned the warehouse, seemed satisfied that it was safe and sound, and never even sensed the kids were there. He turned off the light and closed the door just as a huge burp exploded out of Daniel. Billy's and Stefanie's quiet snickers of nervous appreciation at the outburst changed abruptly to gasps of horror, and the three children listened in stunned silence as the turn of a key and the click of a deadbolt echoed from the other side of the door.

"He did not just lock us in here!" wailed Daniel. He waited a few minutes to make sure the minister was nowhere near the door, then felt his way in the darkness to the doorknob. He closed his hand around the brass knob and gently and silently turned it. The doorknob turned, but the door didn't budge. He pulled and pushed and yanked while twisting the knob back and forth, but the door held steadfastly.

"Shoot! It won't budge!" He finally gave up and dropped his hand. "We're locked in!" He kicked the door and turned around with his arms folded. "We're dead meat. Birdie's granny might as well heat up her stew pot, because we just became roadkill." He glared down to where he knew Stefanie was sitting. "I don't believe this! Why does this always happen to us? We have to find a way out of here," he announced frantically. "Maybe there's another door, or a window we can climb out of."

"Daniel! This is a good thing," exclaimed Stefanie. She stood up, felt her way over to the light switch, and turned it back on. "By the time Mark meets our parents at the King's Arms and they figure out where we are, we'll have plenty of time to look around. Mark knows what to do. It'll take his parents half an hour to figure out what he knows. He excels at confusing them."

"I swear, Stefanie. You're going to get us arrested," yelled Daniel.

"Why? We're not doing anything wrong. First of all, we didn't break in. The door was unlocked. And secondly, all we're going to do is take the stuff on the tickets that belongs to the descendants, like Miss Theo asked us to. Then when we find out who the descendants are, we'll mail the stuff back to them. And who's going to notice that two things were taken out of all these crates that never get opened anyway?"

"We'll just tell everyone that Stefanie was looking for a bathroom. Anyone who knows her will believe that," suggested Billy.

"The only reason Stefanie wants to stay in here and look for the stuff is because someone told her she can't."

"That's not true. I'm just willing to try to find the stuff and return it, which is more than any of the governors or ministers have done."

"My dad's going to flip out when he finds out we're locked in here," Daniel bemoaned. "When I was in the hospital, he told me if I got into any more trouble, he'd come up with a lot harsher punishment than community service."

"As soon as I don't show up for dinner my dad's going to know I'm up to something, whether Mark tells him anything or not," said Billy, who never intentionally missed a meal.

"We're not doing anything wrong," Stephanie insisted. "Besides, Mark will cover for us. He can be really confusing when he wants to be. He does it all the time and gets away with murder."

"Murder is exactly what my parents are going to do to us once we get out of here," Daniel assured them. "We might as well climb into one of those crates, because we're going to be relics by the time they let us out." He looked around and spotted a second light switch a few yards away and turned it on, illuminating a half-dozen more rows of crates. "Great. More of the same."

Billy got up and walked between two rows of shelves. "Well, one thing's for sure. We'll never get through all of this stuff without a list."

"I don't suppose your barrette would open up this door lock, would it?" asked Daniel.

"It's a deadbolt. I don't do deadbolts."

"I hear juvey's not so bad," said Billy, trying to throw some optimism on the situation. "You get your own television set and a college education. I saw it on TV. It was a special called *Crime Pays*."

"Shut up, Billy. If you don't mind, I'd like to find a way out of here so we don't end up in jail. Maybe there's a loading dock at the other end of the storeroom. Or maybe there's a window we can climb out of."

"I'm not leaving without the candlesticks and trowel," said Stefanie obstinately.

"And how exactly do you expect to find them?"

"I don't know. I haven't figured that out yet. I only figured out the getting-in part."

"That's our problem," wailed Daniel. "We never have an exit plan."

Stefanie walked over to the very first row of crates, then wove in and out of the next few rows. "What do you suppose is in all these crates? There must be thousands of dollars worth of stuff. It's so stupid keeping it all locked up like this. It should be out so people can see it."

"Stop worrying about what's in the crates and start looking for a way out of here," Daniel told her frantically.

"Hey! You're a hyraphyte. Maybe you could have one of your ghosts show up and unlock the door."

"I am not a hyraphyte. That man just made all that stuff up. And they're not my ghosts. And they can't unlock doors. And I sure as heck didn't know the minister was going to lock us in here, so stop yelling at me! I'm going to look for a bathroom. Y'all look around."

Daniel checked his watch again. "It's 5:20. We have just over an hour to find a way out of here if we're going to get to the King's Arms in time. Billy, you go down that aisle and see if there's a loading dock. I'll check the other way and see if I can find a way out."

Stefanie was gone less than two minutes when she came running back toward the boys, screaming. "There's another office! Come on!"

Cling to one another fast,

For friends are hard to hold.

To the wind your fears are cast,

Let hearts be brave and bold.

N

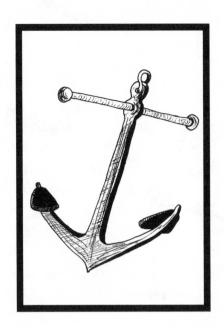

CHAPTER XIV

The boys turned around and raced toward her. "There's an office next to the bathroom," she blurted out breathlessly. "I'll show you." She quickly led them into a small office at the far end of the storeroom. Daniel turned on the small desk lamp and everyone looked around. The first thing Daniel looked for was a window or other exit, but there wasn't one. There was, however, a tall, metal filing cabinet standing in one corner. Stefanie reached for her barrette, picked the lock, and pulled the top drawer open. It was empty. She opened the second drawer and found it lined with empty hanging folders. The same was true for the two bottom drawers. Each hanging folder had a number stapled to the top of it.

"What do you think those numbers are for?" asked Stefanie.

Both boys studied the numbers curiously. Suddenly Billy understood. "Those aren't numbers! They're years!"

"Years?" asked Daniel. He pondered the numbers for a moment and came to the same conclusion. "Look at these. 1812. 1818. 1821." He opened the bottom drawer and flipped through those folders. "1702. 1711. 1718! Bingo."

"What's that number at the bottom of the folder?" asked Stefanie. She pointed to a handwritten number on the bottom, right-hand corner. She checked and saw that each folder with a date at the top had a number on the bottom.

Daniel thought for a moment. "What if those are crate numbers? The 1718 folder has the number 906. Let's see if there's a crate with the number 906 written on it."

Stefanie quickly returned the files to the cabinet and locked it with a twist of her barrette. She then shut off the light and all three left the office. They spread out and raced up and down each aisle, looking at numbers that were stamped on the front of each crate. "Over here!" shouted Billy. He found crate number 906 in the middle of the 30th row on the top shelf. "That's it!" crowed the boy. "We found it!"

"I told you it would be easy," boasted Stefanie.

"I can't believe it! We are so lucky!" shouted Billy.

Daniel stood in the aisle and stared up at the crate. "What's the matter with you two? We're not lucky. We're cursed."

"We are not cursed," Billy told him. "Look! We found the crate we were looking for. It's right in front of us!"

"Think again, brainiac. It's on the top shelf."

"Hmm. Figures," said Stefanie, lifting her head toward the ceiling.

"Criminee. I didn't even think about that. It *would* have to be way up there," sighed Billy.

"Any suggestions, Princess Knows-It-All?"

Stefanie snapped her fingers. "We need a ladder! Everybody spread out."

"This is nuts," mumbled Daniel. He spotted a ladder resting under a window that was barred shut. "Over here!" He waited for Stefanie and Billy to join him and pointed to the window. "So much for climbing out."

"There might be another window," offered Stefanie.

"Not with our luck."

"Come on," said Billy. He lifted one end of the ladder and Daniel took the other. They carried it to the shelf and leaned it up against the crate that was directly below the crate they needed to open.

"That's just great!" observed Daniel. "The ladder doesn't go all the way to the top. Not exactly the best planning on their part."

"That's okay," said Stefanie. She blew into her icy cold hands and appealed to Daniel. "Just climb up as high as you can and pull yourself up the rest of the way. But do it quickly, okay? I'm really cold. There's no heat in here, and I can see my breath."

"Why are you looking at me?" asked Daniel. "I'm not climbing up there."

"Why not? You're the one who found the ladder."

"What's that got to do with anything?"

"I don't know. I just figured you were going to do it."

"Well, I'm not," Daniel informed her steadfastly. "I don't like heights."

"You climb trees," said Billy.

"That's different. Trees are natural. You're supposed to climb trees. Ladders are manmade. Climbing them is unnatural. Besides, I'm the one who climbed into the church and practically broke my ankle. It's your turn to get hurt," he told Billy.

"I don't like heights either," admitted the boy.

"Then don't look down."

"Just hurry it up," Stefanie urged Billy. "It's getting late and I'm freezing."

"Okay, but only because I'm hungry." Billy took a deep breath. His cheeks turned a bright pink and his hands began to sweat. He wiped his damp palms on his pants, then grabbed the sides of the aluminum ladder and climbed up the first three rungs. He looked down. "I can't do this."

"Yes, you can. Just don't look down," Daniel encouraged him. "Just keep climbing until you get to the top."

"Maybe we should think about this," said Billy as he climbed another five rungs. He was grabbing the ladder so tightly, his knuckles turned white. "Oh God. It's wobbling."

"It's aluminum. It's supposed to wobble. Don't worry, I'm footing it. It'll be fine. Just keep going. You climbed down the ladder at the widow's house."

"That's because it was connected to something!" Billy's shaking made the ladder wobble even more. As he climbed higher and higher, he kept his eye on crate number 906. The ladder's highest rung came three feet short of the top shelf. When he got to the top rung, he carefully stepped onto it with both feet and grabbed hold of the edge of the shelf that lay just below the desired crate.

"You're doing great!" shouted Stefanie.

Billy listened to the encouragement from below. It was now or never. He placed his right foot on the lip of the shelf just below the crate directly in front of him, but the bottom of his sneaker was smooth and his foot slid off, nearly sending him sailing to the floor. Stefanie screamed. "Shut up," Daniel told her, "you'll scare him."

"It's a little late for that, don't you think?" whispered Stefanie.

Billy caught his breath and tried again. This time he placed just the front tip of his shoe on the edge of the shelf. He managed to hang on long enough to reach up and grab hold of the top edge of the desired crate. "Oh God," wailed Billy.

"You're almost there!" shouted Daniel. "Why did you stop climbing?"

"I'm thinking."

"About what?"

"Dying."

"They're going to kill us as soon as they find us anyway, so you might as well keep climbing," figured Daniel.

"Don't tell him that!" hissed Stefanie. She looked up at Billy. "Could you hurry it up, please? It's really cold in here. And I forgot to pee when I found the other office."

"Go now," Daniel told her.

"I can't. I have to wait until we get to the restaurant."

"Why?"

"Because it's too cold in here. I can't pee when I'm this cold. It freezes on the way out."

"Oh gross! Stefanie, that's disgusting."

"You started it."

"Could y'all shut up!" shouted Billy. He took another deep breath, reached for the top edge of the crate with his other hand, and pushed off the ladder and onto the lip of the shelf with his left foot.

"All right!" cheered Daniel. "Good work!"

Billy looked to his right. There was a vertical pole not two feet away. If he could grab hold of that pole, he'd be stable for a time. As he took his first, clumsy step, Stefanie and Daniel raised their hands in the air as if they were going to catch him if he fell. It was just a reflex action, for there was no way on earth they could break his fall if he did come tumbling down.

"Keep going!" Stefanie encouraged him. "You're doing great!"

"You already said that!" shouted Billy. He stared straight ahead at the crate in front of him as he slithered sideways. The crate still smelled of pine. He was only inches away from the metal post. All he had to do was grab the post and he'd be home free. Licking his dried lips, he turned his head to the right and glared at the pole, wishing it would somehow float toward him. "You can do it," he told himself. His fingertips hurt from hanging onto the lip of the crate, and sweat poured down his face and into his eyes. "Great. Now I can't see." He blinked a few times, shaking loose the sweat, then glared at the pole. "Just do it, you big sissy," he told himself out loud.

Before he could talk himself out of it, he let go of the top lip with his right hand and wrapped his aching fingers around the metal pole. Billy screamed. Daniel screamed. And Stefanie screamed. Billy's right hand clung to the pole for dear life as he gasped for breath. "Thank goodness," he congratulated himself. Slowly, he inched his feet and left hand over to the right side of the crate, where he grabbed the pole with both hands and had good, solid steel beneath his feet. He let out a sigh of relief. Daniel and Stefanie applauded.

"Now what?" he called down.

"You have to get on top of the crate," said Stefanie.

Billy surveyed the situation. He inched himself to the side of the crate and was rewarded with the sight of a horizontal strip of wood in the center of the crate's back panel. "This, I know how to do," said the avid horseback rider. He put the inside edge of his right shoe on the wooden strip and swung his left leg up and over the top of the crate, where he finally sat, balanced. The first rule of riding was that you always mounted a horse from the left, not the right. But considering his situation, he figured his instructor would have understood.

"Yes!" shouted Stefanie. She and Daniel applauded and shouted jubilantly. Billy wiped the sweat from his face. "Thank you," he said, addressing the heavens. He looked over the side and shrieked. "Criminee, it's high up here. Okay, now what?"

"Open the crate!" shouted Stefanie.

Billy stood up and tried several different ways to pry open the top, but the solid wooden cover wouldn't budge. "The wood's too thick and it's nailed shut."

"Try jumping up and down on it!" suggested Daniel. "Maybe you can break it open."

"Are you nuts?"

"Try it!" called Stefanie. "You might be able to break it open."

Billy closed his eyes. He prayed he wouldn't get dizzy and lose his balance. He looked around for something to hold on to and grabbed the steel rafter directly above him. First he pounded on the cover with one foot. When that didn't work, he struck up enough courage to jump up and down. "It's not working!"

"Keep jumping!" shouted Daniel.

"Criminee." Billy jumped again and again. Finally after several minutes there was a loud crack, and his right foot went straight through a top plank. "Ouch! Shoot!"

"What happened?"

"My foot went through the top!"

"That's great! Pull it out and reach inside for the stuff!" directed Daniel.

"Uh-oh."

"What's the matter?"

"My foot's stuck."

"What do you mean, it's stuck?" asked Daniel. "Just pull it out!"

"It won't come out," grunted Billy. He pushed onto the top of the crate and pulled as hard as he could, but his leg was wedged between two pieces of the broken plank. "It's really stuck!"

"Well, we can't get the stuff out if your foot's in there," complained Stefanie.

"I didn't get it stuck on purpose!"

Daniel looked at his watch. It was 6:00. "We are so not getting out of here on time."

Stefanie turned to Daniel urgently. "You have to go up there and help him!"

"Excuse me?"

"You have to go up there and help him get his leg out of the crate."

"Why don't *you* go help him? This was all your idea."

"It wasn't my idea for him to get his foot stuck. Besides, I'm not strong enough to help. Come on, Daniel. If you don't go up there, we'll be here all night. Then it really will be your fault."

"How come it always ends up my fault?"

Stefanie fluttered her eyelashes. "Because you're such a great guy."

"I hate you," said Daniel.

"Yeah. But only on Fridays."

"I should have said, 'Not me'," hollered Billy.

"What?"

"When Daniel said it was my turn to get hurt, I should have said, 'Not me.'"

"I didn't mean it," said Daniel. Now he felt terrible for saying it. He stared up at Billy, who was still desperately trying to pull his leg out of the crate. "Shoot!" Daniel rubbed his nervous, sweaty hands on his pants, then took hold of the sides of the ladder. He stepped up with one foot and looked over at Stefanie. "Foot the ladder for me," he told her, "and don't let go. Not for anything!"

"Fine. Just hurry up."

Daniel was halfway up the ladder when he looked down to see if Stefanie was still footing it. A sudden wave of dizziness came over him and he lost his balance. Stefanie screamed as Daniel floundered for a moment, then regained his footing. "Don't do that!" shouted the girl. "You scared me to death!"

"I scared *you*?" freaked Daniel. He caught his breath and continued to climb. When he reached the top rung, he grabbed hold of the top of the crate below Billy and stepped onto the ledge of the shelf. Following his friend's lead, he worked his way to the pole on the right. He rested a moment, then put the inside of his right sneaker onto the same strip of wood and swung his left leg up and over the crate. Daniel was shorter than Billy, so when he stood up, he could barely reach the overhead rafter. He stood still for a moment, wheezing.

"Don't just stand there!" shouted Stefanie. "Hurry up and help him!"

"Do you mind?" complained Daniel, giving her a nasty look. His hands were bright red from gripping first the ladder, then the crate, and he was sweating profusely. He finally caught his breath and surveyed his friend's predicament. "Man, you're really stuck." He reached over and grabbed Billy's leg just above the knee and tried pulling it out of the crate, but to no avail. "Ugh, it won't budge!"

"I told you," said Billy. "What do we do now?"

"I don't know," said Daniel.

"I thought you had a plan," said Billy.

"My plan was to pull your leg out. Hey, genius!" he called down. "Any more bright ideas?"

"See if you can break the lid with your hand!"

"I'd like to break your neck with my hand!" Daniel reached down and tugged at the broken piece of lid. That wouldn't budge either. "It's no use. The wood is too thick."

"Can you feel the candlestick with your foot?" Stefanie asked Billy.

"Give it a rest, Stefanie."

"I can't even feel my foot," shouted Billy. "My whole leg's asleep." Daniel tried once more to pull Billy's leg out, getting it to raise and lower a few inches at a time. Suddenly, Billy and Daniel noticed blood seeping through Billy's blue jeans.

"Oh, no! I'm bleeding!" panicked Billy. "My leg's cut."

"It's probably just a scrape," Daniel assured him. "It's not gushing or anything. Stefanie, go back to that office and see if you can find a hammer and a bandage."

"What for?"

"To break open the crate and bandage Billy's leg. Hurry!"

Stefanie ran back into the small office, then returned to the foot of the ladder. "I found a screwdriver."

"Good. Bring it up."

"Say what?"

"Bring it up."

"No. You come down and get it."

"Stop arguing and bring it up."

"I can't. I'm too scared. Besides, there's nobody to foot the ladder."

"I swear, Stefanie, you drive me nuts. I'm not coming down for the screwdriver. You have to bring it up, so just do it!"

"Somebody do something!" screamed Billy. "My foot is dead."

"I'll throw it up to you!" shouted Stefanie. She stood away from the shelving and flung the screwdriver as high as she could. It bounced off the front panel of a crate that was perched on the second shelf, then fell back down to the floor with a loud clank. Stefanie picked it up and flung it back into the air. This time it hit the ladder and bounced off.

Stefanie had just tossed the screwdriver into the air for a third time when a small, brown mouse zipped out from underneath the shelving and scampered across the top of her shoe. Stefanie let out a blood-curdling scream and jumped onto the first rung of the ladder, just as the screwdriver plummeted back down to the floor, missing her head by an eighth of an inch. She grabbed her head and leaped up to the second rung as another mouse scampered toward her. "Mice!" screamed the girl, as one tiny creature scuttled after another as if they were about to jump ship.

Totally freaked, Stefanie climbed the third rung and bent over to see if there were any more mice. She unexpectedly lost her balance and fell sideways, pulling the ladder with her. She jumped off the ladder as it slid down the wall of crates and crashed onto the floor beneath it with an earsplitting explosion. Stefanie squealed as she jumped out of the way. All three children clasped their hands over their ears as the sound reverberated throughout the warehouse.

When the clanging stopped and the children recovered their hearing, Daniel bristled. "What did you do?"

Stefanie looked up. Her ears were still ringing. "It wasn't my fault. It was an accident."

"You're an accident!" yelled Daniel. "And it was *your* fault. It's always your fault. This whole day is your fault. Billy and I being stuck up here is your fault. If you had brought the screwdriver up here like I asked you to, the ladder wouldn't have fallen down and we wouldn't be stuck up here. I still don't have the screwdriver and now there's no way down!"

"We'll have to wait for someone to find us," Billy said with a great, long sigh. "It would have been a really nice dinner."

"Will you shut up about the dinner!" begged Daniel.

"What do you think they'll do to us now that we've broken one of their crates?" asked the older boy.

"I don't want to think about what my parents are going to do," fretted Daniel.

"They might send us to juvenile jail," Billy said optimistically. "I had a cousin who went to juvenile jail for throwing cherry bombs in his neighbor's toilet. Blew the bowl and the window right out of the house."

"I remember that," said Daniel. "This isn't half as bad as that was. Maybe they'll just give us a warning."

"Hey!" shouted Stefanie.

The boys looked down.

"I have an idea. I'll be right back."

"Where are you going? Stefanie!" Daniel watched her jog away. "Hey! Where are you going?"

Stefanie ran back toward the small office. She remembered seeing something when she returned for the screwdriver. "Beautiful," she said with a smile. There, parked up against the wall, was a shiny, new, yellow-and-green forklift. She stared at the machine and bit her lip. She reached for her diamond pendant and swung it on its chain thoughtfully. "You can do this," she told herself. She took a moment, then climbed aboard.

The yellow leather seat was wide and cushy. She could reach all the pedals, but wasn't sure what any of the buttons were for. She'd figure it out. The key was in the ignition. "Good so far," she told herself out loud. "All I have to do is turn on the motor, aim the forklift up the right aisle, turn left at the 13th row, drive to the front of the crate, then work the ladder that's attached to the front." She blew into her cold hands. "How hard can it be? I know how to steer a boat. This can't be much different than a boat."

Stefanie wiggled into her seat and grabbed hold of the steering wheel. Turning the key slowly in the ignition, she jumped when the lift roared to life. "Oh, good.

Headlights." She wet her lips. "Here goes." She pressed her foot onto the accelerator and the forklift lunged forward, but immediately jerked back. "Ouch!" She turned her head and stretched her neck. "That hurt." She tried again. She pressed her foot onto the accelerator and, once again, the forklift lunged forward and jerked back. "Ouch! Darn it!"

She looked around and saw that the forklift was being charged and the electric plug was still pushed into the wall socket. She paused for a moment, then turned off the motor, went to the wall, and reached for the plug. She pulled and pulled, grunting and tugging, but to no avail. She even braced her feet up against the wall as she pulled with all her might, but the struggle was useless. The plug was locked into the wall, but good.

She paused again, then got back into her seat. She turned the motor back on, pressed her foot down on the pedal, and held it there. The forklift jerked forward and backward, giving Stefanie a ride that would rival any ride at an amusement park, while the motor continued to roar and the wheels spun in place. "Oh yuck!" She wrinkled her nose as nasty-smelling smoke rose up from the tires, followed by a sudden loud *pop*. The forklift lunged forward, and a huge spark of light erupted from the wall as the lift broke free.

Stefanie and the lift shot forward, heading straight into the shelf of crates directly in front of her, just as all of the lights in the storeroom went out. "Ouch!" cried the girl. She rubbed her neck and turned her head back and forth. "Criminee. Whiplash!" She looked around as the emergency lights came on, bathing the warehouse in a soft red haze. "That's better." She let her eyes adjust, then put the forklift into reverse and hit the accelerator. She banged into the wall behind her. "Ouch!" There was a sick, grinding noise as she changed gears once more.

Next she threw the lift into drive and aimed for the right aisle. As she came toward the second row of crated antiques and relics, she collided with the corner of that aisle with such force that the entire shelf shook. Several of the crates inched forward on their shelves. "Shoot. That's not good."

Once again she tried backing up and then going forward. This time she hit the same shelf so hard, it sent the fronts of several crates on the far side of the row over the edge. Stefanie slapped a hand to her forehead. "Just don't fall off," she pleaded with the crates. She took a deep breath and backed up again, this time stopping short of the wall. After congratulating herself, she put the forklift into forward gear and zigzagged up the aisle, scraping the sides of several shelves as she passed them.

"What's that noise?" asked Daniel. He glared through the red haze as the sound grew closer.

"No way!" shouted Billy. "Stefanie, what are you doing?"

Stefanie couldn't hear the boys over the roar of the engine. When she got to the end of their aisle, she made a sharp left turn and rammed full speed into the corner, knocking two crates dangerously close to the edge. She straightened out by moving backward a little, then forward a little, over and over again, until she was facing the right direction.

She stopped for a moment, then looked up and grinned and waved to the boys. "Forklift!" she screamed over the motor. She steered the lift straight toward them and pulled to a stop in front. They gawked open mouthed as Stefanie gunned the motor and rolled back and forth until the front of the lift faced the crate to the right of theirs. Stefanie looked down and spied the button that said *ladder*. "Here we go."

Stefanie rubbed her hands together, wiggled her fingers out in front of her face, aimed her forefinger at the yellow button, and pushed. Like magic, the ladder on the front of the lift began to unfold and move upward. "All right!" crowed the girl, applauding herself. She pressed the accelerator and lunged forward, hoping to get a little closer to the crates. Moving too fast, she rammed into the shelf. The entire shelf wobbled. Billy grabbed the steel girder above him to keep from falling off. Daniel grabbed hold of Billy for the same reason.

"Stop it before you kill us!" hollered Daniel.

"I'm getting you down!" shouted Stefanie. She changed gears, once again making a horrible grinding noise, and rammed into the shelf behind her. This time she knocked two crates completely off the shelf and onto the floor. "Wait there!" she called to the boys.

"Where are you going?" hollered Daniel. "What do you mean, wait here?" He looked at Billy. "Where does she think we're going to wait?"

Stefanie jumped off the still-running forklift and ran to the other side of the shelves behind her. She stared down at the crates that had slid forward and dropped off the bottom shelf. "Good. Nothing spilled out." She raced back to the forklift and climbed back in. "Nothing spilled out!" she told them.

"What?"

"Never mind!" Stefanie quickly changed gears and slowly inched closer to Billy and Daniel. When she tapped their shelf, she put on the brake even though the lift was still a few feet to their right. Again she pressed the button and the ladder rose higher.

Suddenly there was a loud hissing noise, a *thunk*, and the ladder jammed. Stefanie tried every button there was to push, but nothing happened. "The ladder won't go any higher! You'll have to swing over to the top of the ladder and then come down to get the screwdriver!"

"You want me to *what*?" screamed Daniel.

"Climb down and get the screwdriver!"

"She wants you to climb down and get the screwdriver," said Billy.

"I heard her, you dimwitter!" shrieked the boy. "I don't believe this. All she had to do was bring the screwdriver up the ladder when I asked her to, and we wouldn't be in this mess."

"It's not your foot that's stuck in the box," argued Billy. "Go get the screwdriver before I bleed to death!"

Daniel growled. "How am I supposed to get to the ladder? Fly?"

"Just hold the end of the shelf and lower yourself, then swing over to the ladder. You did it at the church. The ladder's only about four or five feet down."

"When I did it at the church, I knocked over the stack of chairs, knocked the candle out of the candleholder, and caught the whole church on fire. So if you have any other bright ideas, keep them to yourself." Daniel slid off the top of the crate and wedged his feet on the side of the shelf, only inches from the edge. He slowly crouched down and lowered his right leg while clinging tightly to the pole to his right.

"Move farther right!" shouted Stefanie.

"Your right or my right?" shouted the boy.

"They're the same right!"

Daniel blindly swung his right leg in search of the top rung of the forklift ladder.

"You have to go farther right!" hollered Stefanie.

"I can't move it any farther! Move the truck!"

"I can't. I'm wedged in. Move your foot!"

Daniel swung his leg back and forth, causing the entire shelf to sway. He suddenly let out a scream as he groped for new footing. His feet were so far apart, he was practically doing the splits. His right foot eventually found an inch of space to rest on, so he froze in place.

"Bring the ladder closer," he squealed in a pleading voice.

"Okay, okay. I'll try." Stefanie was shaking. She put the lift into reverse and hit the accelerator. This time she crashed into the shelving behind her with such force, the ladder on the front of the lift collapsed and folded with a powerful and loud *thunk*. She pressed the button to open it back up, but the electricity failed and the entire forklift turned off.

"What happened?" yelled Daniel.

"I don't know. It turned off!"

"Well, turn it back on!"

"I can't. It won't go back on." Stefanie turned the key over and over again, but the motor refused to turn over. She tried smacking the machine, but that only resulted in a hurt hand. She looked up and saw Daniel sprawled out on the side of the shelf like a four-legged spider holding on to its web for dear life. He was screaming about falling, while Billy stood above him yelling at his own leg. He continued to try and yank his leg out of the crate, while blood oozed down into his ankle like cold sweat. Stefanie sat in the forklift pushing buttons and hollering for Daniel to stop yelling at her.

All of a sudden, the door to the storeroom flung open and several rows of lights turned back on. Dr. Hardison, Todd Garrish dragging Mark, and Sergeant Bernard of the Williamsburg police department raced up the side aisle until they reached the three bandits. "Good lord!" exclaimed Dr. Hardison.

Billy stopped tugging on his leg and looked down. "Uh-oh," whispered the boy. "Busted."

Push and tread, the wheel turns 'round,

Churning fire from sea and sound.

Digging deep, thrusting arms,

Melted sand and men disarmed.

Timeless end. Endless time.

Churning up the sandy brine.

Davy Jones the key does hold,

Where souls are lost and hearts are cold.

CHAPTER XV

L anterns glistening like the glow of a thousand fireflies hung from the distant decks of ghost ships scattered up and down North Carolina's Outer Banks. Stitched and restitched masts were tightly furled for the night, wound like summer cocoons and tied with hemp rope. Pirate ghosts rested in cramped quarters on hammocks that hung between ships' beams. Down in the hold, other pirate apparitions drank spirits as they played cards and sang, some dancing to a fiddler's tunes, spilling their drinks onto wide-planked floors and tables. Most of the ghostly images fleshed out in the beam of candlelight, while others faded from view completely as they stepped back into the darkness of deck corners. Blackbeard, king of pirates alive and dead, sat in the captain's quarters with his long, muscular legs stretched out before him, downing black-powdered ale and smoking his hearty clay pipe.

Always ready for action, he wore his trusty pistols and knives across his chest, while his cutlass and sword hung off duty by his side. He had entrusted the top deck to Israel Hands and quartermaster William Howard. His night crew of 120 souls stood watch, scattered among the ropes, yet for all of his preparation, he was deeply troubled. He puffed on his pipe and gazed distantly into nothingness as he thought hard about the four children from Ocracoke Island. He had sent his candle maker, Simple, on a mission, and Simple had reported back that the children had found the third trunk. But it was after the children broke into the warehouse that Teach spoke to Simple of his concerns.

"There be no connection at present 'tween the prize and the ticketed loot," mused Blackbeard. "But the children must be kept at bay. Ye must see to it that they n'er behold the secret that lies within me buried trunk. Let us see if the tickets bring them full circle. If not, it shall only postpone the inevitable. We must wait and see if the plundered goods yield a pathway to the chair. Then I shall decide on the merits of sharing the treasure within the wall."

He took a deep, reflective sigh. "I should not have buried the prize and trunk where I did. There may come a time when I shall need to solicit the widow's help. The secret that has been a sleeping bear for 300 years is in danger of being awakened from its slumber. There are things that lie in wait, Simple, that should n'er see the light of day."

"One more thing, captain."

"Out with it."

"The lassie is lightning."

"Are ye sure?" asked Blackbeard.

"Aye, sir."

Blackbeard paused. "Thank ye, Simple. Away with ye."

Mrs. McNemmish lay in her own quarters and thought about the courageous children who granted her wish for a burial at sea. Visions of pirating and sailing with her uncle lured her to sleep. When day broke, she found Captain Teach on the bridge looking through a telescope. He was focused on two ships off the coast of Ocracoke, their guns blazing, smoke rising, wood shattering, and men falling into the sea. He was envious. The widow nearly skipped over to see him, she was that excited. She stood behind him and grinned, waiting to be noticed. In time Blackbeard felt her gaze upon the back of his neck, lowered his telescope, and turned. "Ah, good morn, madam. Are ye well?"

"Aye, sir. Most well." Mrs. McNemmish bit her lower lip like she had when she was a young girl. "Excuse me, sir, but I was wondering . . ."

"Were ye, now?" teased the captain. "And what were ye wonderin' about?"

"Davy Jones's locker."

"Ah!" Teach was surprised and delighted by the inquiry. "I expected a quiz on marksmanship or swordsmanship," exclaimed the giant, "but Davy Jones's locker, indeed."

"Is it true, what you said? Did the pirates who were mean to the ladies really end up in the locker?"

"'Tis true enough," nodded Blackbeard. He stroked his thick, black beard and chuckled at his eager student. "Tales of Davy Jones's locker are an ocean deep and an ocean wide. Recalling them would be both pleasurable and most enlightening." He leaned against the rail and pondered long and hard before beckoning to the widow. "Follow me, McNemmish. There is something I wish to share with ye."

He led the woman off the main deck and down into the privacy of his personal cabin. Blackbeard walked over to a huge sea trunk with his initials proudly displayed on the polished brass front lock. The words *For the devil's own eyes* were carved on the brass plate above the lock, along with the etching of the skeleton and image of his flag. He slowly pushed back the cover and opened the chest. He reached inside and pulled out a large piece of oiled cloth. He laid the cloth on a table and unwrapped it. Inside was a large shard of glass about a foot long and six inches wide that branched out like the silhouette of a tree. It reflected his large features as he peered into it. "When ye peruse the looking glass, what do ye see?" he asked Theodora as he held the glass in front of her.

The widow smiled. In the glass she appeared young and pretty, with strawberry-blond hair and satiny skin. She showed no signs of what 96 years of life on earth had left upon her face. She brushed the soft wisps of hair off her cheek, righted her collar, and fluffed her skirt. "I see a young, eager ghost pirate waiting to walk in her captain's shoes."

"Aye. That you would see, tho' they be mighty big boots for such wee feet. What else do ye see in the mirror?"

Mrs. McNemmish looked closely. She looked at herself, then looked on either side of herself. "I see the room that is behind me."

Edward Teach nodded. "Aye. That ye do. Now watch ye this." He walked across the room to a flowered china bowl and matching pitcher. "Come, mate. Look into the pitcher. What do ye see?"

Mrs. McNemmish walked to the pitcher and bowl and peered inside. "Water."

"Aye, mate. Water. But not just any water. Water from the Bermuda Triangle! I collected it meself." There was a certain softness and gaiety to his being that the widow had never seen. He faced her, turning serious for the moment. "As a member of the Brethren of the sea, can ye keep a secret?"

"Aye, sir, most assuredly. If you trust me with a secret, I swear to you it will stay a part of me forever, never to be revealed."

Blackbeard nodded. He lowered his voice. "The water in that pitcher is not for washing. 'Tis for the mirror."

"The mirror?"

"Shh!" Blackbeard plunged his hand into the pitcher and withdrew a fistful of water. He shook his hand over the mirror, sprinkling it with drops from the Bermuda Triangle. He then lifted the wet mirror and held it in front of the widow. Her image was distorted more than the first time, due to the rivulets of water streaming down the wavy glass. "What do ye see when ye look in the mirror now, McNemmish? Tell me, for I am giddy with anticipation."

The young widow knit her eyebrows. She didn't understand the request, but did as she was asked. Once again she peered at her own reflection. "I see the same lady in the prime of her life, eager to please her captain."

"What else?" asked Teach.

Theodora looked beyond her own image at the cabin

behind her. Her eyes focused on the window that over-looked the coastline of Springer's Point. Then something changed. Her reflection was the same, but in the reflection behind her, sand dunes and sea oats replaced the captain's cabin. There was water surrounding Springer's Point, and the sound was crowded with fishing crafts. She stood mesmerized by the vision.

Suddenly, the images of Ocracoke that lay behind her in the mirror transformed and became the images that spread out in front of her. She took a tentative step forward and realized she was home. She was standing on South Point Beach. She turned and faced one direction and saw the Ocracoke Lighthouse gleaming in the morning sun, and the tall blue water tower near Berkley Mansion. She turned to the other side and saw the pristine ghost town of Portsmouth Island. Behind her, protected by fencing, great black-backed gulls nested in the day's freshly spilled sunlight while two long-necked egrets fished in the shallows of a warm tidal pool.

Mrs. McNemmish's bare heels sank into the soft cool sand. She wriggled her toes and dug them deep into the spongy basin. She giggled out loud as the oozing sand squished between her toes. She looked up as herring gulls squealed overhead. Something caught her attention out of the corner of her eye. She walked toward what she thought was a blackened log used in a beach fire.

As she approached the log, she shrieked with delight. It wasn't a log at all. It was a young seal sunning itself, resting lazily on its side. Mrs. McNemmish smiled down at it, but the seal was unaware of her presence. Even when she squatted down and looked straight into its chocolate-milk eyes, the animal was unmoved. Mrs. McNemmish realized she was simply an observer in this mirror trick, but her visit was satisfactory and she was glad she was there.

The young seal waited another five minutes or so, then hobbled back into the ocean. Theodora looked up. For a brief moment she saw the ghost lights of the *Queen Anne's Revenge* and a small dingy headed in her direction. But then the picture faded. She was back in the captain's quarters peering into the glass mirror Teach was still holding in front of her. The mirror had dried. She looked up at the captain. He was smiling down at her.

"What did ye see?"

"I saw Ocracoke. I was there! I stood on the beach with my feet sunk deep in the sand. I saw your ship's lights and a dingy waiting to take me to you. How . . . ?"

"'Tis one of the greatest mysteries of the sea, McNemmish. I'm only beginning to know its wonders and value. Had I not nearly drowned in the Graveyard of the Atlantic, and had Davy Jones not sent me back up to the here and now, I would never have known about this magical glass, nor the pleasures it brings me."

"May I touch it?" asked the widow. She reached out and fingered the glass reverently. She shook her head and gazed up at Teach. "I don't understand. Where did the mirror come from? How does it work?"

Blackbeard wrapped the mirror back into its oiled cloth, then tucked it back into the huge pirate chest. He pulled his pistols out of their holsters, placed them close at hand on the table, then sat down in his rocking chair with his coat thrown open. He unclipped his sword and sheath and laid them on the table beside his guns. He removed his hat and placed it on his sword. "In 1716, I left the world of a privateer and began me journey as a pirate under

Captain Hornigold. Soon after that, I acquired a French ship and named her the *Queen Anne's Revenge*. After a fortnight at sea, I took me leave of the *Queen Anne's Revenge*, leaving Jack Rackham in charge."

"We were just off the coast of Bermuda at the time, and the weather had turned foul. Forty-foot waves slammed the ship and thrust us eastward toward land. Several of me men and I were on a smaller boat, having gone out for freshwater green turtles and game for food. There were twelve of us altogether. There was plenty of grog prior to the boat ride and we had just plundered a merchantman with amazing prizes on board, so spirits were high. I had booty for me men, for Governor Eden who allowed me safe passage, and for the colonists upon me return to the Carolinas.

"About halfway to the island, the storm got ugly. Lightning filled the sky, spreading its tentacles down to the sea, turning dark into light, then thundering with such fierceness, the sea shook with fear. As we came closer to the island, we were hit by a wave that threw us headlong onto a bulge of hard sand that jutted up near the hem of the shore. There was no way to navigate the mound for we never saw it, and we were surprised by the crash. The dingy was smashed, and all hands were thrown to the waves and undercurrent. Aye, three of me men drowned before we were rescued."

"But here lies the amazement," Blackbeard continued. "Before I was rescued, I hit me head on the side of the dingy and, unconscious, sank to the bottom of the sea. When I awoke, I was without me senses and too stunned to move. I remember lying there, me bloody body achy and numb. Me eyes stared blankly through the dim light.

I wanted to swim but couldn't. Me muscles had turned to liquid lead. I just lay on the bottom of the ocean floor with me eyes half open and too aimless even to wander. Me breath was leaving me and I felt death reach in with its hand and take hold of me throat. In that very moment when fear turns to inevitability, I saw what no man before me or after me has ever set eyes upon. I tell ye, Theodora, I saw for meself the poor wretched souls who forever dwell in Davy Jones's locker!"

"No! You didn't!"

"Aye, mate. I did!" Blackbeard's eyes were huge with amazement as he related the story to his great-grandniece. He motioned for the widow to sit closer, then he lit a pipe for himself and one for her. Both breathed in the fragrance as they savored every moment of the tale.

"I was as stunned as ye be now," continued the animated storyteller. "I saw for meself the thousands of piteous pirates who are condemned for eternity to turn the giant wheel of the earth's anchor."

Mrs. McNemmish was awed. "You don't say," she murmured.

"Aye, I do. Think of it, McNemmish. Deep in the center of the planet, fire and brimstone roar like a trapped sun pressing against the walls of the earth. Heat and fire lick through the walls and layers of the planet, rising toward the deepest waters of the sea. Below the satiny sand, below the fish and coral, the heat rises and turns the hottest sand closest to the fire into glass."

"Glass!" exclaimed McNemmish.

"Aye. A million miles of glass below the sand, heated by the ball of flame beneath it."

The widow was thunderstruck.

"Below the great Bermuda Triangle, a round of glass is cut and etched by the pirates sent to Davy Jones's locker. These poor scoundrels are bound for eternity, circling forever, as they push the anchor wheel that holds the two halves of the earth together and keeps the planet from flying off into space." Blackbeard took a sip of ale and offered the same to the widow. She accepted graciously. He continued.

"While I was lying in the sand above the glass, Davy Jones spied me. He opened his mouth to speak and his deep voice echoed like whale song, filling the ocean with resounding order. 'Ye are the King of Pirates,' he says to me. 'Ye are not mine to have. Ye are to survive this turn of events and keep the real mastery of the sea alive! But upon yer death, ye will sail the ghost ship *Queen Anne's Revenge*, where ye will reign as Pirate King for eternity.'"

"In me struggle to survive and rise back up to the top of the water, I reached out for help. Davy Jones placed a shard of the thick ocean glass into my hand, then pushed me to the surface. His resounding voice filled me head. 'Peer into the glass and see the skin and bones that encase yer soul. Look not away and see that you are alive, then as time moves the planets, learn its ways.'"

Blackbeard shook his thick head of black, curly hair. "To this day I know not why Davy Jones behaved thus, Theodora. I have never shown the glass to a soul before today. I learned of its magic and value long after I had it, quite by accident. I took it out of me chest and examined it to ponder me good luck the day of the crash. It was then I discovered the glass was more than a mirror. It was magic, Theodora.

"I was contemplating the matter when one of me crew entered me cabin, soaked from the Bermuda waters. He had been washed by an exuberant wave and begged forgiveness for his appearance. As I listened to his report, I hid me piece of glass behind me back, not wanting to share with him me fortune or story. When he left me cabin, I noticed that drops of seawater had spilled onto the shard, for he had reached over me head with his dripping hand to snatch a bug from the air. This is where me story begins.

"When I had peered into the mirror prior to the seaman's visit, I saw the background of me own quarters, including a stein from me favorite tavern. But as I peered into the wet mirror, the scene changed to the orderly in Falmouth where I had pilfered the stein. The harder I stared at the background, the faster the scene became me foreground. Me breath was startled out of me as I took me first step forward.

"Ah, Theodora! Sweet lavender ladies were all around me with their ample bodies, sweet smiles, and laughing eyes. And there was ale and lively conversation all around. I stayed and drank heartily, then played darts. I would have taken a player for a quid, but I was not to be seen. I was a fly on the wall, to watch and enjoy, but not to participate. I heard much conversation about the great pirate Blackbeard and had me a fine laugh. But when I saw me own reflection in a mirror on the wall, I found meself back in me own cabin on me own ship, for the mystical glass had dried."

"I was enthralled, McNemmish," Blackbeard said. "Amazed, I was! Now in the witching hours of darkness, or the gray of a stormy day, I peer into the wetted mirror and see the background of me past, and I walk forward into the vision. Think of it, McNemmish. I can visit the days when pirating put fear into every sailor and adventurer, when looting opened the way to riches, and swordplay decided the winnings. For ghost ship battles are but a shadow of what used to be, when plundering was ripe for the fitful pirate. But returning to me past is a treasure worth reliving. 'Tis others returning to me past that has me vexed."

"Is that the prize?" asked Theodora in a whisper. "Is the mirror the secret?"

Blackbeard saddened. "If only it were, Theodora." He shook his head gravely. "I knew the mirror was something beyond price or reason, so I hid it with the prize where I thought no one would ever find it and where I would someday retrieve it and move it to a more secluded place. 'Tis only in death that I can return to a time past and enjoy the glass before the day I hid it. Time is but a game to ghosts and spirits. 'Tis a trade fer the right to truly pirate."

Our hands dug deep in golden coins,

We rained doubloons upon our heads,

We touched the pirate deep within,

And heard what whispering

ghosts have said.

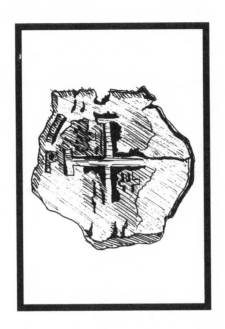

CHAPTER XVI

"What in blazes were you thinking?" bristled Sergeant Bernard. He was a big, burly man who Daniel figured had eaten far more than his share of jelly-filled doughnuts.

The four kids from Ocracoke cowered and squirmed in their seats as the sergeant paced up and down in front of them in the lobby of the Williamsburg police station. He stopped and stared down at Billy's leg, which was bandaged and had an ice bag strapped to it. He continued pacing. "I can't even begin to think of the damage you might have caused. You made an absolute mess of the storeroom! You dented at least four rows of shelving, caused a short in the lights, and set off every emergency bell from this station to the curator's office at William and Mary! Not to mention the crate you actually broke!"

He stopped walking and pointed to each kid separately as if he were going to choose one of them to be his personal Christmas turkey. "Do you have any idea of the repercussions this is going to have? Do you have a clue to the trouble you would have caused if any of those artifacts had been broken? For all I know, you did break some."

He stood poised with his hands on his hips just inches above his side arm. "The antiques in that storeroom, the antiques you so recklessly jiggled about in those crates, are absolutely positively priceless! They can't be replaced! They're one of a kind!" He pressed his large right hand against the wall, bent over, and planted his face six inches in front of Daniel's. "We had to bring the Williamsburg fire department into the storeroom to get you and your friend down off the shelf!" He sprayed Daniel's face with every word that began with the letter *f.* "Would either of you like to tell me what would have happened if there had been a real emergency while our firefighters were saving your two hides?"

"No, sir," squealed both boys.

"Well then, let me enlighten you." He left the wall and planted himself in front of Stefanie and Mark. "If there had been a real emergency somewhere in town, our firefighters would have been preoccupied rescuing your butts! And you!" he shrieked directly at Stefanie. "You climbed onto a piece of machinery you had no business touching, slammed into I-don't-know-how-many racks, jostled I-don't-know-how-many crates, and managed to push four of them off the edge of the shelf."

"Yeah, but they didn't open," Stefanie reminded him.

Sergeant Bernard wasn't in the mood. He shut her up with a look she recognized. Her father had used it on several occasions. "Those crates are sealed for a reason!" the police officer growled. "Everything that got shaken will have to be unpacked and repacked."

"Yeah, but then you'll know what's in them," offered Stefanie.

Sergeant Bernard narrowed his eyes at her, then studied each child one at a time for at least five seconds—long enough to keep all of them sweating. "Well?" he exploded. "Do you have anything you'd like to say? Because if I don't hear some kind of explanation, I just might recommend 28 days in juvenile detention for the lot of you. And in case you're not counting, that means spending the holidays in jail!"

Daniel gulped. "We were looking for the candlesticks and trowel," he peeped.

"What candlesticks and trowel?"

"The ones we have to return to the descendants of the families who lost them," Billy explained quietly.

Mark put up a finger as if to say something. Stefanie regarded him, then nodded. She turned and addressed the sergeant. "Mark said that it was in Miss Theo's will, and the law says you're supposed to do what's in somebody's will, so it wasn't even our fault."

"Well, that certainly explains nothing," growled the sergeant.

"Could I . . .?" began Todd.

"No, you can't," barked the police officer. "I want these children to explain to me exactly what they were doing in the warehouse."

"We just did!" yelped Stefanie. "If you'd stop yelling long enough to listen, we'll tell you."

"Oh Lordy," sighed Todd.

Daniel leaned over and spoke in a loud whisper. "Shut up, Stefanie. You'll just make things worse."

"No, no. If the young lady has something to say, I want to hear it."

"No, you don't," mumbled Todd.

"First of all, we already explained everything to Dr. Hardison," expounded Stefanie.

"Good. Now you can explain it to me," ordered the sergeant.

Stefanie took a deep breath, as if she were planning to stay underwater for five minutes. "It's like this," she began. "Mrs. McNemmish wrote these poems that told us to look for a key. A real key, not a hint key. So we found it in a Snow Duck. Then Mr. Springer took the other key and opened a drawer in the bank and took out Theodora's will. In the will she said to take the tickets—oh yeah, they were in the Snow Duck, too—to Williamsburg and find what was on the tickets and return the stuff to the descendants of the people who lost the stuff 300 years ago when the pirates took it. The tickets were for two candlesticks and a silver trowel. Only, y'all have the candlesticks and the trowel locked up because Governor Spottswood took them away from Melanie Smyth and brought them here. So we came here to get the stuff and take it back to the island so we can return it to the descendants and stop doing community service, except for the other stuff we did, which we have to do the hours for anyway.

And everything would have been okay if Daniel had come back down for the screwdriver instead of me throwing it up there, and then I jumped on the bottom of the ladder because you have mice. Did you know you have mice? Well, you do. And they're not the little pretty white mice you buy at a store, they're the brown kind that can give you malaria and stuff that we don't have on the island because we have so many cats. It's not that I don't like little animals. I have a hedgehog named Peedles because his fur is like pins and needles and I like him, especially when he rolls around in that little ball and bumps into things, which is sort of the way I bumped into things in the warehouse because I couldn't steer the forklift any better than Peedles."

Sergeant Bernard's jaw dropped. He took a breath as if Stefanie had taken him underwater with her. He waved his hands about and looked confused. "You're already doing community service? What for?"

"Oh geez," sighed Todd.

"For taking our parents' boats, breaking into a church, catching it on fire, and stealing Mrs. McNemmish's coffin. It doesn't matter," explained Stefanie. "She disappeared anyway."

"Good God! I hope you're kidding."

"They're not," moaned Todd.

Sergeant Bernard shook his head. "And you honestly thought you could find candlesticks and a trowel in a warehouse full of antiquities that go back 400 years."

"We did!" exclaimed Billy. "They're in the crate my foot got stuck in."

"You're telling me that out of all the crates in that storeroom, you found the one crate that contains the candlesticks and trowel you were looking for?"

The kids nodded enthusiastically.

The sergeant rubbed his forehead. "Be that as it may, it gave you no right to go into that room and mess around!" Sergeant Bernard took a breather. "Well I don't know what to do with the four of you. The truth is, I should haul the lot of you off to court and let you explain it to a judge. This whole story is incredulous."

"What does *incredulous* mean?" whispered Billy.

"He doesn't know whether to believe us or not," Daniel whispered back.

"Oh."

"It's really Dr. Hardison's fault," Stefanie said, pointing to the man who was standing quietly in a corner of the hallway.

"My fault?" asked the minister.

"How's that?" asked the sergeant.

"We wouldn't have gone looking for the stuff if the minister had shown it to us in the first place. He said it was 'sticky.'"

"'Sticky' doesn't begin to describe your situation," grumbled the sergeant. "You sneaked into a locked storeroom in Colonial Williamsburg and tried to steal artifacts! Trained burglars don't even try that." He turned to Mark. "And what do you have to say for yourself? I understand you kept Dr. Hardison's attention while the others sneaked into the warehouse. That makes you an accessory to the fact."

Mark looked down and stared at his lap, then looked over at Billy.

"Mark doesn't talk," Billy explained to the police officer. "Besides, the storeroom wasn't locked, so we really didn't break into it."

"That's not the point!" shouted the sergeant.

"I'm sure the other kids put Mark up to his part of it," volunteered Todd.

Mark shook his head vehemently.

"He said he did it himself," Stefanie interpreted.

"He did, did he? Well, I guess he'll be joining you in juvey."

"Look, is that really necessary?" asked Todd. "They didn't take anything."

"They sneaked into the room, they broke the crate, they dented the forklift, they did I-don't-know-how-much damage, and they're already serving community service hours for stealing a coffin, of all things. So unless I get an explanation I can understand, maybe a stay in juvenile hall is what they need."

"All we were trying to do was look at the candlesticks and the silver trowel to see if we could find out who they belong to! We weren't trying to steal them," Daniel explained. "Well, not exactly."

Stefanie appealed to Dr. Hardison. "The stuff in that crate doesn't belong to you! It doesn't belong to Williamsburg. It belongs to the descendants of the people who lost the stuff to pirates." She turned her attention back to Sergeant Bernard. "Mrs. McNemmish told us to give the candlesticks and the trowel back to the families who are supposed to have them. I don't see why we're in trouble for trying to return stolen booty that never belonged here in the first place."

Sergeant Bernard responded before Dr. Hardison had the chance. "Look here. I don't know who this Mrs. McNemmish is or where she came up with this cocka-mamie idea, but it certainly doesn't give any of you the right to go into a locked or unlocked storeroom to look for the stuff."

"Todd said y'all are just saying that because you're bureaucrats," said Stefanie. "That's someone who gets in the way of doing the right thing."

"Oh my God," gasped Todd. He closed his eyes and swallowed. "Tell me she didn't just say that."

Sergeant Bernard looked like a bolt of lightning had just shot through his nervous system. He stood stone still for several seconds with knit eyebrows. Then suddenly, without any warning, he exploded in laughter. He laughed so hard and so loud that he frightened the children. At first he couldn't even catch his breath. His legs began to wobble and his eyes sprung a leak. He tried to stop laughing, but that ended up in a series of giggles and hiccoughs. Finally, he slammed a fist down on his desk, gave one last hoop, and attempted to take control. "That is the best definition of a bureaucrat I have ever heard," he howled.

He continued to snicker for a few moments, then regained his composure. "Whew. That was good." He took out his handkerchief and blew his nose. "That still doesn't give you the right to go into the storeroom and look for the items on your own. Those antiques don't belong to you. They're not yours for the looking or the taking. They are the property of the state of Virginia."

"No, they're not," insisted Stefanie. "They belong to the families of the people who lost them."

"The people who lost them have been dead for 300 years!" exclaimed Dr. Hardison.

"That never stopped her before," uttered Daniel.

"That's enough, Daniel," Todd told his son.

"Could I say something?" said Billy.

Everyone turned their heads to face the tall, blond-haired boy who usually stayed out of such conflicts.

"Sure. Why not?" agreed the sergeant. "Everyone else has had a chance."

"See, we found this trunk in Mrs. McNemmish's house. Stefanie kicked it because it didn't have any of the good stuff in it. Well, actually it did, but she was looking for diamonds. Anyway, when she kicked it, the bottom fell through, and there was a ladder in it that led to a tunnel, which this jerk named Zeek Beacon locked us into. He's in jail now. When we were in the tunnel, we found another trunk and right near it was a Snow Duck. That's a duck Mrs. McNemmish made out of seashells and passed out every Halloween. This Snow Duck was huge and had a key and two tickets inside of it."

"I think we covered that," sighed the sergeant.

"I know, but there's more," Billy told him excitedly.

"Go ahead."

"The tickets were from a plundering that happened on June 25, 1718. How neat is that! Real tickets from a real pirate looting. Anyway, when we got rescued from the tunnel after the tree caught on fire, they read Theodora's Last Will and Testament. It said that the tickets were from her great-great-grandsomething, Melanie Smyth. Melanie didn't get to keep what was on the tickets because Governor Spottswood took the stuff away from her, but she kept the tickets as a souvenir. When Mrs. McNemmish died, she put in her will that whoever found the tickets should go to Williamsburg, find the stuff Melanie Smyth took off the boat, and return the items to the descendants of the people who lost them in the first place.

So now we're trying to get the stuff back, find out who

lost the stuff in the first place, and give it back to their descendants. And since y'all aren't doing anything with the stuff, and you're not trying to find the descendants yourselves and we are, isn't there a law or something you can pass so we can take the stuff and find the people and give it all back?"

Dr. Hardison stepped forward out of his corner and scratched his head. "Look, I think what you children are trying to do is remarkable. I do. It's a lovely thought, and I can understand you wanting to fulfill Mrs. McNemmish's will. But even if you had proof that you were the actual descendant of one of the blokes who lost the items, you'd have to go through the governor before you could take anything off the property."

"Why?" asked Todd. "It would seem to me you'd want to return pilfered items to their rightful owners. And the truth is, Stefanie is related to Melanie Smyth, who was in actual possession of the candlesticks and trowel before the governor took them away from her. So in actuality, they were, for a few minutes anyway, once belonging to Stefanie's family."

"Don't you think that's a little far-fetched?" asked the sergeant.

"I'm afraid I have to agree with Sergeant Bernard," responded Dr. Hardison. "Even if you actually located one of the descendants, what transpires next would totally depend on the governor. It is the law. Let me see if I can get a message to his Honor, run your story by him, and see what he says. Don't hold your breath. I doubt I'll get through to him before you leave Williamsburg." He addressed Todd. "Why don't you give me a call tomorrow, say, late morning. I should know something by then. In the meantime," he asked the kids. "Do you think you can stay out of trouble and out of the storeroom?"

The children nodded.

"I'm not going to press any charges," he informed the officer. "But you lads had better straighten up your act or it sounds like you will end up in jail."

Sergeant Bernard didn't look as forgiving. "I don't know. You seem to be so taken with things that happened in the past, maybe it's a good idea to give you a taste of the past by sticking you in the stocks for an afternoon."

"I've already been there," said Daniel, giving Mark and Billy a dirty look.

"All right," said the sergeant. "I'll let you go. But if I see the four of you doing anything but sightseeing while you're in Williamsburg, I'm going to haul you back in here and press charges myself. Is that understood?"

"Yes, sir."

"You didn't really steal a coffin, did you?" When the kids answered that they really had, the sergeant shook his head. "All right," he told them, "get going. And keep your noses clean. I *mean it.*"

The four children scrambled out of their seats so fast, Billy knocked his over. Recovering, he plowed through the police station door along with his three friends. Todd and the Minister of Antiquities joined them outside.

Daniel looked at his father from a distance. "Are we grounded?"

"Grounded?! Are you grounded?!" erupted Todd. "Are you kidding?! Grounding doesn't begin to describe what you're facing!" He threw his arms up in the air. "I don't know! I don't know what to do with y'all! I wouldn't know where to begin!

"I'll tell you one thing," he promised all four children. "You're not leaving my sight while we're in Williamsburg. How am I supposed to explain your leg to your father?" he asked Billy. "How could you break into the storeroom like that? What? Breaking into churches and boatsheds isn't thrilling enough?"

He pointed to Dr. Hardison. "I think you owe the minister an apology," he told all four children. "Do you know how many antiques and relics are in that warehouse? Do y'all have any idea what could have happened while you were in there? It's a miracle Daniel didn't fall off that shelf and break his neck."

He looked at Stefanie. "You could have been electrocuted! Look what y'all got Mark involved in! You know what? Forget it. I don't even want to think about any of it. I'm going to have nightmares for the rest of my life!"

He shook his head and glared at Daniel disapprovingly. "Not one word to your mother. She'll freak if she finds out. I don't want any of you to say anything to anyone. Is that understood?" The kids were too stunned to answer, so they all nodded in agreement.

Todd shook hands with the minister, who was fighting a grin, and told him that he'd give him a call the following morning after 10:00. Each of the children stepped forward and apologized with a handshake.

"Hopefully I'll be able to reach the governor by then," Dr. Hardison told Todd. "Good luck," he told the children. "I think you're going to need it."

Daniel watched the minister walk away, then turned to his father. "What do we do now?"

"Well, we missed dinner at the King's Arms, thanks to you guys. We'll have to pick up the others, tell them that we were detained, and then find a place to eat. Then I suggest you take a long, hard swim and get some of that excess energy used up while I take something for my headache." He paused for a moment. "You actually found the right crate?"

Daniel smiled. "Yes, sir."

Todd stared at the kids and shook his head. "Impressive."

Time cannot be held.

Like a soft breeze or gusty wind,

It floats through us and around us.

We cannot clasp time in our hands.

But find a seashell,

and know a life once existed.

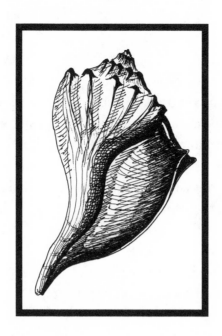

CHAPTER XVII

After breakfast the following morning, Todd received a phone call from the Minister of Antiquities.

"Well?" Marylee asked him eagerly.

"It seems Dr. Hardison spoke with the governor. He's given us permission to see what's inside the crate."

"All right!" shouted the kids.

"But!" elaborated Todd. "We can't take anything off the property, even if we do find what we're looking for."

"Why not?" asked Stefanie.

"He didn't say, but let's not push our luck." He addressed the others. "I'll take Daniel, Billy, Stefanie, and Mark back to the minister's office. Y'all stay with the tour and we'll catch up with you later."

"Why can't we go with you?" asked Matt.

"I wish you could all be there," admitted Todd, "but I think we better do things the way the minister wants us to."

When Todd and the children arrived at the minister's office, they found Dr. Hardison in the storeroom. A man seated behind the wheel of the repaired-but-dented forklift was removing the broken crate from the top shelf. When it was lowered to the floor, Billy blushed at the large crack his foot had made. "I hope I didn't step on anything breakable," he whispered to Daniel.

"I didn't think about that," admitted Daniel.

Dr. Hardison took out his walkie-talkie and asked for several other workmen to join him in the storeroom. Minutes later, the crate was carried into his office. It was placed in the center of the room on a latch-hook rug depicting the governor's mansion. The front door was locked and the curtains drawn. When the workmen left the room, the storeroom door was bolted.

"I have to admit this is really exciting," the minister told the kids. "It's the first time a curator's ever been allowed to look inside one of these crates."

"Can we open it now?" Stefanie urged him.

"Yes, let's." Dr. Hardison went to his desk and picked up the crowbar he had placed there earlier. He slipped the flat end of the tool under one side of the cover and pressed down. The lid opened with a loud *pop*. He did the same for the second side. It was then that he realized his hands were sweating and his heart was racing. He was as eager as the children to see what treasures lay waiting inside.

Everyone watched intently as the minister slowly and timidly reached into the crate and began pulling out handfuls of sand, dried grass, and oiled sailing cloth. His hand swam through the packing material until his fingers touched something solid wrapped in cloth. He pulled it out.

He gently unwrapped the item and held it up for everyone to see. "It's a chalice! It's magnificent!" exclaimed the minister. It was sterling silver and stood eight inches high. Its stem and rim were painted in gold leaf, as were the strings of ivy painted around the center.

"What's it worth?" asked Stefanie.

"That depends," explained the minister. "It could be worth a couple of hundred dollars or a lot more. I'd have to know where it came from to determine its value."

"Why?" asked Billy.

"Well, let's say it once belonged to an influential family, or royalty! That would make it worth thousands."

"Royalty," said Stefanie. "How cool would that be?"

"Anything's possible."

"Look at this," said Daniel. He reached into the sawdust and pulled out a small piece of newspaper that hadn't decomposed with time. "There's a date on it," he said squinting at the oddly shaped letters. "May 11, 1718!"

"No kidding?" Dr. Hardison gently took the piece of paper and examined it. "This was probably the only paper available when the items were packed. So now we know the items were packed sometime on or after May 11, 1718, which means it could have been June 25th. Your first piece of the mystery."

After everyone had taken a look at the paper, the minister placed it in a plastic bag and labeled it. He then took the goblet and the piece of paper over to a shelf he had cleared earlier that morning for the recovered items. He returned to the crate and reached in for a second bundle. He carefully unwrapped the oiled cloth and held the item out in front of him. It was a sphere measuring nine inches in diameter, covered in gold leaf and encrusted in precious jewels.

"What is it?" asked Billy.

"It's the head of a church scepter. This one would have been used in a high church, probably Catholic."

"Where's the rest of it?" asked Daniel.

"In the crate, I imagine," said the minister.

"What's it worth?" asked Stefanie.

"Again that depends on where it came from. The gold and jewels make it either English or Spanish. Face value alone would put it at tens of thousands of dollars." He handed the ornate globe to Billy, then rummaged through the crate looking for the rod. He pulled out two long, thin bundles that were each wrapped in oiled cloth. He unwound the cloth and revealed two gold-plated rods, each three feet long. The two rods fit together. On the end of one of the rods, a tiny spike protruded which connected to the gold sphere. There were jewels on the top third of the connecting rods and filigree on the bottom two-thirds. When all three pieces were in place, the minister stood admiring it. "I've never seen a scepter like this one."

Daniel peered into the crate and saw another piece of newspaper. He held it out to Dr. Hardison who was returning from placing the scepter on the shelf. "I can make out the word *Virginia*," said the minister. "That's where the newspaper came from, but probably not where the governor packed the crate."

"Why's that?" asked Todd.

"Pirates weren't concerned about the safety of the stuff they pilfered. Not unless they already knew the value of the cache. For practical purposes, they just stowed it until they got where they were going. But Governor Spottswood might have had his men protect the stash before moving it here. Wrapping it in oiled cloth would have been the right thing to do. Newspapers and oiled cloth were hard to come by back then, so he would have probably collected the newspaper and cloth in Virginia before heading down to Carolina."

"Was the scepter on the same ship as the candlesticks and trowel?" asked Billy.

"There's no way of telling until we see everything that's in the crate."

Dr. Hardison slipped the piece of newspaper into a bag and set it by the scepter on the shelf. He returned to the crate and pulled out another small bundle. He unwrapped it and gasped. "Whoa! A solid gold chalice! This is brilliant!"

Stefanie's eyes widened. "How much is that worth?"

Dr. Hardison laughed. "Your guess is as good as mine. A lot, I know that much. Wait a minute." He scrutinized three small letters that were etched, one on top of the other, on the bottom of the cup. "I'll be darned."

"What?" asked everyone.

Dr. Hardison ran to his desk and brought back his hand-held magnifying glass. "These are monographed letters! See here. It says HRM!" He gave each of the children the magnifying glass so they could see for themselves.

"You're kidding! HRM?" asked Todd.

"Who's HRM?" asked Daniel after his turn with the magnifier.

"The 'who' is His Royal Majesty," gloated Dr. Hardison. He was nearly giddy with excitement.

"No fooling!" cried Billy. "His Royal Majesty!"

"Maybe it means Her Royal Majesty," Stefanie was quick to declare.

"Absolutely," the minister acquiesced.

"So you're saying this stuff could have belonged to royalty?" Daniel asked to clarify the information.

"That's exactly what I'm saying."

"Criminee!"

"If the chalice belonged to royalty, that would make it worth a whole lot more, wouldn't it?" supposed Stefanie.

Daniel rolled his eyes. "God, Stefanie. Give it a break. Can't you say anything but, 'What's it worth?'"

"Don't be so quick to criticize. The truth is, the chalice would be worth a great deal more if it once belonged to royalty. But which royal family is the question."

The next item unwrapped appeared to be a large golden box. The front and back were designed in hard gold filigree featuring tiny figures of people and animals. Both sides were sprinkled with precious jewels. It stood fifteen inches high and was twelve inches wide. One of the four-inch-thick sides was designed with the same hard gold filigree, but the other three sides were plain and painted in a shiny gold.

"Dear God," gasped the minister. His jaw dropped open and he put a hand on his chest. "This is no box," he whispered in awe. He took a moment to process the treasure while reverently running his fingers over a portion of the filigree. He looked up at the others with an expression of utter amazement. "It's a Bible!" He gently placed the golden Bible on top of one of his glass counters and gingerly opened it to the first page. "Look at this, kids." He pointed to a date at the bottom of the first page. "This

Bible is a thousand years old! It was hand scripted in 1016! Just look at the detail on the cover and how well the pages have stayed preserved."

"How is that possible?" asked Todd. "The pages should have turned to dust centuries ago."

Dr. Hardison smiled. "The paper in those days wasn't made with acid, and the gold-painted edges prevented the pages from disintegrating."

Stefanie admired the gold artwork and tiny jewels. "What's it worth?" she asked the minister.

"Stefanie, for crying out loud!" wailed Daniel. Mark giggled, but Dr. Hardison remained patient with the question. "It's priceless," he told her, "absolutely priceless."

"Priceless," sighed Stefanie. She placed her hands on her hips and grimaced at the minister. "You know what priceless means, don't you? It means no one's buying. To be priceless, something has to be an antique in a museum where people can come and pay to see it. You keep this stuff in a crate, which makes it worthless, not priceless. Which, in my opinion, is really stupid, because this entire place is a museum, and all you'd have to do is put the stuff out in your museum for people to see to make it priceless, which means it would be worth more to the people who are going to get it back because they're the descendants of the people who lost it. Why would they want something that's been left in a crate making it worthless when they could have something priceless?"

Dr. Hardison raised his eyebrows and wore a look of astonishment, which was becoming his custom when listening to anything Stefanie had to say. "Actually, you have a point."

Mark pointed to the Bible, then looked up at the minister and shrugged.

"Mark wants to know who the Bible belonged to," explained Billy.

The minister thumbed through the first several pages. "It doesn't say. But it's becoming pretty obvious that all of these things came from a church. We have to be careful not to automatically assume they came from the same church, or a royal church. The Bible is written in Latin, so it could have come from anywhere. But the filigree on the Bible has an English cross on it, so it's probably of English origin. It might have belonged to English royalty."

"If we can prove that all of this stuff came from the Church of England or Westminster Abbey, wouldn't there be a list somewhere of all the stolen items?" asked Todd. "Surely the curators at the Abbey must have made some kind of complaint if a robbery took place."

Mark tapped Daniel on the shoulder, sporting a confused expression.

"Mark wants to know what Westminster Abbey is," interpreted Daniel.

"Oh! Yes, I see. Well, Westminster Abbey is the name of the church where English royalty attend services. It's very old and very prestigious. Most of the royal marriages and funerals take place there."

The next item unpacked was a polished wooden box the size of a shoebox. Some of the wood had rotted away, but there was enough of the cover left to see a partial carving of a lion. Dr. Hardison opened the box.

"Wow! What is all that stuff?" asked Daniel.

"Let's see, shall we?" Dr. Hardison lifted out the first item. He examined it closely. "This is a cardinal's ring!"

He picked up a second ring and shook his head in disbelief. "This one belonged to a bishop!"

"If these things are from the Abbey or any other royal church, the thieves really cleaned them out," observed Todd.

"What are all those gold things in the box?" asked Billy.

Dr. Hardison picked one up and examined it. "They're golden body parts."

"Body parts!" Stefanie wrinkled her nose. "Why would somebody steal golden body parts? That's as weird as stealing a finger stuck in a wall because the rest of the skeleton fell apart."

"Excuse me?" asked the minister.

"Don't go there," Daniel told him.

"Stealing golden replicas makes a lot of sense," explained Dr. Hardison. "In many churches, parishioners purchase golden body parts for someone who is sick. They say a prayer for the person, then put the golden replica of the body part that's sick on the wall. For instance, if someone had a bad knee, a family member or friend would purchase a golden knee, pray for the knee to heal, then nail the trinket to the wall."

He peered into the box, then jumbled them around with his hand. "There must be over a hundred of them in here. All the pirates had to do was melt down the gold and put the money in their pockets. I'm surprised Governor Spottswood didn't do that." He paused for a moment.

"You know, most of the pirated loot was spent or sold at auction. Sometimes the governor would split the prize money with the pirate or promise him safe passage, allowing him to continue his attacks and looting. Governor

Eden of North Carolina was famous for befriending
Blackbeard and collecting a share of his pirated loot. Then
he'd sell the stuff and keep the money. That's why there are
so few artifacts from that time period."

Daniel mulled this around in his head. It didn't make
sense. "Why would Governor Spottswood take the stuff
away from the pirates and bring it to Williamsburg to be
stuck on a shelf? Wouldn't he have sold the stuff and split
the money? Especially if it said HRM. Why didn't he just
hold it for ransom or sell it all as fast as he could?"

"It's possible Spottswood brought the goods back here
to sell or use for ransom, but for some unforeseen reason,
never got to trade it or collect the ransom. Then after he
was replaced at the governor's mansion, the stuff was
packed away, eventually ending up in our storeroom."

"I still don't see what the point is of having all this stuff
if you don't even know you have it," said Stefanie.

"You make a good argument," admitted the minister.

The next half hour was spent opening more oiled-cloth
packages, revealing more golden articles from the royal
church. There were incense boxes, more chalices, gold
communion plates, crosses, statues, and other church
items of every shape and size. Almost all had the mono-
gram emblazoned on them. "I'm going to talk with the
governor and the board of trustees about displaying these
things," the minister told Stefanie. "It does make me curious about what's in all those other crates."

Stefanie brightened. "I have a brilliant idea."

"Uh-oh," thought the boys.

"Let's open them all up! We'll get the guy who knows
how to drive the forklift to bring us the crates one at a

time, and we'll go through them and unwrap the stuff! We'll tell the governor that we didn't know which crate was the one we were supposed to open, so we opened all of them. It's a great idea. Let's do it!"

"Whoa! Nobody said anything about opening any other crates," said Dr. Hardison. "It's bad enough we may have to repack some of the crates you knocked into yesterday. But as far as you children are concerned, the governor gave you permission to view the items in this crate and none other. I'd like to keep my job, if you don't mind." He took a deep, cleansing breath, then dove back into the crate.

As he began to unwrap the next item, Stefanie started. Her heart suddenly quickened and her hands turned to ice. She was trembling. Mark gave her a sharp glance. He felt it, too.

Stefanie inched closer to the minister and stared intently at his hands as he unfolded the cloth. Everything around her seemed to be moving in slow motion. Her eyes were fixated, and she was unable to break her stare. She licked her lips and clasped her diamond necklace between her fingers. Her polished, blue fingernail flew into her mouth. Whatever the minister was unwrapping was unnerving her. She gasped audibly when Dr. Hardison displayed a sterling-silver-and-crystal candlestick.

Stefanie could barely find her voice. "That's it," she whispered. For a split second, she was back on the beach with Simple, waiting to plunder the grounded ship. She could smell his breath and hear the commotion around her. She finally blinked. She reached out and timidly touched the hazy, deep-red crystal glass at the top of the candlestick. Then she looked at Daniel and Billy. "This was Melanie Smyth's candlestick." She looked at Mark. He already knew.

Daniel stared at Stefanie with total amazement. "Wow! She's speechless! What a treat."

"I can't believe we actually found the real candlestick," said Billy. "Is this really the candlestick on the ticket?"

"It might be," said the minister. "Let's see if there's a second one."

Stefanie retreated into herself for a moment. She thought back to all that had happened because of Mrs. McNemmish's two tickets. And now, after 300 years, the actual item Melanie Smyth had taken off the grounded ship was in their grasp. It proved that land pirating had existed. It proved that the stories she and the others had grown up hearing were true.

"May I?" asked Todd. He reached for the candlestick and held it for a moment. "You know what's amazing? One minute, someone in 1718 is holding this very candlestick, and then 300 years later, we're holding the very same item. It's like it was passed through time, uniting us with the people on the beach that day." He handed the ticket and the candlestick to Dr. Hardison. The minister compared the back of the ticket to the bottom of the candlestick. There were several matching marks on both. One looked like a crescent moon, one looked like the small letter *e*, and one looked like the Roman numeral two. "It's a perfect match."

Stefanie asked to hold the candlestick and examined it closely. As she held it, she noticed a tiny, etched marking on the edge of the crystal. "What's this?" she asked Dr. Hardison, pointing with a nail-bitten finger.

The minister took the candlestick, picked up his magnifying glass, and examined the etching. "I'll be darned." He looked up and took in all the children. "It says HRM. It's royalty!"

"All right!" shouted Daniel. "It had to have come from the same church!"

Dr. Hardison smiled at Stefanie. "The price tag just went up."

While the minister and the boys went back to the crate, Stefanie walked away with the candlestick. She shut her eyes and blocked out the sights and sounds of the room. She could smell the salty air of the ocean and taste it on her lips. In the distance, she saw a tall ship running aground on Nags Head. A swarm of pirates was parading around the island, drinking, singing, and dancing around lit fires. There were sea chests full of jewels and doubloons. Loot was strewn everywhere. And then she saw a face. A pretty face under a bonnet. The petite woman had wispy blond hair and blue eyes. She was holding two candlesticks and a . . . .

Mark tapped her shoulder and she jumped. She opened her eyes. Her finger was resting on one of the ancient fingerprints. She couldn't see it, but she knew it was there. A chill ran up her spine and out her arms. She had seen Melanie Smyth. Again.

Mark took hold of the candlestick and closed his eyes. He didn't get the same kind of pictures Stefanie did because he hadn't shared her dream. Yet his own mind took him sailing back in time, and he wished he could have just one peek at reality. He handed it back to Stefanie.

"Put it on the shelf," Daniel told her.

"What?"

"Put the candlestick on the shelf. What's the matter with you?"

"Nothing."

"You are so weird," said Daniel.

Stefanie leaned in close to him and whispered, "I saw her."

"You saw who?" asked Daniel.

"Melanie Smyth! I saw her!"

"There is something really mentally wrong with you," Daniel told her.

"No, there isn't. I saw Melanie Smyth holding the candlesticks and the tickets!"

"What do you want me to do about it?" asked Daniel.

"I didn't say you should do anything about it. I simply said I saw her!"

"Well, try staying with the living for a change."

"Stefanie, why don't you put the candlestick on the shelf and help us look for the rest of the items?" said the minister.

Daniel followed Stefanie to the shelf. "Hey! Melanie Smyth isn't here now, is she?" he whispered anxiously.

"No, you twit brain. She's on the beach 300 years ago."

"You know that, and I'm the twit brain?"

After uncovering many more items belonging to church and royalty, the second candlestick was located. The minister checked the base of the item and found it to match the markings on both the ticket and the first candlestick. "And finally," he announced a few minutes later. He unwrapped and held up a sterling silver masonry tool. "The trowel!"

"All right!" shouted Daniel. Mark, Todd, and Stefanie applauded.

"Looks like a great big cake cutter," said Billy. He looked closely at the filigree which covered the entire trowel, front and back. "What's this?" He showed Dr. Hardison scripted letters in the center of the bottom of the trowel.

"The scripted letters are the initials of the silversmith who made the trowel. He would have been in the favor of the king or queen to be given such an honor." He paused for a moment. "I can't be 100% positive, but it looks like these items all came from the same place. My guess is they were stolen out of Westminster Abbey. And if these items bearing HRM belonged to the royal family at the time, then they still belong to the royal family today. If we're right, you should be able to find out something about the robbery." Dr. Hardison thought for a moment. "You might start by writing an email to the Abbey to ask the curators if any of them know anything about a robbery that took place around 1718. Don't tip your hand. Let them tell you what was stolen."

"If the stuff does belong to the church and we can prove it, do you think the governor will let us return it?" asked Billy.

"Wouldn't that be amazing!" exclaimed Dr. Hardison. He went to his desk and brought back four pads of paper and four pencils. "Go ahead and record all of the stuff we uncovered today, the ones that have HRM on them and any other markings. Then when you get back to the island, start composing a letter to Westminster Abbey. I'm sure one of your parents can help you track down the right person. In the meantime, I'll go through the rest of the crate and email you any items that may still be in there. By doing this, we'll have documentation to offer the governor the next time we approach him." The children agreed and spent the next few minutes taking notes they'd need to begin their research.

Dr. Hardison made copies of the pieces of ancient newspaper, as well as a copy of the grounding tickets. He gave the original tickets back to Todd and the copies of the papers to the kids.

"We did it!" squealed Stefanie.

Todd chuckled and looked at the four children with amazement. "You really did."

"Positively brilliant!" gloated Dr. Hardison. "Not at all proper, but positively brilliant!" He shook hands with each of the children and bid them goodbye. "Good luck with your research."

The kids took one last look at all of the items that had come out of the crate, then said goodbye and left the office.

"Well, I have to admit, this was one remarkable experience," admitted Todd. He put his hand around his son's shoulders and squeezed him just shy of breaking his collarbone. "Break into one more thing, steal one more thing, or destroy one more thing, and I'll bury the four of you in a crate myself."

As they walked toward the tour bus, Stefanie walked next to Daniel and elbowed his side. "So, what do you think the trowel's worth?"

Memory comes in all shapes and forms.
Peer at a photograph and see yourself
in your grandfather's eyes.
Pour from a precious pitcher and
remember a favorite aunt who poured
you water as a child.
Hold out your hand and admire
the silver ring that was worn by
your great-grandmother.
When you do, history melts into
the present and the link is secured.

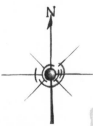

CHAPTER XVIII

James Leonard slammed down the phone, then banged his fist on the table. His pencil cup jumped. So did Harold. "They saw the loot!" he screamed at his partner. "Those four, filthy little cockroaches saw the loot!"

"Take it easy," said Harold. He leaned back in his oversized chair and shoved a half-lit cigar into his mouth. His shirtsleeves were rolled up, and the smell of body odor permeated the air around him. "How do you know they saw the stuff? Who told you?"

"Trent Larson. He knows one of the guys in Williamsburg who brought the crate into the minister's office so the kids could open it. This is not happening!" he raved. He plopped down into his chair and rapped

239

his pencil nervously until it broke. "It cost me 100 bucks to find out I've been wasting my time for a quarter of a century. How's that for payback?" He picked up his pencil cup and threw it across the room. "Little turds."

Harold sipped coffee from a stained cup, then set it down gingerly. He looked at James and spoke in a controlled voice. "Tell me about the crate."

"It was one of the crates from the vault. Some workman used a forklift to get it off the shelf so he could bring it into Hardison's office. He said that one of the kids damaged it trying to get the crate down himself, or herself. Whatever."

"Damaged what? The crate?"

"Yes! No! The forklift! He said that one of the kids tried to use the forklift and banged it up so much, it's ready for the junkyard. Then some others kids climbed up the shelving, stood on top of the crate, and broke it. After that, Hardison and those blasted thumb suckers opened it. Opened it!"

"How did the kids know which crate to open?" asked Harold.

"I don't know! Do you know how long I've been asking to research those crates?"

"Yes, I know how long. I've been at this game longer than you have."

James placed his elbows on his desk, then put his well-coiffed head between his hands. "What if it really was a grounding crate? What if it was one of Spottswood's crates?"

"Didn't Trent say?"

"He didn't know. He just said it was one of the crates. It could have been anything, for crying out loud! But it could have been one of Spottswood's. Look, I know there are pirated goods in that warehouse. I feel it with every fiber of my body. I just can't prove it. All I need is one item that matches one of the robberies we tracked. Just one!"

"You're preaching to the choir," Harold reminded him. His head was spinning with questions and disbelief. "How did they get into the storeroom in the first place?"

"Trent said the kids somehow tricked Hardison into not looking, then sneaked into the storeroom. He inadvertently locked them in."

"You've got to be kidding!" spat Harold. "And no one knows which of the crates the kids chose to open, or why?"

James Leonard closed his eyes and sighed. "No. And my contact didn't say which shelf it came off of, either. The guy on the forklift who took the crate down wouldn't tell him. Apparently, Hardison called the governor and asked if the kids could see what was inside. He relayed the kids' cock-and-bull story about returning the relics to the descendants who lost them. It's the same story the Associated Press picked up." He chuckled sarcastically. "Like that's going to happen." Again he slammed his fist down on the table. "Can you believe those nosy little insects were allowed to see what came out of that crate? I've asked six governors if I could look inside those crates! Six! Twenty-five years of begging. Now these four termites from Ocracoke come along and WHAM, they're taken to the minister's office to pop open a crate! I'd like to choke them."

"Did they take the stuff back to the island with them?"

"I don't know."

Harold rubbed his forehead. "Did anyone else see the stuff that came out of the crate? Any of the workmen?"

"I don't think so."

"Well, did anyone hear anything?" screamed Harold.

James shook his head. "No one was close enough to listen in. Dr. Hardison made sure of that."

Harold sighed. He sat and closed his eyes. He needed to think. A moment later, he bit down on his cigar and growled. "Go back down to the island and talk to the kids. Get them to tell you what was in the crate."

"Forget it. The whole island is probably on alert. No one's going to let me get close to those kids. Besides, one of the parents knows me, and he won't give an inch. Did I mention I was escorted to the ferry and practically pushed off the island when I was down there? You said it. They don't like strangers. They don't like tourists. And they don't like questions. They also have this telepathy-thing going on. They knew I was there to ask questions before I even arrived. What happens if the governor gives those nose-picking cherubs permission to return the loot to the descendants of the owners? What then? We have buyers all over the world waiting for that stuff. How do we keep those kids from shipping it overseas?"

Harold pulled out his nail clipper and started on his toes. He tapped his cigar on the ashtray but missed the cup, allowing the ashes to fall on his desk. He stuck the remainder of the cigar back into his mouth. Then he considered the question. "If the kids are allowed to return the loot, getting the stuff away from the kids on this end is out of the question. They won't be the ones shipping it. We may have to find out where the stuff is going and take possession of it on the receiving end. Stay in touch with your contact in Williamsburg, and let me know the second he hears anything about the minister's plans."

"Those kids are trouble," raved James. "If they get chummy with the people on the other end, it could get complicated."

"Don't you worry about the children," said Harold. "I've never met a kid I couldn't persuade to my way of thinking. Bribery and threats go a long way."

Blackbeard folded the mirror back into the oiled cloth and had just tucked it away in his trunk when there was a knock on his cabin door.

"Enter!"

Simple stepped into the cabin and closed the door behind him. He saluted Teach and tipped his hat at Mrs. McNemmish. "They've discovered the Abbey's misfortune," he reported to his captain. "They've seen Spottswood's cache."

Blackbeard let out a vocal sigh, then stroked his long, thick beard. He paced back and forth across the cabin, his hands clasped behind his back, his eyes staring down at the floor. Suddenly he stopped and looked up at the messenger. He approached the man and spoke into his ear. "Belay their venture to me trunk. Keep them from finding the stow. Later it may prove an unexpected resolve. If this bit of fortune leads them to the Abbey, they may trip upon the connection. If they do, we'll have need to protect me prize. I must think of a way to insure the outcome. Anything else?"

"Thar be men interfering, sir."

Blackbeard nodded. "Keep me informed."

"Aye, sir. Ma'am." Simple saluted and left the cabin.

Mrs. McNemmish noticed the captain appeared both concerned and thoughtful. "Anything wrong?"

"'Tis too soon to tell," he told the widow. "Perhaps in time I will entertain ye with a tale."

"I would like that," said the widow, but her demeanor had turned somber. She sensed the captain's problem had something to do with her death and the four children. Blackbeard appeared to read his niece's mind. "Don't ye fret yerself, miss. Simple is a good man and a decent pirate. Together we shall see this through."

Those who seek what lies within

Shall ever be in danger's grasp.

Turn thy heads, peer not inside,

Let not this vision be your last.

N

CHAPTER XIX

After the four families returned to the island, Stefanie phoned Daniel. "Are you going back down to the tunnel tonight?"

"No!"

"Why not?"

"Because I'm tired, and we have school tomorrow."

"But you have to go back down there tonight. Y'all have to start getting the trunk out of the wall before anyone else finds it."

"Anyone, who?"

"The engineers from Wilmington."

"I don't think they're coming here tomorrow, or we would have heard about it. And I doubt the tunnel is likely to collapse any more now than a week ago.

Besides, there is no 'y'all.' It's all of us or none of us. You even raised your hand, remember?"

"What if Billy and Mark want to go down? Will you go then?"

"You're a pain, you know that? Hang up. I'll call you right back."

Stefanie sat on her bed with her legs crossed, staring at the phone. She grabbed it the second it rang. "Well?"

"Billy said he'd go if I go and then went to tell Mark. I'm going to sleep. Meet us at the tree before midnight. We have to hide until Teddy finishes his run. And listen: leave your ghosts at home. We wouldn't want a hyraphyte throwing a party down there."

"I'm not a hyraphyte." Stefanie fell asleep wondering what to wear to an evening of dirt, spiderwebs, bats, and sludge water. But the mystery of the third trunk swept her away into sweet dreams.

Eleven-thirty crept into the four bedrooms far sooner than the kids expected. One by one, they dragged themselves out of bed and outside into the chilly night air. It was cold and overcast, and a thick mist covered the bike route. Mark had trouble seeing, even with the flashlight in front of his bike, so he waited for Daniel and followed him to the Bobby Garrish tree. Stefanie walked in and out of her house three times before finally deciding to go. She met the boys at the Schoolhouse Road entrance to Howard Street, where they stowed their bikes in the closest graveyard.

"Hiding in a graveyard at midnight isn't exactly my kind of fun," chattered Stefanie.

"It was your idea, so stop complaining."

"I saw on television you can get typhoid fever by standing in tunnel water," whispered Stefanie, while shivering in a crouched position. "They said if you get an infection from the dirty water, it can fester and get all pussy in your blood, and then you get a fever and your veins blow up and you die."

"That's a 'not me,'" Billy whispered out loud.

"That's not true," Daniel informed her. "Mostly you get junk like dysentery, the creeping crud, and the trots."

"Wow. That makes me feel a whole lot better," Stefanie remarked sarcastically.

"Shut up, y'all," whispered Billy. "It's bad enough down there without y'all describing it."

"Are you going to complain the whole time we're down there?" Daniel asked Stefanie.

"You shouldn't have invited me if you don't like me complaining."

"You're right. My mistake."

"No problem. I can leave?"

"No, you can't."

"Then stop complaining," said Stefanie.

"I don't complain," argued Daniel.

"You just did."

Billy glanced over at the both of them. "I think you should stop mommicking before someone hears us!"

At that moment, Mark clapped his hands and put a finger to his mouth for everyone to be quiet. He pointed to a string of dead leaves forming tiny twisters that danced up and down Howard Street. Mark used his forefinger to make tiny circles near the side of his head.

Stefanie leaned forward. "Where is she?"

Mark pointed to the path about fifteen feet away.

"Can you see her?" asked Daniel.

Mark nodded.

Stefanie grabbed Billy's arm and scooted closer to the road. "There she is!" The two older boys saw her as well.

The ghost of Mad Mag was skipping up and down the sandy road. She had her foot bandaged and a self-inflicted brand on her forehead, and she was swinging a boiling pot of cooked cat to be served for her husband's dinner.

"If I see Blackbeard walking around here without his head, I'm out of here," said Billy.

The specter disappeared when Teddy drove his car down Howard Street, checking to make sure everything was as it should be. When he passed by the Bobby Garrish tree, Mustard went berserk in the back seat.

"Oh no!" gasped Daniel.

Teddy stopped the car. The kids watched in agony as the sheriff turned in his seat and faced Mustard. They could see him talking to the dog, but couldn't hear what he was saying through the closed window. The next thing the kids knew, Teddy stepped out of the car, turned on his flashlight and checked around the street, small cottages, and rows of gravestones. Mustard was clawing at the window and wouldn't shut up.

"He smells us," whispered Billy.

"I don't smell," objected Stefanie.

"Everybody smells," said Daniel.

Teddy walked back to the car and spoke through the closed window. "Are you seeing ghosts again, boy? You see Mad Mag out here?" He took one more look around, then got back into his car and drove away.

Daniel closed his eyes and sighed. "I hate that dog. He's going to give me a heart attack by the time I'm fifteen."

"At least we didn't get caught," Stefanie sighed gratefully.

"Yeah, well, that's a first."

Everyone waited another five minutes, then stood up and climbed out of the graveyard. Billy quickly tied the rope around the girth of the tree, while Daniel pulled the planks off the front. He then dropped two of the lit flashlights onto the dirt mound below.

"At least we've done this before," rationalized Billy. He slid under the tree, grabbed hold of the rope, and climbed down. The others followed.

"It's not as dusty this time," said Daniel as they proceeded toward the hidden trunk. "We must have let some fresh air in when we took the planks off."

"Yeah? Well, it still smells," grimaced Stefanie.

Billy's eyes wandered to the ceiling, where bats were clinging to the edge of the walls. They started peeping as soon as they saw light, and several flew from one side to the other. Billy dropped to the floor and covered his head. "Leave me alone!" he begged. He kept a close eye on them until they quieted. When he stood back up, he pressed his hand against the wall for balance.

There was a sudden, loud crack and the cement gave way under his hand. Billy's entire arm fell through the wall, consumed by the empty space, finally coming to a stop when his hand reached a piece of ship's piling deep inside. "Ouch!"

Stefanie screamed into her hand. "Oh my God! It's falling apart!"

Daniel panicked as well, as he reached over and pulled Billy out of the wall. Billy was clutching what looked like someone's arm bone. He shuddered and threw it on the ground. "Those people from Wilmington better get down here soon, or there won't be a tunnel."

"Maybe we should get out of here. Now!" Stefanie emphasized.

"We just have to be careful, that's all," said Billy, rubbing the scrapes on his arm.

"No. We should just forget about the trunk until someone comes down here and fixes the place."

"We'll be okay. I promise," Billy assured her. "We're almost there. We just have to stay together. If the walls and ceiling haven't collapsed by now, I doubt they'll collapse tonight."

"What if the trunk isn't really a treasure chest?" asked Stefanie as she shuffled behind Billy. "What if we just thought it was a treasure chest because it looked like one, but it really isn't one? Don't you think Miss Theo would have written one of her poems about another treasure chest if there was another one down here? She knew everything that went on down here, and she didn't say one word about another treasure chest. What if we're down here to break into a third trunk and there isn't a third trunk? This whole trip could be for nothing."

"First of all, you're the one who insisted we come back down here tonight. And secondly, maybe Mrs. McNemmish didn't know there was another trunk. She couldn't have written a poem about it if she didn't know there was anything to write about."

"I'm positive it's a trunk," Billy insisted.

"How do you know?" asked Stefanie.

"I just know."

"How do you know?"

"The treasure fairy told him," said Daniel.

"The treasure fairy told him?" repeated Stefanie snidely.

"Yeah. The treasure fairy told him. Ghosts talk to you and treasure fairies talk to Billy."

"You are so weird," remarked Billy.

"Me or Stefanie?" asked Daniel.

"It's a toss-up."

"What's that noise?" freaked Stefanie. Just as the children turned a corner, they were greeted by a squishy sort of sloshing noise that grew louder and closer. Billy aimed his flashlight straight ahead and down the long corridor. A white ball of some kind was rolling toward them. He jumped to the side and let out a yelp when a human skull rolled past him and came to a stop at Mark's feet. Mark's eyes flew open and he slithered closer to Stefanie.

Stefanie stood paralyzed, her eyes bulging. "It's a head! It's somebody's head!"

"It's a skull," said Billy. "You've seen skulls before."

"Not without their bodies!"

"Where'd it come from?" wondered Daniel. The words were barely out of his mouth, when a second skull sloshed down the tunnel floor, landing at his feet. A third skull followed.

"Someone's bowling with skeleton skulls," said Billy. "That's just plain rude."

"Someone? Someone, who? There's nobody down here but us," Daniel assured them.

"Oh, gross!" wailed Stefanie. A fourth and fifth skull squished down the tunnel floor, stopping right in front of her feet. "Make it stop!"

"I can't make it stop. I don't know what made it start."

Daniel aimed his flashlight at the crumbling, oppressive walls and ceiling. "The wall must be disintegrating.

The skeletons buried inside the walls must be falling out."

"What skeletons buried inside the walls?"

"I don't know what skeletons! You're the first one who brought it up. Maybe it's their heads that rolled off."

Mark lifted his hands and waved them like radar dishes.

"Mark thinks it's a warning," said Billy. "He thinks my falling through the wall was a sign."

Stefanie sneered at Daniel. "I'm glad you think that's so funny."

"I don't think it's funny."

"Then why did you laugh?"

"I didn't laugh."

"Yes, you did. Right after Billy said that Mark thinks it's a sign."

"I didn't laugh!"

"Yes, you did. I heard you."

"Stefanie, why would I laugh?"

"Well, somebody laughed, and since it wasn't me, Mark, or Billy, it had to have been you."

"Maybe you laughed, and didn't know you did it."

Stefanie freaked as more laughter echoed throughout the tunnel. "You had to have heard that," she told the boys.

Billy leaned over and whispered into her ear. "I didn't hear it either," he told her gently. "Maybe it's your nerves."

"None of you heard someone laughing?"

Mark and Billy shook their heads.

Daniel stared down at the skulls. "Look, I really don't want to know if you heard those empty skulls laughing, because the waiter in Williamsburg said you are some kind of ghost magnet. So please, just shut up about it. It's bad enough walking through a damp, stinky, crumbling, filthy underground tunnel without you adding to my paranoia."

"Just don't tell me to shut up when I hear laughing and you're too stubborn to admit you heard it, too," Stefanie retorted. "Now, I want to go home! We need to go home! Mark's right. Somebody or something doesn't want us to start digging that trunk out of the wall. Maybe the skulls are telling us that the walls will start collapsing and hundreds of their bodies will fall out and land on us until we're buried in bone stuff, and no one will find us until we petrify, and they won't be able to tell our bones from the other bones except by our teeth. Or maybe somebody followed us down here and as soon as we show them where the trunk is, they're going to kill us anyway, and we'll still end up in a bone heap with dead pirates and empty skulls."

"No one is down here except us. They would have had to use the rope, and no one has passed us. And there's only one empty skull around here, and you're wearing it!"

"You know, if there are ghosts trying to keep us away, that must mean the stuff in the trunk is worth tons of money," figured Billy. "We just have to be careful and do only a little digging at a time. We'll sneak down here until we get the chest out of the wall, collect the treasure, and then you won't ever have to come back. Okay?"

Stefanie pointed her flashlight at the face of one of the skulls. "Don't look at me that way," she addressed its hollow eye sockets.

Daniel stepped back. "Please tell me there's no ghost in that head!"

Stefanie kicked it away. "No. Just a bad sense of humor."

I jest with thee and tell ye things

Of priceless wares and diamond rings,

When all we know is what we see,

Depends upon whose eyes they be.

Simon says—a children's game

Will light the way with flickering flame,

And lead us all to secrets deep

And we shall always secrets keep.

CHAPTER XX

Almost immediately after the attack of the rolling skulls, Mark stopped them and pointed up ahead.

"Now what?" fretted Daniel.

"I think he sees something," said Billy.

"What? What do you see?" shrieked Stefanie. Her nerves were so on edge that she jumped at everything.

Mark looked at her and shrugged.

"Did you see something move?" asked Billy.

Again, Mark pointed up ahead.

Billy stretched his neck and tried to focus his flashlight beam where Mark was pointing. "I don't see anything."

Mark pushed Billy's hand down so the flashlight beam faced the ground. Then he pointed up ahead.

"Wait a minute," said Daniel, "there is something moving."

Everyone strained to see a tiny flicker of light hovering in midair about 20 feet in front of them.

"How in the world did you see that?" marveled Billy. "You can barely see your own hand in front of your face."

Mark shrugged.

"So, what is it?" asked Daniel.

"It must be the person who rolled the heads," said Stefanie. "I told you there was someone else down here."

Mark tapped Stefanie on her shoulder and shook his head. He was sure no one else was down there.

"Then who rolled the heads?"

Mark pointed.

"That's a big help," grumbled Daniel.

The foursome huddled together and shuffled forward as if their eight legs were bound together. As they slowly inched their way down the dark path, Billy realized what they were seeing. "It's a flame!"

"Fire?" panicked Stefanie.

"No, just a flame. It's a candle flame without the candle."

"How can you have a candle flame without a candle?" asked Daniel.

"I don't know. I didn't put it there. Come on," whispered Billy. He led the group through soggy sand, crumbling ceilings, and back toward the stench of rotten seaweed as they approached the end of the corridor. Everyone used their dryer sheets to ward off the smell. Stefanie yelped when off in the distance a loud *snap* was followed by a second flickering candle flame. Within seconds after that, the tunnel came alive with snapping and glistening firelight. Patches of seashell cement sparkled and glittered all around them. Reflections of the candle flames glowed in the smallest of water puddles.

"It's beautiful," sighed Stefanie.

"It's spooky," uttered Daniel. The lump set firmly in the center of his throat made it hard to breathe and impossible to swallow. His old friend, claustrophobia, was on its way to becoming a full-blown panic attack. "It's like watching a really scary horror film, only we're in it."

"Yeah. *Nightmare Under Howard Street*," said Billy.

"Very funny." Daniel shoved Billy forward. "Find out where the flames go."

"Why me?"

"Because you're the oldest."

"That's not my fault." Billy looked at his hand and realized his flashlight beam was shaking. "Hello!" he peeped. "Is somebody down here?" He called timidly at first, but no one answered. He tried again, a little louder. "Hello? Meehonkey! Is anybody down here?"

From the distance, another skull sloshed down the pathway, landing right at the tip of Billy's shoe. Stefanie's stomach leaped into her throat. She thought for sure she was going to either faint or puke. Her insides were tied in a knot. Pulling together all the nerve she had, she scooted around Daniel and stood beside Billy. She clung to his coat sleeve as she blinked in the abundance of tiny flames. "Whoa! Look at that," she said, pointing straight ahead.

"Look at what?" trembled Daniel.

"That shadow person."

"What shadow person?" gulped Billy.

"That shadow person," insisted Stefanie.

Billy and Daniel looked where she was pointing, then looked at her. "We don't see anything." They looked at Mark, who shrugged.

Stefanie encouraged Billy to take a few more steps closer to the candle flames, while she clung to his sleeve. Suddenly she stopped, let out a very long, very loud sigh, and placed her hands on her hips. "I don't believe it. It's you!" she said accusingly. She stopped and glared at the man who was seated on a barrel, whittling candles. The moment he saw Stefanie, he grinned and blew out the flames.

"What happened?" gasped Billy.

"The flames went out," exclaimed Daniel.

"I know they went out. I saw them go out. I was asking why they went out."

"What do you care why they went out, when we don't even know why they went on!"

Stefanie shook her head and scowled. "He blew them out," she said, pointing straight ahead with a disgusted grunt.

"He, who?" Daniel narrowed his eyes and aimed his flashlight beam straight ahead. "I don't see anyone."

Stefanie aimed Daniel's light at the floor. "He's right there. You can't see him if you aim your light at him."

Billy thrust his neck forward and focused where Stefanie was pointing, but he didn't see anyone, with or without a light.

Daniel suddenly realized what was happening and groaned. "Forget it, Billy. She's pointing to a ghost." He turned to Stefanie. "I told you not to bring any ghosts with you. Why can't you use an anti-ghost deodorant or something?"

"I didn't bring a ghost down here, you idiot. He showed up on his own."

"I don't see a ghost," said Billy.

"Of course you don't see a ghost. Normal people don't see ghosts except for the ghosts who live on the island, like Mad Mag. Everyone sees her. Only hyraphytes see off-island ghosts!"

"Shut up, Daniel. I'm not a hyraphyte! And even if I was one, I wouldn't go around inviting off-island ghosts everywhere I went." Stefanie turned to the ghost and crossed her arms in front of her. "I remember you. You were in my dream. What are you doing here?"

"What's who doing here?" asked Daniel. "Who are you talking to? What dream?"

"I told you, I'm talking to him," pointed Stefanie.

"I still don't see anyone," admitted Billy, making a sincere effort to see what Stefanie saw.

"He's right there, sitting on a barrel," insisted Stefanie.

"What barrel?" asked Billy.

"She's talking to a dead person sitting on an invisible barrel," Daniel reminded him. "So quit trying to see anything."

"Well, who is he?" Billy asked her.

Stefanie rolled her eyes. "Billy, this is Simple. Simple, this is Billy, Daniel, and Mark," she said, pointing to each boy in turn.

"Simple?" laughed Daniel. "Like Simple Simon?"

"Who's Simple Simon?" asked Billy.

"It's a nursery rhyme, for heaven's sake. Didn't anyone ever read nursery rhymes to you?"

"I don't know. I can't remember back that far. What's he doing here?" Billy asked Stefanie.

"I already asked him that. Didn't you hear me ask him that?" She turned to Simple. "What are you doing here?"

"Me captain sent me."

"Oh, great." She turned to her friends. "Blackbeard sent him."

"Blackbeard?" shrieked Billy.

"This is so bogus," grumbled Daniel.

Stefanie noticed that Simple had all of his candle-making equipment laid out on the floor, blocking their way down the corridor.

"Did you roll those heads at us?" she asked him.

"Aye. 'Twas a bloody good yarn, was it not?" chuckled Simple. "Got yer attention."

"It was stupid," Stefanie told him. She looked down at his things. "You're in our way."

"Aye, lassie. 'Tis me job."

"What did he say?" asked Daniel.

"He said it's his job," said Stefanie.

"What's his job?"

"To be in our way."

"Be in our way, where?" asked Billy.

"I'm to keep ye from the trunk," Simple informed the girl.

"Which trunk?" asked Stefanie, knowing perfectly well which trunk.

"The trunk in the wall," said Simple.

"Why?" asked Stefanie.

"Why, what? Which trunk?" asked Daniel.

"Why is he keeping us from the trunk in the wall," explained Stefanie to the boys.

"The trunk in the wall?" asked Daniel. "What about the trunk in the wall?"

"Simple says that it's his job to block our way to the trunk in the wall," repeated Stefanie, "and that's why he put all of his stuff in the middle of the floor. He wants us to trip over it."

"That's nuts! How can he be in our way if you're the only one who can see him?"

Stefanie stepped back toward the wall and folded her arms across her chest. "Go ahead," she invited Daniel. "Try and get past him."

"Wait a minute. Let's think about this," said Billy with growing anticipation. He turned to Stefanie. "How come we could see the flames, but we can't see him or the barrel or the stuff on the floor?"

"It's spectral choice," said Simple. "Ye sees what I mean ye to sees."

"He said it's his choice. We see what he wants us to see," repeated Stefanie.

"Well, what did he say about the stuff on the ground?" asked Daniel.

"I just told you. He wants us to trip on it, so we can't get to the trunk."

Daniel was not amused. "I think you're making the whole thing up. I'm telling you, there's no one there." When Stefanie said nothing in response, Daniel took a timid step forward. As he did, Simple stuck out his foot. Daniel tripped over his foot, then slid along the floor of the tunnel and rolled across the path of lined-up candles. His arms flapped furiously as he tried to keep himself upright, but he finally lost his balance and fell flat on his face.

Mark laughed, Billy gasped, and Stefanie giggled. "Told you."

"That wasn't funny," remarked Daniel with injured pride. He pushed himself up from the floor and wiped the mud off his face and jacket. "Your ghost has a nasty sense of humor."

"He's not my ghost," giggled Stefanie.

"Why doesn't he want us to get to the trunk?" asked Billy.

"'Tis a danger for ye to behold what lies within. Me captain doesn't know if ye are ready," answered the specter.

"He said it's dangerous for us to see what's inside the trunk, and he doesn't know if we're ready. Or Blackbeard doesn't know. Or something like that," explained Stefanie.

"That's ridiculous," objected Daniel. "We're standing here listening to someone who isn't really here. Ask him if he took our stuff."

"He can hear you," sighed Stefanie. "He's dead, not deaf."

"Well, what did he say?"

"He didn't say anything. Give him a chance." She looked at Simple. "Well, did you?"

"Nay, mate. I'm here to guard ye, not pilfer from ye."

"He said no."

"Ask him what's so special about the trunk," requested Billy.

"I told you. He's dead, not deaf. Ask him yourself."

Simple looked up from his candle trimming. "'Tis a great, guarded secret," he replied.

"He said it's a great, guarded secret," reported Stefanie. She looked at Simple. "What kind of secret?"

"A secret that goes back thousands of years. 'Twould

bring great peril to those who saw it. 'Tis Blackbeard's biggest fear, which is why he is undecided."

"Undecided about what?" asked Stefanie.

"I have not been privy to his indecision," said Simple.

"What is he saying?" asked Daniel.

"Shh! What if we see what's in the trunk but don't take the stuff? What if we just look inside? Blackbeard can't object to that," said Stefanie.

"Stefanie!" insisted Daniel. "Blackbeard can't object to anything. He's dead. Simple is dead. How can two dead people stop us from digging out the trunk?"

"He stopped you from getting to it," Billy reminded him.

Simple stopped his candle whittling and looked up at the girl. "The trunk belongs to me captain," he explained. "If ye dig it out without proper permission, he'll have yer head." He smiled his toothless smile, then went back to his candles.

Stefanie rubbed her neck with her hand. "Then it *is* a treasure chest."

"Of course it's a treasure chest," exclaimed Daniel. "Why else would he be guarding it from us?"

"Yeah, but I think it's some kind of special treasure," said Stefanie. "He said Blackbeard would have my head if I took whatever's inside of it."

"Tell him he can have it," said Daniel.

"Cute."

"Well, I think it's funny coming from a guy who doesn't have a head," kidded Daniel.

"Don't say stuff like that. Blackbeard might be listening in," worried Billy.

Daniel peered in the direction Stefanie was addressing. "Excuse me, Simple. Can I go to the trunk now?"

"Ye have been warned," he told the boy. "Even if I let ye pass, I cannot let ye touch the trunk."

"He says 'Ye have been warned, and even if I let ye pass, I cannot let ye touch the trunk.'" Stefanie waited along with the others for Simple's response.

"Well?" asked Daniel.

"He's thinking," said Stefanie.

"This is nuts," said Daniel.

"I don't think we should be arguing with a ghost that works for Blackbeard," observed Billy.

Stefanie watched as Simple made a gesture, with his hand pointing in the direction of the treasure chest. "He's letting us go."

"It's about time," sniffed Daniel.

Stefanie thanked him and took a timid step past the spirited ghost. This time Simple didn't trip anyone. He packed up his things and followed the children the rest of the way through the corridors, until they reached the opening with the second trunk in plain view.

"Finally," said Billy. He aimed his flashlight at the wall where they had patched it, then opened his backpack and removed his father's pickax.

"Uh, uh, uh," warned Simple with a wag of his finger and a shake of his head.

"Stop!" hollered Stefanie.

"Now what?" asked Daniel.

"I told ye. Ye may look, but not touch," said Simple.

"He said we could look, but not touch," repeated Stefanie.

"Then we might as well go home," said Billy.

Simple continued his whittling. "Now if that trunk be mine, I would let ye chop away, I would," he told Stefanie. "But the trunk and all its worth belong to the pirate Blackbeard. The master does not want the trunk disturbed."

"Is he talking?" asked Daniel.

Stefanie nodded. "He says that if the trunk were his, he'd let us chop away, but it belongs to Blackbeard, and Blackbeard doesn't want it disturbed."

Daniel was getting upset. "What does he expect us to do? Find Blackbeard and ask his permission?"

"Brilliant! Capital idea!" hailed Simple. "He's on his ship. Shall I fetch him?"

"Simple says Blackbeard's on his ship. Do you want him to go get Blackbeard?"

"I was just kidding. This isn't Blackbeard's tunnel anymore. It belongs to the people of Ocracoke."

Simple looked up from his candle-making equipment and smirked. "Have ye found the Blood of Moritangia?"

"The Blood of Moritangia?" asked Stefanie.

"What's the Blood of Moritangia?" asked Billy and Daniel together.

"I don't know," said Stefanie. "Simple asked me if I found it." She turned to the ghost. "Is that what's in the trunk?"

"Nay, mate. All that's in that trunk is a red herring."

What was once a pirate's cache

Now becomes a child's task.

Beware ye bold and curious teen,

Some riches should remain unseen.

N

CHAPTER XXI

Stefanie glared at Simple. "You've got to be kidding. That's the big secret?"

"What?" asked the boys.

"He says there's a red herring in the trunk."

"A fish? There's a fish in the trunk?" erupted Daniel. "Are you telling us he won't let us open the trunk because there's a fish in it? That's moronic! That's the most moronic thing I've ever heard in my entire life! Tell Simple I think he and Blackbeard are out of their invisible minds."

"I think you just did," whispered Billy.

Simple took a whittled candle and hung it in midair, snapped his fingers, and the tiny flame flickered above the wax. "I can't let ye open the trunk," he informed Stefanie. "Yer lives would be at risk if ye beheld what lies within."

"You said it was a fish. Trust me, we're not going to eat it."

"He wants us to eat the fish?" asked Daniel.

"I said 'twas a red herring," said Simple.

"He said it's a red herring," said Stefanie.

"I'm not afraid of herring," said Daniel. "My grandfather eats herring."

"Maybe it's the smell," guessed Billy.

"This whole place smells," said Stefanie.

Simple grinned, then collected his candles. "Suppose I fetch the captain. What say ye then?"

"He wants to know if he should fetch the captain," reported Stefanie.

"The more the merrier," said Daniel.

"I don't think you should be sarcastic with a ghost," Stefanie told him. "It's bad luck."

Daniel ignored her. And he ignored Simple. He grabbed his father's relic-digging knife out of his coat pocket, lifted his hand, then lowered it. "I don't know what to do. We're arguing with a ghost who's representing another ghost. Why would Blackbeard and Simple be so secretive if the only thing in the trunk is a red herring?"

"Uh-oh." Stefanie stopped and looked around.

"Now what's wrong?" asked Billy.

"Simple's gone."

"Good riddance," said Daniel.

Stefanie thought otherwise. "What if he went to get Blackbeard? I've met the man and he scares me."

Now everyone stopped and gawked at the girl. "What

do you mean, you met the man? You met Blackbeard?" Billy asked her.

"Sort of. It was in the same dream where I met Simple. Blackbeard made me sell tickets to a plundering while we were on the way to Williamsburg."

"He made you sell tickets to a plundering on the way to Williamsburg," repeated Daniel, making sure he had heard her correctly.

"Yeah."

"On the way to Williamsburg?"

"Yeah."

"Where were we?" asked Daniel.

"I don't know. On your way to Williamsburg."

"So you were in two places at the same time?" asked Billy.

"Sort of."

Daniel knit his eyebrows. "I don't think you should tell too many people about that if I were you," he advised.

Stefanie pretended not to hear him. "Actually, I was pretty good. Nobody bought any of my tickets at the first house, but then I started telling people that Blackbeard would burn down their houses and pillage them if they didn't buy my tickets, so I sold every one. Then I got to go onto the ship and pick something I wanted from the pirated loot after all the sword fighting and gun shooting were over. I ate my apple because this creep of a man was staring at me. I tried to shoot the gun, but I shot a sand dune instead and landed on my backside, so Simple shot him for me. I think that's how it went."

There was stunned silence for a moment, then Daniel asked, "Where's the stuff you took off the ship?"

Stefanie smiled. "I let Melanie Smyth have it."

"You let Melanie Smyth have it!" repeated Daniel. "Oh! That's right. You said you met her when we were in the minister's office and you were holding the candlestick." He shook his head, looking greatly concerned. "You need help," he told her. "Maybe when your lung collapsed, part of your brain matter went with it. I'll tell you what, though. Next time we have a church raffle, you should definitely sign up for ticket sales. Just tell them you'll get a ghost to burn down their houses if they don't buy a ticket. That should go over big."

Stefanie was about to answer, but then she placed her finger on her lips. "Shh!"

"What's wrong?" whispered Daniel.

"Simple's back."

"Oh, God. Did he bring Blackbeard?" panicked Billy.

"I don't think so."

Daniel relaxed. For someone who didn't believe in Stefanie's ghosts, he was certainly freaked out by them. "What does he want?"

Simple wiggled a finger, beckoning Stefanie to approach him. "It seems the tides have turned, though I have not been privy to explanation," he told the young girl quietly. "Someone has taken to ye, Mary Reed, so I am to make ye a deal."

"Okay, that's it!" shouted Stefanie, now exasperated. "My name is Stefanie Austin, not Mary Reed. Mary Reed is what you called me in my dream. She was a pirate when you were a pirate. Maybe she's a pirate on a different ghost ship than you're on, and I hope you find her, I really do, because you seem to like her an awful lot.

"But I'm not Mary Reed. I'm a kid. I'm only13 years

old, and I'm stuck down here with these three dingbatters because we found a third trunk when we weren't even supposed to be down here. The only reason we came down here is because we were afraid somebody stole our stuff out of the second trunk, and guess what? They did. So now we have a chance to open a third trunk to see if there is anything in there we can have to replace the stuff that was taken out of the second trunk, which really should still be down here, because the people from Wilmington haven't come yet.

"So if you don't mind, I, Stefanie Austin, not Mary Reed, would like to go back to digging out the trunk, even if it is only a red herring." She stopped for a moment and caught her breath. Daniel's eyes were wide with curiosity as he stared at the girl screaming at the wall. He didn't know whether to laugh or rush her to a doctor.

Suddenly, Simple's offer to make a deal entered Stefanie's consciousness and she asked the wall, "What deal?"

"Your ghost wants to make a deal?" asked Billy.

"Yes."

"This should be interesting," thought Daniel. "What kind of a deal?"

Simple was still looking at Stefanie with nothing short of amazement when he came out of his stupor. He had never heard such a ranting come out in so eloquent or animated a manner. "I call ye Mary Reed as a compliment, me lady. 'Tis her ye remind me of. I did not have the pleasure of sharing yer dream. But, 'tis true, the trunk contains a red herring."

"He's talking about fish again," reported Stefanie.

"No, child. A red herring is not a fish."

"Then what is it?"

"What's what?" queried Daniel.

"A red herring," said Stefanie.

"It's a fish," said Daniel.

"'Tis not a fish!" hollered the ghost.

"Then what is it?" piped the girl.

"What's what?" asked Billy.

"A red herring," said Stefanie. "Simple says it's not a fish."

"Then what is it?" asked Daniel. "Ask him what it is!"

"I've been asking him what it is! Didn't y'all hear me asking him what it is?"

"'Tis a false clue," explained Simple. "'Tis a thing that makes ye think y'are looking fer one thing, but ye find another."

Stefanie studied the spirit and frowned. "I don't get it."

"What don't you get?" asked Daniel.

"Shh," said Stefanie, "he's explaining."

"A red herring masks what ye are lookin' fer. It takes ye away from the real thing. 'Tis meant to lead ye astray."

Stefanie still looked confused.

"Well, what did he say?" asked Daniel and Billy together.

"It's confusing."

"Try," Daniel urged her.

"He said a red herring is something that's there instead of the real thing being there, and that when you see the thing that's really there, it really isn't the thing you're looking for, but it's there to confuse you."

"He said that?" asked Daniel.

"Not exactly."

"Well what exactly!" hollered Daniel.

"Stop yelling. I told you, it's confusing. Whatever is in the trunk is hiding what we think is in the trunk."

"But we don't know what's in the trunk, so how can it be different than what we think is in the trunk?" asked Billy.

"Exactly," said Stefanie.

"Exactly what?" screamed Daniel.

Stefanie grumbled and tried once again to explain. "The thing that's in the trunk isn't the real prize, it's just pretending to be the real prize. The real prize is somewhere else, but you're supposed to think the real prize is in the trunk, even though it's not."

"Nay," said Simple. "The red herring is that thing that is leading ye astray."

"Oh. I got it wrong," she told the boys. "The thing inside the trunk is leading us astray."

"Aye," said Simple.

Stefanie smiled, having satisfactorily recited the correct answer. "He says I got it right."

"I'm really confused," confessed Billy.

"Wait a minute. If the thing in the trunk isn't really the prize, what difference does it make if we see what's in the trunk?" inquired Daniel.

"If it's not the prize, why even look in the trunk?" asked Billy.

Mark had been silently thinking during the entire conversation. He pointed to the area Stefanie looked at when she spoke to Simple and shrugged.

"Mark wants to know . . ." Stefanie began.

"'Tis all right. I understand the child," said Simple. "Ye have permission to peek inside the trunk, but the trunk stays in the wall. Then ye must cover up the wall so no one will ever find it or know what's inside of it. 'Tis a grave warning. No one must ever find the trunk or see its contents."

"What did he say?" asked the boys.

"Then I guess we can't keep what's in it?" assumed Stefanie.

"Ye assume correctly."

"Stefanie! What's the deal?" asked Daniel.

Stefanie sighed. "We can peek in the trunk, but the trunk stays in the wall. Then we have to cover it back up.

"What's the point if the real treasure isn't inside the trunk?"

"How should I know?" confessed Stefanie. "But we have permission to take a peek."

"How are we supposed to take a peek if we're not allowed to take the trunk out of the wall?" asked Billy.

Stefanie glanced at Simple. "Good question."

"'Tis a means," said Simple.

"He said there's a means," reported Stefanie.

"Maybe Blackbeard is sentimental about this trunk," suggested Billy. "Maybe it has another lady inside of it."

Stefanie looked at Simple. "What would happen to us if we kept what was in the trunk, since it's not the real prize?"

Simple smiled coyly. "'Tis your choice. Your fate."

"What did he say?"

"He said it's our choice and our fate."

"Very deep," said Billy.

"How are we supposed to break into the trunk without taking it out of the wall?" repeated Daniel.

"Let's break into the wall until we find enough of the trunk to punch a hole in it, then peek in with our flashlights," suggested Billy.

"Fine with me," said Daniel. He picked up the pickax and struck the first blow into the wall near the corner of the trunk. He stopped and looked at the others. "Hello!"

Stefanie looked up. Another piece of the ceiling broke loose and fell to the floor. She was growing more and more nervous by the minute. "Hurry up. I want to get out of here. Besides, I'm tired of dealing with ghosts." She turned to Simple. "No offense."

"Could y'all stop yapping and help?" asked Billy.

"Sorry." For the next fifteen minutes, everyone went back to work, chipping and scraping, slowly and carefully, trying to prevent any part of the wall from caving in. Billy chipped away at the higher parts of the wall, while the younger kids chopped and dug around the lower parts.

"Do you mind?" Stefanie hissed at Billy. "You're dropping cement all over me!"

"I'm the only one who can reach up here," he apologized.

"Well, look before you chop."

The children stopped working every few minutes to make certain the wall was still holding. Finally, an entire corner of the trunk was revealed, along with a two-foot square of side section.

"It really is a treasure chest," said Stefanie, sounding delightfully surprised.

"I knew it," cheered Billy.

Just then, a large chunk of ceiling and upper wall fell onto the children, revealing more empty pockets where the cement was breaking off. The kids brushed themselves off and looked up. "That's not good," admitted Billy.

"Let's just stay away from the wall and punch a hole in the side of the trunk," suggested Daniel. He took his father's relic-hunting knife and began to carefully jab at the side of the trunk. "I still don't get this choice or red herring thing. I think we should take the stuff out of the trunk and take it home with us. Otherwise we'll end up with nothing, since all of our other stuff was stolen."

"Simple said the treasure isn't in the trunk," said Billy. "Besides, we have our seeds."

"I know. And the pirate's den. I just want one thing from the treasure chest that I can keep, even if it's not worth anything. I mean, Blackbeard did put whatever's in the trunk in there. That makes it kind of neat." Daniel looked at his watch. "We better work fast or we'll have to come back down."

"No way I'm coming back down," mumbled Stefanie. "Let's just do it now and get it over with. Then I'm going to sleep for a week."

Mark agreed. His eyelids were growing heavy, and he was practically falling asleep on his feet as he aimed two of the flashlights in the direction of the trunk. Daniel, Stefanie, and Billy worked as quickly as they could without disturbing the wall around the trunk. The side of the chest was much thicker than they had suspected, even with decay, and it took 20 minutes before Daniel punched a hole through the wood. It took another half hour to bore a hole big enough to look through without damaging anything that might be on the inside of the chest.

"Hand me a flashlight," Daniel told Mark. Daniel lifted the flashlight and flooded the opening with light. Leaning in, he peered inside. He blinked a few times, strained his neck forward, and took a second look. This time, he turned his head and spoke to the area where Stefanie had conversed with Simple. "What gives?" he asked the blank space.

"He's not here," said Stefanie.

"Well, get him back!" said Daniel.

"I can't get him back. He's not a cell phone call. He's a ghost that comes and goes when he feels like it."

"What's in there?" Billy asked Daniel.

"Take a look."

Billy put his face up to the side of the trunk and gaped into the hole. He, too, took a second look. "There's nothing in there. It's empty."

"Empty? What do you mean?" asked Stefanie. She rushed up to the hole and peered inside. After she stood there saying nothing for a few moments, Mark tapped her on the shoulder. She moved over and let Mark take a look, then she put her face back up to the hole. She finally backed up and sat down on the wet floor with a loud thud. "Figures."

Mark thought for a moment, laid his hand on the portion of trunk that was exposed, then indicated to Daniel that he should reach inside.

Daniel was ticked. "What's the point?" But he figured he had nothing to lose, so he walked in front of Stefanie, reached into the hole with his long arm, and felt around the floor of the trunk. "Wait a minute! There is something in here!" He reached as hard as he could with his fingertips, and grabbed hold of something cold, somewhat round, thick, and rough to the touch. He pulled it out. "This is the red herring? This is what all the fuss was about?"

Billy reached way down into the side of the trunk and pulled out several more red herrings. "This is Blackbeard's big secret?"

Mark reached over and took one of the items out of Billy's hand and stared at it. It meant something, he was sure.

"At least we know what a red herring is," stated Billy philosophically.

"Yeah. Lucky us," moaned Stefanie. She stood up and gazed at the object in Daniel's hand. "It's a brick."

Daniel shooed Billy away from the hole, pulled out two more bricks, and laid them on the cover of the large, empty trunk that still sat in the hallway. "Look at them! Bricks! All this work, all that stuff with Simple, and Blackbeard was about bricks!"

"They don't look like regular bricks," said Billy, examining one closely. "They're different. Older, I think."

Stefanie picked one up and turned it around in her hand. The top of it flaked like hardened sand. "Billy's right. It's not like the bricks they use for building houses here on the island. It's choppier. And round. See how the bottom is flat. Maybe it's the kind of bricks they made 300 years ago."

Mark brought the brick he was holding over to Daniel, then pointed to the ceiling.

"The ceiling doesn't have any bricks," Daniel told him.

Mark shook his head and pointed up again.

"Oh, my gosh! He's right! I recognize these bricks," she told the others. "They're the bricks Blackbeard used as the base of his trading post in the cove."

Mark nodded.

Daniel studied the bricks with new interest. "They're exactly like the bricks beside the well and lookout tree underneath the ivy. But why would Blackbeard, or whoever, put bricks in the trunk, then hide the trunk inside of the wall? What's so secretive about these bricks?"

"Oooh! Maybe there's something inside of them," imagined Stefanie.

"They could have gold in them," ventured Billy.

"Or diamonds," hoped Stefanie.

Billy placed one of the bricks on the floor and grabbed the pickax. "Stand back, everyone." With one good swing, he brought the pickax down into the center of the brick. The solid clay structure shattered. Everyone rushed forward with their flashlights and scrutinized the small pieces.

"There's nothing in them but dirt and clay," complained Stefanie.

"No gold," sighed Billy.

"No nothing," said Daniel.

"Well, we better clean it up so no one finds it," said Stefanie.

While Billy scooped up the pieces and put them back into the trunk, Daniel paced back and forth. "So someone, we think Blackbeard, took the bricks out of the cove, stuck them in this trunk, hid the trunk, and did what? We just proved they're not worth anything."

"Maybe he put something in the cove where the bricks used to be, then hid the bricks so no one would know that he had switched them," suggested Billy.

"Like what?" asked Stefanie.

Daniel looked at his watch. "I don't know, but we'll have to figure it out tomorrow. Let's get out of here." He stuffed the bricks back into the side of the trunk, then the four of them used the chunks of cement to patch the hole as quickly as they could, using wet sand and bits of cement to seal it shut. But the job was far from satisfactory. "We'll have to come back down and fix the wall," Daniel told Billy. "Anybody who sees the wall will know it's been hacked."

As the kids picked up their flashlights to leave, there was a sudden tremor in the tunnel. Sand and seashell cement fell like thick dust from the ceiling, covering the children. A loud, grinding noise followed. The kids grabbed each other for comfort. "What's happening?" panicked Stefanie.

"Look!" cried Daniel. He aimed his shaky flashlight at the wall. Sand and cement from the wall and ceiling near the exposed chest began to swirl and ooze, filling in the gaps the children had left behind. As the four children watched in stunned amazement, the wall completely repaired itself, covering all hints of entry.

Slowly the swirling and vibration ceased. Stefanie turned and faced the back wall. Simple was standing, whittling and grinning through the darkness. "Thanks, maties," he called out loud. Then in a flash, he disappeared.

"What was all that about?" gasped Daniel, still gaping at the patched wall.

"I have no idea," said Stefanie with a slight grin. "Can we leave now? I really have to get out of here."

"Let me guess," yawned Daniel. "You have to pee."

Deep beneath the pirate's cove,

Where earth is rich and soil deep,

There lies among the English vine

The bricks once tread upon by Teach.

Three hundred years its ivy coat

Has hidden steps once used for trade.

Sandstone secrets hide within.

Standing guard is Sam Jones's grave.

N

CHAPTER XXII

The children dragged themselves to school that morning and spent their time in class yawning and fighting to stay awake. They perked up slightly when teachers and schoolmates alike swarmed around them, asking questions about their trip to Williamsburg and their search for the ticketed items. Before they left Williamsburg, Todd had instructed them on what they could and could not talk about. Unfortunately, they had to leave out the really juicy parts concerning their most recent acts of crime and punishment. Mostly they were limited to saying how privileged they were to actually see the candlesticks and trowel. No one spoke about the great crate fiasco, but the word *hyraphyte* spread like poison ivy, thanks to Daniel. Now kids who had grown up with Stefanie saw her in a new light—stranger than usual.

When the lunch bell rang, the four children hopped onto their bikes and sped away from the school. They made sure no one followed them, then quickly rode down the long dirt trail beside Tubba's house toward Blackbeard's Cove. They ditched their bikes behind high thickets, then walked toward the center of the cove.

"There are 80 cemeteries on Ocracoke," Billy mentioned. "Why do you think Sam Jones picked the center of Blackbeard's Cove to be buried?"

"He was eccentric," Stefanie chimed in. "That's right before your arteries harden. Besides, it's 80 cemeteries plus one."

"What do you mean?" asked Daniel, pulling his face back from the fiercely blowing leaves.

Stefanie stopped in front of Sam Jones's grave and pointed. The post standing upright next to the gravestone read *Ikey D*. "How many other islanders do you know who are buried with their horse?"

The closer they walked to the spot where Blackbeard was known to have had his trading post, the windier it became. The ivy flooring seemed to come alive, wrapping itself around the children's shoes, and brittle winter sticks flew through the cove, smacking their faces with the bite of a green-headed fly.

"Is it extra freaky in here today, or what?" Stefanie mentioned to the others.

"I'm with you," admitted Billy. Mark nodded agreement.

"It's just your imagination," Daniel told them. He wouldn't admit it, but the woods were definitely making him uncomfortable. "Come on, let's get this over with." Daniel led the way toward the remaining base of Blackbeard's trading post, where he knew old bricks, like the ones they found in the hidden trunk, were still in the ground. As the children got closer to their goal, the wind continued to strengthen. All four sensed an

overwhelming dread they had never felt before when walking through the cove. Above them, gnarled tree limbs creaked and moaned, like dozens of old wooden rocking chairs, rocking above them on squeaky floorboards. The sun, which had shone all morning, now hid behind a thunderous gray cloud that had turned the sky a slate gray ash.

Stefanie didn't see any ghosts, but she sure felt them everywhere. And they weren't happy.

"Maybe Sam Jones doesn't want us here," whispered Billy.

"He never minded us being here before. Let's just look for the bricks and get out of here."

"I don't want to be late getting back to school," worried Billy. But the truth was, the wind and biting air mixed with the creaking and darting sticks were unsettling, and he was eager to leave. Everyone looked in earnest for the bricks beneath the ivy, but the ivy had grown so thick and entwined over the 300 years, that it was almost impossible to separate the vines. The only visible bricks that matched the ones in the treasure chest were above ground near the cement cistern.

"We have to go back," Stefanie announced urgently. A flying stick had hit her leg, which had begun to bleed.

"We will in a minute," persisted Daniel. "Keep looking." All four continued crawling on their hands and knees while pushing back the dense vines and interlaced thicket, but nothing was uncovered except for dirt and sand.

"We're going to be late for school," repeated Billy.

"I'm not leaving until I find out what he hid here," obsessed Daniel. "It's important."

"What exactly are we looking for?" asked Billy, darting a flying stick.

"Something that's in the ground where the bricks used to be." Lunch hour was almost over when Daniel let out a yelp. "Over here. I found something." He waited for the others to join him, then pointed to the outer edge of the brick foundation. He pulled a brick out of his pocket and compared the two.

"Where did you get that?" shrieked Stefanie.

"I took it out of the trunk."

"You weren't supposed to do that! Simple said not to do that!"

"You told us Simple said it was our choice whether or not to keep the red herring. So I kept one. Besides, who's to know it's a brick from the trunk and not a brick from the cove? At least we've proven it's a match."

"We already knew that," said Stefanie.

"Well, now we know it again."

"Maybe Simple played a joke on us," suggested Billy. "Maybe the thing about the bricks being a red herring is a lie, and there really isn't any treasure. Maybe Stefanie's ghosts are getting one big laugh."

"They're not my ghosts!" objected the girl.

"Yeah? Well, they're still laughing."

"There's something in this cove where those bricks used to be. I'm sure of it," insisted Daniel. He checked the time and resigned himself to the fact that they were going to be late returning to school. "We might as well keep looking."

"Maybe Blackbeard just had too many bricks and, as a joke, buried the extras," said Billy.

"I don't think Blackbeard made jokes," said Stefanie. "He didn't have a very good sense of humor when I met him."

"You didn't meet Blackbeard," Daniel told her.

"Yes, I did. I met him in my dream the same day I met Simple. That's why I was selling tickets."

"Please don't start that again."

"Hey, I found something." Billy had weeded through several feet of ivy and brick, when he uncovered something unusual. "Look at this, y'all." The moment he called to the others, a scorching flash of lightning lit the sky directly above him. It was accompanied by an earsplitting crash of thunder. The four kids covered their ears, then rushed toward Billy.

"We need to get out of here," shouted Stefanie.

"Look at this first," hollered Billy. The wind was so loud he had to yell over it, and the thunder had left his own ears ringing.

"What is it?" Stefanie could barely hear her own voice over the rattling of tree limbs and a second burst of lightning and thunder.

"It's a pink rock!" yelled Billy. He ducked and covered his head as a sturdy branch from the tree right above him broke loose and dropped to the ground, hitting him squarely on the shoulder. "Ouch! That hurt!"

Daniel's eyes went from Billy's shoulder to the ground where his friend had been pointing. "That's it? That's the great discovery? The bricks were replaced by a big, pink rock?"

"Yeah, but look at it!" hollered Billy, climbing back up to his feet. "It's a really big rock, and it's pink! That must mean something. Blackbeard must have taken the bricks out of the ground just so he could bury it here."

"That's crazy! Why would any sane person take bricks out of the cove and replace it with a pink rock?"

"Maybe he wasn't sane when he did it," Stefanie shouted over the wind and thunder. "Maybe he was drunk."

"That's the first thing you've said that makes sense."

Billy kept glancing down at the rock. Curious, he tapped it with his foot. The moment he touched the rock with the tip of his shoe, another streak of lightning flashed across the sky, followed by an awesomely angry burst of thunder. A swirl of dead leaves rose up from the cove and danced around the feet of the four children. Stefanie noticed that the ivy appeared to be closing in on them. While Daniel, Stefanie, and Billy gaped at the creeping ivy, Mark stayed fixated on the pink rock. There was something mystifying about it. He couldn't put his finger on it, but he sensed it was much more than it appeared to be.

"Please, can we get out of here!" screamed Stefanie.

"Good idea! Come on, let's go!" hollered Daniel.

Mark ignored the others and knelt beside the rock. He stared at it without expression. When Billy went to help him up, Mark pushed him away.

"We have to go!" shouted Billy.

Mark wouldn't move. Suddenly, he placed his hand on top of the pink stone. He pulled it back quickly, rocked back on his heels, and thought for a moment.

"Let's go, Mark," Stefanie begged him. She was terrified of being hit by a flying branch. "We have to get out of here before someone gets hurt!"

But Mark wouldn't listen. Without taking his eyes off the stone, he removed a Boy Scout knife from his pocket, reached out, and scratched the top of the rock. Soft ribbons of bright blue sparks rose off the top of the stone as a deafening crash of thunder exploded just feet above his head. The blast knocked Stefanie to the ground.

"What's happening?" freaked Billy. "Where did those lights come from?"

"The stone!" Daniel grabbed the back of Mark's coat, but Mark yanked it out of his hand. "Mark, come on! We have to get out of here!" yelled Daniel.

Mark shooed him away angrily. He raised the tip of his knife in the air and brought it down with such force that a small chip of the stone flew off, landing in the palm of his other hand. A zigzagged spike of blue lightning shot up and out of the large stone and followed the path into Mark's palm, illuminating the chip and knocking the youngster unconscious. As he fell to the ground, the sky opened and rain poured down in buckets.

"Oh, my God! Is he dead?" panicked Stefanie.

"I don't know. Grab his legs!" Billy shouted to Daniel. The boys picked Mark up off the ground and fought their way through wind and rain back to the cove entrance.

Stefanie climbed to her feet, nervously kicked ivy and sand back over the pink stone, then ran to catch up with the boys. When they reached the edge of the cove, the storm began to wane, and they placed Mark on the soaked ground. Stefanie sat down beside him and placed the boy's head in her lap. A few minutes later he woke up.

"Thank goodness," heaved Billy.

The small chip of stone was still tightly clenched in Mark's stinging palm.

"Are you okay?" asked Stefanie, while dripping onto his face.

Mark thought for a moment, then nodded that he was fine.

"What was all that about?" gasped Daniel. He and Billy collapsed to the ground next to Stefanie and Mark.

"Lightning shot out of that rock!" exclaimed Billy. "And what was with that storm? I thought we were toast."

Daniel glowered at Mark. "We could have been killed," he admonished the boy.

"He didn't know the rock was going to shoot lightning," Stefanie replied, defending the youngster. She helped Mark to his feet, then all four walked into the thicket to reclaim their bikes. "Now that's weird," Stefanie noticed as she looked up at the sky. The sun was shining and there wasn't a cloud in sight. No wind was coming from the cove. "What happened to the storm?"

"Who cares. Let's just get out of here," said Daniel.

The foursome returned to school 25 minutes late and soaking wet.

"What happened to you?" asked the principal as she greeted them by the front door.

"Uh . . ." Daniel looked at the others, "we were going to have lunch over by the sound."

"And?"

Billy stood dripping on the floor when Daniel looked at him. "You tell her."

Barbara Scarborough turned her attention to Billy. "Well?"

"Oh! Well, we were taking our bikes by the path near Tubba's house and Mark got there ahead of us."

"And he can't see very well, so he rode right into the sound," explained Daniel. "The three of us," he pointed to himself, Billy, and Stefanie, "dove in after him because he doesn't swim very well, and we had to get his bike out of the water."

"And him! We had to get him out of the water," added Stefanie. "And then we had to look for his glasses, which took most of the time, and that's why we're all wet and late."

Barbara forced herself not to smile. "Is that what happened, Mark?"

Mark's eyes widened and he searched his friends for an answer. No one looked at him. He looked back at his principal, blushed, and nodded.

"Is that 'yes' that's what happened, or 'yes' if you say so?" asked Barbara.

Mark shrugged. He was shivering from the cold.

"Never mind. Just go home and change your clothes, then come back to school. And don't dawdle."

"Smooth," Stefanie told the boys. "Really smooth."

'Tis troubling, these secret tales
Of legends past that now prevail.
Things unknown that lie in state
Wait for knowledge to yield one's fate.
A secret sleeps, time passes by
Until the life of one does die.
That death alone shall queries make,
The secret thus must n'er awake.

CHAPTER XXIII

The children returned and finished the school day, then met at the library to work on their community service. When they were finally alone, they leaped out of their seats and rushed Mark.

"Let me see it," Daniel asked excitedly.

Mark reached into his pocket and pulled out the small chip of pink stone. He laid it on his desk. At first they just stared at it, then Billy got up the courage to pick it up.

"Is it hot?" asked Stefanie.

"No. It's just a piece of stone."

Daniel took the chip and placed it in his palm. "Yeah, well, it's one possessed piece of stone."

Billy took the chip and examined it closely. It was rough on the top side with some moss that had grown onto it. The underside was smoother and clean. It was pink and had a sparkle to it. "What kind of stone is this?"

"Maybe it's a moon rock," suggested Stefanie with eyes wide.

"Moon rock?" laughed Daniel. "Get real! How could Blackbeard hide a moon rock if the astronauts hadn't been to the moon yet?"

"It's pretty hard to 'get real' when you're talking about a stone that shoots lightning and makes the wind blow!" argued the girl.

"She's got a point," said the oldest.

"Thank you, Billy."

Mark clicked on his computer and searched for information about rocks. Several websites came up, but they all contained descriptions, not pictures.

"Wait a second." Stefanie trotted over to the bookshelves. "There has to be a book on rocks somewhere in here." It only took a minute to locate a book on rocks in the geology section.

The boys joined her at her desk. "It doesn't look like shale or slate," said Billy, making a comparison to the pink chip. He flipped to several other pages. "It's not granite, or quartzite, or basalt."

"Here it is," Daniel pointed out. He looked at the others quizzically. "It's sandstone. Listen to this, 'Sandstone is a sedimentary rock composed of feldspar and quartz and is often found in deserts.' Deserts? Why would Blackbeard take a piece of sandstone out of the desert and bury it on Ocracoke Island? And why would he hide the bricks he took out of the cove, so no one would know he planted a piece of sandstone? That's crazy, even for Blackbeard."

"It has to be valuable," surmised Stefanie.

"Sandstone isn't valuable," said Daniel.

"Daniel, it's a piece of sandstone that spits lightning, makes thunder, blows trees, and creeps out dead ghosts who didn't want us to find it!"

Daniel glared at her. "Ghosts are dead."

"Some are deader than others," explained Stefanie.

"How can a ghost be a deader ghost?"

"There are see-through ghosts who are just ghosts, like Mad Mag, and there are non-see-through-ghosts-who-look-alive-even-though-they're-dead ghosts, like the guy on the steps in Williamsburg," said Stefanie.

"Which ones didn't want us to find the rock?"

"The non-see-through ghosts."

"If it was a non-see-through ghost, how come the rest of us couldn't see him?"

"How should I know?"

"So, was the ghost in the tunnel a dead ghost or a deader ghost?" asked Daniel. "And what about the ghosts on the island that everybody sees, even the tourists?"

"They're see-through ghosts."

"Then how come you don't have to be a hyraphyte to see the see-through ghosts?"

"How should I know! Do I look like a ghost expert? Ask Philip. He's met them all."

"Criminee! What difference does it make?" exploded Billy. "If Blackbeard took the time to dig up the bricks and hide them so he could bury the sandstone, it has to be valuable. Otherwise, it's just stupid."

"And what about the Blood of Moritangia stuff Simple asked about before he told us about the red herring? Maybe that's part of the pink stone, too," added Stefanie.

"Or maybe it's something from the same church robbery as the candlesticks and trowel," suggested Billy.

"The Blood of Moritangia," repeated Daniel. "I wonder what it is."

"We could ask Dr. Hardison about it," said Billy.

"We should keep our mouths shut about it," Daniel stated emphatically. "At least until we try to find out what it is on our own."

"How are we supposed to do that?" asked Stefanie.

Mark was already busy at the computer. He looked up the Blood of Moritangia and waited to see what came up on his screen. A few seconds later, a short paragraph appeared. He rapped on his desk for everyone to come and read.

Stefanie read out loud. "'The legend of the Blood of Moritangia has never been proven. It is believed to be a valuable ring that once belonged to the Knights Templar.' I wonder who they were."

"I don't know. We'll have to look them up, too," said Daniel.

Stefanie continued reading out loud. "'The Blood of Moritangia is said to contain the key to a thousand-year-old mystery.'"

"How cool is that?" said Billy.

"Yeah, but it doesn't tell us anything," said Daniel. "Maybe it was one of the rings we found in that box full of golden body parts."

"Keep reading," said Billy.

"'The legendary ring was once described in a Templar scroll as being a band of solid gold with eighteen perfectly matched rubies perched on one side. The rubies were believed to have been a gift from the king of Burma to the king of Egypt, for they were valued far and above diamonds. The word *ruby* is called *ratnaraj* and translates as *king of gemstones*. The ruby is said to be the most precious of the twelve stones God created. The Bible says that only wisdom is more precious than rubies. The legend continues to say that the ring worn by the Knights Templar was a gift from the king of Egypt to the king of England, but was intercepted by the French, who gave it to the Templars for safekeeping. It is said that the ruby at the top was the same ruby God commanded be placed around Aaron's neck.'"

Stefanie stopped reading and covered her mouth with her hand. She stared at the screen, speechless.

Daniel read and reread the information three times. "Eighteen rubies," he croaked. "On a gold band."

"Is anybody else thinking what I'm thinking?" whispered Billy.

Mark sat at his computer, staring at the screen and nodding in slow motion.

"She did say it was from Blackbeard's booty," Stefanie reminded everyone.

Daniel turned to Stefanie. "You're sure it had eighteen rubies? You're positive?"

"Trust me. I counted them about a bazillion times."

Daniel plopped down in his seat. "What do we do now?"

"Nothing." Billy folded his arms and looked thoughtful. "It's the widow's ring and it's in the widow's casket. No one ever has to know about this."

Blackbeard stormed across the deck, kicking and smacking members of his crew, shooting several, leaving limbs with gaping see-through holes. He grabbed a rope and leaped onto his deck rail, where he fired his guns into the air. Mrs. McNemmish stayed a good distance away and watched the angry tirade.

"Thar getting too close!" thundered Blackbeard. "I did not want the children to know what was in the trunk! Now they know about the ring and the prize!" His eyes blazed with anger. He jumped down and reached out with his hand, lifting Simple into the air by his throat. He slammed him up against the railing and threatened to throw him overboard. "Ye were told to keep them away from the trunk, not to show them what lay within the walls! What say ye?"

Simple gagged under the clutch of his captain's hand. "She . . . she . . . she . . . ."

"Spit it out, man!" shouted Blackbeard, "or I'll have yer head on the bowsprit."

"I asked him to show the children what was in the trunk," came a soft voice from behind. Blackbeard removed his hand and let Simple slump to the floor. He turned and faced the flushed, young widow. "Ye told him to tell the children? I gave orders they were not to know what lay in that trunk until I deemed it necessary. I told ye the dangers of them knowing."

Mrs. McNemmish sighed. "Forgive me for intruding, Edward, but Simple told me the children found the trunk. He knew I was concerned about them. They were going to dig the trunk out of the wall. I was afraid the tunnel would collapse on them. They could have been killed. I couldn't take that chance."

Blackbeard paced back and forth, giving Simple an angry look each time he passed the man. He looked at Theodora sadly. "Knowing has put them in grave danger."

"Not knowing would have put them in more danger." Mrs. McNemmish laid a tender hand on the giant's arm. "What's in the trunk, Edward? What is so frightening for them to find out?"

Blackbeard had feared the time would come when he might have to share this information with his grandniece. He thought hard and long before responding. He took Theodora by the arm and escorted her to his private cabin. He bade Simple to follow them. When they were inside his private quarters, he sat down, let out a long sigh, then lifted his concerned expression toward the widow.

"Thar be bricks in the trunk. Bricks from the cove."

"Bricks?" exclaimed the widow. "What could possibly be so important or so threatening about bricks?"

"'Tis what the bricks have replaced, madam. I knew if they found the bricks, they would search for what took their place. Truth is, anyone finding the trunk would have found me prize. 'Tis the reason yer death vexed me so."

"Did they find what replaced the bricks?" questioned Mrs. McNemmish.

"Aye. They did."

"If you don't mind me asking, what did they find?"

Blackbeard looked at Simple. He then looked at the widow and sighed deeply. "'Tis a block of sandstone."

Mrs. McNemmish was utterly confused. "A block of sandstone?"

"Aye."

Theodora swept back her strawberry wisps of hair and studied the buccaneer now pacing back and forth in front of her, twirling a gun handle in his hand. "Edward? Is there something special about the sandstone? Is there something hidden inside of it?"

Blackbeard stopped pacing and chuckled at the widow's suggestion. "Nay, mate. But I best say no more." He stood quietly for a moment, then added a warning. "Theodora, if the children speak of what they have found, it could, in time, lead to a catastrophe. Knowledge of the thing would bring consternation around the world. 'Twould prove the end of a legend." He placed a finger over the widow's lips. "Say not what ye know to be true, madam." He looked at his man Simple. "You disobeyed a direct order. I would have ye shot to death if ye were not already dead."

Simple stretched his neck. Blackbeard's large, tight hand had left its mark. "Excuse me fer sayin' so," stammered Simple, "but ye have never spoken with the lass Stefanie except in her dream, and she is a persistent little moppet. She could make a spider spinning circles dizzy. Nay, the widow is right. Them kids would have cut the trunk out of the wall. They would have been crushed when the tunnel collapsed." He did add a piece of optimistic information. "'Tis true they found the sandstone, but they have no knowledge of what it is they have found or what to do with the thing. They know not of its history or value."

Blackbeard had one fear: that someone else would find what the children had found and, in turn, discover the prize. "If the treasure is discovered and the secret truth ascertained, the world will turn the cove and the island upside down, and the heavens above will show their anger."

Whether it be pirate or child,

A thing remains a thing until

knowledge is imparted.

A stone is just a stone until

it has a history.

A ring is just a ring until

we know its bearer.

Walk with me down sandy paths

and rocky lanes,

And we shall search for buried truth.

CHAPTER XXIV

M rs. McNemmish waited for Simple to leave the captain's quarters. She took a moment and gathered up her courage. "I was wondering," she began timidly, "if you might be able to tell me something about the sandstone, without revealing its mystery. For instance, where did it come from?"

Blackbeard sat with his feet apart, his arms resting on his legs, and his head bent down. "'Tis a long story, mate."

"I have nothing but time," said Theodora.

Blackbeard got up and walked to the window. He looked out onto the water. "I was a young privateer in the royal navy. I came upon two ships of pirates fighting it out off the coast of Madeira. I trailed the two ships and surprised one of them by turning broadside and firing straight on. We overpowered the crew and claimed the ship and all its loot. We then turned about and defeated the second ship, which eventually burned and sank to the bottom of the sea.

"Later, I swung meself over to the first pirate ship we had captured and sailed it back to England. While on board, I went below and searched the stow and captain's quarters for any concealed booty. I discovered, hidden on the underside of the captain's personal desk, an ancient map. It wasn't like any map I had ever seen. It was written on hand-washed paper and had strange writing and symbols, with the date 1067 penned near the edge. In the center of the map was a single square with two symbols beside it. One was the Star of David, a Jewish symbol, and the other a cross, the symbol for Christianity.

"I then perused the series of dashes which I took to be roads. On the bottom of the map, almost invisible to the eye, was the word *scone*. When I turned the map over, I saw two lines of words written in the same foreign language. I searched for a long while before finding someone who could translate them for me. The words on the front of the map read, 'Created by the hand of God.' The words written on the back of the map read, 'Created by the hand of man.' I was enthralled, madam. I had no choice but to find out what it was I had tripped upon.

"I kept the map a secret all the years I was with the navy. When I joined the pirates and acquired me own ship, I waited for the right time to take out the map and secretly follow where it led. I took along three of me best mates.

I knew of Scone, Scotland, so I began there. We hid me ship where no one would find it, then traveled afoot. After a fortnight of searching, we came across a rocky fence in the shape of the dashes on the map. We followed the stones, which led to the remains of a small, stone church. We went inside the remaining walls, and after much searching, discovered an opening that led to an underground labyrinth of caves. Both the tunnel and caves were pitch black. I sent one of me men back for branches and oilcloth. We lit the ends of the branches and used them as torches to guide us through the underground.

"After a time, we entered the first cave. It took us deeper into the ground. At the end of one cave, another cave began. It seemed we were on a false trail. We were in the caves for many hours, when we came across two men standing guard of a large boulder leading to the entrance of the next cave. The men were elderly, with long white beards and pale skin from having been swallowed by the earth for such a long time. They both wore long, white robes that bore the sign of the red cross. Their heads were covered by mail helmets, they wore white gloves, and they carried with them ornate swords and axes.

"Meself and me three men struck a pose with our swords, hoping the guardians would give up, but they fought hard to defend the boulder. I must admit, they were very adept with their swords and gave me and me men a good fight. In the end, we took their lives and slit their throats. But they died honorably, so we gave them a proper Christian burial with stones for tombstones and etched crosses. Before we buried them, I noticed that one of the knights had a magnificent ruby ring on the smallest finger of his right hand. I took the ring and kept possession of it until I gave it to one of me wives."

Mrs. McNemmish cleared her throat and hid her embarrassment. "Aye. The ring."

"After we buried the guards, we pushed the boulder aside and entered the protected cave. In the center of the cave, surrounded by candles, golden chalices, and bowls of holy water, was a single pink block of sandstone. I was mystified and looked around. I saw that the stone walls bore the same strange writings as did the ancient map. 'Tis then I knew we had followed the map to its conclusion. There be nothing more in the cave, only the sandstone."

"I wondered to meself what precious block of stone could this be, that it is hidden and guarded by two swordsmen of such fine caliber." He looked back at the widow. "I sent one of me men for a wheeled cart, and we carried the stone away from the caves and loaded it onto me ship." He stared into deep space, his eyes growing large, then he looked down into his two giant, black-powder-stained palms. "It was magic or some form of devilish trick, madam. But each time we touched the thing with pointed steel, daggers of blue lightning shot out from its surface, and thunder rolled above us! Then, when all was quiet, the stone began to weep. Drops of water, clear and crisp, rained down from its pores. So curious was I, that I tasted the tears." He looked up and gazed into the widow's eyes. "They were sweet, Theodora! As sweet and clear as snow upon one's tongue."

"We took great care of the stone and carried it ever so cautiously into the cove," Blackbeard continued. "There I removed several of me bricks from the base of me trading post and planted the mysterious block of sandstone. At first I thought of me own neck, and that I would use the thing as a bartering tool to keep me head from the gallows.

"But truth be known, Theodora, there was something so magical, so mystifying about the stone that I wanted no one to find it. I thought it best stay hidden as it had been in Scone. I thought the thing to be so brilliant and so important that I buried the bricks replaced by the sandstone where no one would find them. I couldn't take the chance that someone would go above to the cove and seek what I had buried in the bricks' stead. It was years later that fortune smiled upon me, and I ascertained what it was I had sought and recovered. Both the ruby-cluster ring and the sandstone are legendary and valued above all riches."

"But you still won't say what it is," smiled Mrs. McNemmish.

"Nay, mate. Not even to ye. Not yet, anyway. I've kept the map hidden all these years. No one but ye and I know of its existence."

"Well, I doubt the children will think too hard on a piece of sandstone," she assured her captain. "My quest should keep them quite busy. But I thank you for sharing the story."

"'Tis yer quest that has me stymied, me lady."

The widow left the captain's cabin and walked back up onto the deck. Perhaps she'd learn more in time. Time was the one thing a ghost could play upon.

"Billy's right about the ring," said Daniel. "We have to swear never to tell anyone about it. Just leave it where it is and forget about it. Zeek should never have taken it from the widow."

"The Blood of Moritangia. I wonder what it's worth," daydreamed Stefanie.

"Gee, what a surprise," mocked Daniel.

"All I know is that it's a good thing Zeek didn't keep it," said Billy.

"Zeek!" Stefanie flew out of her chair. "We have to dig it up!"

"Dig what up?" asked Billy.

"The ring! We have to dig the ring up!"

"Are you insane? That's the most harebrained idea you've had yet!" Daniel spoke in a whisper, trying to hush her up. "We are not digging the widow's ring back up! Forget it! I mean it, Stefanie. Leave it alone!"

"Listen to me! We have to get the ring out of the casket. Now!" Stefanie was practically hyperventilating. Mark jumped out of his seat and nodded aggressively.

Suddenly Billy shot a hand to his forehead. "Oh, my gosh! They're right! We have to get it out of the casket before Zeek sends someone to the graveyard to dig it up first!"

"Have you all lost your minds? We do not have to take the ring out of the casket. Zeek doesn't even know it's there."

"Yes, he does," said Stefanie in a terrified voice. "Don't you think Birdie or one of his buddies told him where it was buried right after the funeral?"

"Oh, man," sighed Daniel. "I never even thought about that." He looked at the others. "At least he doesn't know it's the Blood of Moritangia, or how much it's worth. We don't even know that."

"Zeek knew the ring was worth a lot. His friend up in Avon told him that. That's why he went back to the widow's house and asked for the rest of the treasure. Miss Theo told us that much herself. And we know the ring's historic and that a lot of people are looking for it," added Billy. "Even Simple asked us if we had found it."

"Zeek wants that ring back really badly. If he had his friends rob the tunnel, the casket could be next," reckoned Stefanie.

"I think we should stick to the stuff we're supposed to be doing, like finding the people at Westminster Abbey to see if the candlesticks and trowel belong to them," stated Daniel. "I don't know about y'all, but I don't want to get into any more trouble than I'm already in by digging up Miss Theo's coffin."

"It's not about the coffin," Stefanie reminded him. "It's about what's in the coffin. It's about the ring. We need to dig up the ring and protect it from Zeek's baboons."

Daniel was ready to pull his hair out. "Can we finish doing the Westminster Abbey stuff first? Then we can take the ring out of the coffin. If it's gone, we'll know who took it and send my dad over to the jail to shake the truth out of Zeek."

"Oh, sure. We're really going to tell your dad we dug up Mrs. McNemmish's second coffin after stealing her first one," Stefanie challenged him.

"I'm with Stefanie on that one," said Billy. Mark added his two cents with a huge nod.

"Fine. We won't tell my dad."

"Fine!" said Stefanie.

"Fine!" said Daniel.

"Wampus cat!"

"Dingbat!"

For the next few afternoons, the kids researched everything they could about Westminster Abbey. "Maybe that piece of sandstone came from the Abbey," suggested Daniel. "That would make sense. And it would make the stone special, although I doubt they used a stone that spews fire. That would definitely have made the news."

"Listen to this," read Stefanie. "Westminster Abbey has its own graveyard just for poets!"

"Actually, that makes sense. People didn't watch television or go to the movies back then. And they stopped feeding people to the lions way earlier. So writers and poets were the entertainers. They were the famous people, like Shakespeare." Billy searched the same website and copied the email address of the Abbey curator's office. "Do you think we should tell them what we found?"

"Dr. Hardison said for them to tell us," said Daniel. "I think we should give a clue about one of the items, and see if they can match up any of the other items that were in the same box."

"Agreed," said Billy. He, Mark, and Stefanie stood behind Daniel as he composed a letter to the director of history in the curator's office at Westminster Abbey. The letter explained that they had come across a Bible in a golden cover that was printed in 1016. He then asked whether or not the Abbey had ever lost such a Bible or any other items on or about 1718. Daniel took a second, then pressed *send*.

The response came almost immediately. It read, "Dear Daniel. My name is Mr. Davenport Warrant."

"Who names their kid Davenport?" snickered Billy.

"Rich people," said Stefanie.

Daniel continued. "'I am one of the historical society's curators at Westminster Abbey in London, England. We are very interested in your email concerning the golden Bible that was printed in 1016. The Abbey had such a Bible several hundred years ago, but it was stolen early in the 18th century and was never recovered. It is written on thick hand-washed paper with a slight purple tint. Three sides of the Bible are decorated in gold and gems, while the edges of the paper are simply painted gold.

"Many of the Abbey's possessions disappeared around the same time. Two of the items were rings. One was a bishop's ring and the other belonged to a cardinal. We would be very interested to know where you discovered the Bible, and if you might send a picture of it so we might identify it. Thank you for your interest, honesty, and inquiry. Yours truly, Mr. Davenport Warrant.'"

"It sounds like their Bible," said Billy.

"And their rings," added Stefanie. "I guess we'll have to call Dr. Hardison and ask him to send a picture."

"Wait a minute." Daniel reached for his backpack and rummaged through it. He pulled out a small piece of paper. "I have Dr. Hardison's email." He placed it on the desk next to his computer and typed in the minister's email address. He forwarded the Abbey curator's message to the Minister of Antiquities in Williamsburg and asked Dr. Hardison to keep them informed when he found out anything.

Dr. Hardison emailed back the next day. It read, "Good sleuthing. I'll email a photo to Mr. Warrant right away."

"This could be it," Daniel told the others excitedly. "If everything in the crate belongs to Westminster Abbey, our job is done!"

"All right!" shouted Stefanie.

"That was easy," said Billy. He paused for a moment, then looked at the others. "What about the ring?"

"What about the ring?" asked Daniel.

"If the other stuff is theirs, shouldn't we tell them about the ring?"

"No!" Stefanie looked like she was going to suffer another bout of apoplexy. "We decided to dig it up and hide it! That's it!"

"We didn't actually decide to do that," said Daniel.

"Yes, we did."

"What if they come right out and ask about the Blood of Moritangia?" Billy asked her.

"I don't care! The ring stays here!"

There was no more discussion for two days until the kids received an email from Dr. Hardison saying that the Bible did indeed belong to Westminster Abbey. He added that the other items found in the crate were part of the same robbery and also belonged to the Abbey. "They would love to meet the four of you someday and thank you in person for finding their stolen property," wrote Dr. Hardison. "I have also spoken with the governor of Virginia. You will be happy to know that he is making arrangements for the items to be returned to the Abbey. This will be the first time in 300 years that any of the pirated loot from the 1700s will be returned to their actual owners. Apparently, the royal family has been informed of your discovery and is thrilled. We are keeping the discovery and identity of the items private, and will not be informing the press. I suggest you do the same. You have done a brilliant job and the entire world a service."

"The royal family knows about us," Stefanie repeated dreamily. "That makes us, that makes us . . ."

"Peons," said Daniel. "It doesn't make us anything, so you can climb off your white horse."

"Well, I think it's great!" cheered Billy. "Congratulations to us."

Mark rapped on his computer and called them over.

"Uh-oh. There's another page," said Billy, reading, "'Although the governor is extremely pleased at the outcome, he is distressed by your actions while here in Williamsburg. He has decided that you need a lesson in the importance of antiques and colonial relics and is, therefore, assigning the four of you to an archaeological dig for one month during your summer vacation. Arrangements will be made at a different time. Once again, thank you for your persistence and congratulations on the outcome. Yours, Dr. Paul Hardison.'"

"No!" screamed Daniel. "This did not just happen!" He glared at Stefanie with darts propelling from his eyeballs. "All you had to do was bring me the stupid screwdriver! Who cares what color the mice were? All you had to do was climb the stupid ladder. But, oh no! You see a mouse and jump on the ladder and knock it down. Then you steal a forklift and maroon Billy and me on top of the crate! Now, as soon as we finish our community service, we have more community service!"

Stefanie stared at him and blinked.

"Nobody said you had to listen to me. You usually never listen to me. It's not my fault y'all listened to me. It's your own faults you listened to me. And anyway, we found the stuff." Stefanie turned away and sat with a sullen expression on her face.

Daniel glared at her. "Now what's the matter? Did you forget to rob a bank?"

"I wanted to send the candlesticks and trowel back to the Abbey myself. Now we'll never see the stuff again. At least they didn't ask about the ring."

"We still don't know which pirate stole the stuff and which pirate got grounded," added Billy.

"What difference does that make?" asked Daniel.

"I don't know. I'm just curious."

Daniel was satisfied with the Westminster Abbey success and didn't want to spend one more second researching the robbery. "We've narrowed it down to Jack Rackham, Stede Bonnet, David Harriot, and Ann Bonny. Who cares which one got stuck?"

"Stede Bonnet!" exclaimed Stefanie. "That's the pirate I saw at Josiah Chowning's!"

"Oh, my gosh! Why didn't you say so?" teased Daniel. "Let's go back to Williamsburg and ask if he's the one who stole the stuff. As a matter of fact, why didn't you ask him when he stopped you on the staircase?"

"First of all, that's a stupid question. Second of all, he was behaving like a complete jerk. Third of all, I had to pee. And fourth of all, that's a stupid question and you're a jerk."

"What about the stone?" asked Billy.

"The Abbey didn't say anything about a stone. I don't think it has anything to do with the robbery," said Daniel.

"Are we going to at least tell the Abbey people about the ring and the stone?" asked Billy.

"No!" Stefanie slammed her hand on her desk dramatically. "No one says anything about the ring. Dr. Hardison didn't ask us about it, and neither did Mr. Warrant."

"It really does belong to the widow," agreed Billy.

Daniel reread the email. "Well, if it is the Blood of Moritangia, no one's connected it to the Abbey. I guess we keep it here."

"Yes! Thank you!" gushed Stefanie. "Let's go dig it up!"

Daniel dropped his head in his hands and whimpered. "I really don't think Zeek is going to have someone dig up the coffin and steal the ring. The graveyard is in the middle of Howard Street. They know they'd get caught."

"You don't think Zeek Beacon is going to remember that the ring he stole from the widow and had to give back when he was arrested, that he knew was worth a lot because he asked someone about it before we found out about the nuts and seeds and he heard all that stuff at the reading of the Last Will and Testament, isn't going to send someone to the graveyard and dig up the empty casket so he can get the ring back, even though he doesn't know what it is and we do?"

Daniel peeked up over his fingertips. He was getting one of his Stefanie headaches.

"Where would we hide it?" asked Billy.

"It would have to be buried where no one would even think to look, but where it would be safe forever," Stefanie mumbled as she paced back and forth behind the row of desks. "I know! We'll hide it in the pirate's den. It's perfect. No one would ever look for it there. No one would even think to look for it there. Then, if anyone gets the bright idea to dig up the casket, it won't be there because we will have already taken it out and buried it somewhere else."

"How do you come up with this stuff?" asked Daniel. "I swear, it must be in your DNA that you just can't wait to get into some kind of trouble."

"Come on, Billy," begged Stefanie. "You could dig it up for me. I promise I won't keep it. I just want to move it."

Billy appealed to Daniel and Mark. "The coffin isn't buried very deep. It's not like it has a body in it and they had to put it six feet under. It's only a foot or two under the ground."

"We'll wake up everybody near the graveyard if we go hacking away at the ground in the middle of the night," argued Daniel.

"No we won't. We'll shovel really quietly, lift the lid, find the ring, then close it back up," Billy said encouragingly. "I bet it doesn't take more than ten minutes."

"Ten minutes!" squawked Daniel. "On what planet?"

"We have to do this," persisted Stefanie. "I just know we have to get it out of the casket and buried where no one can find it before Zeek's stooges get it." She looked at Daniel pleadingly. "I went with y'all into the tunnel. I'm practically a vegetarian because of y'all. I can't even play cow poker because farms have chickens on them and they have bones."

"What?" shrieked Daniel.

"You have to do this," said Stefanie.

"Will you promise to stop pestering me if we do this?" begged Daniel.

"Forever," promised Stefanie.

"I still don't see how we can get away with it. What about Miss Dixie? She lives right across the path, and she's nosy."

"She'll never hear us," Stefanie assured the boys. "She's old. Old people can't hear anything. I think their ear bones disintegrate or something."

Daniel stared at her. "When the aliens dropped you off, did they leave any kind of manual so we can fine tune your brain?"

"I could be right," said Stefanie. "Either every old person on the island is hard of hearing, or they just plain ignore me."

Daniel grinned at Billy. "Nah. Too easy."

Billy tried not to smile, but couldn't help it, so Stefanie punched him in the arm. "Teddy and Mustard do their last rounds at midnight," snickered Billy. "We'll wait until we're sure they're gone, then sneak into the graveyard. If we're really quiet, I think we can get away with it."

"This has to be the dumbest thing we've done so far," insisted Daniel. He looked at Stefanie. "Except for stealing the forklift. That was totally insane. And now, because of you, we have to go back to Williamsburg and do an archaeological dig! Some vacation."

"If you had come down to get the screwdriver, I wouldn't have had to steal the forklift!"

"How come it's always my fault?" asked Daniel.

"Because you're the geek. It's always the geek's fault," Billy informed him pleasantly. "It's a rule."

"Fine."

"Fine."

At 12:30, when the children were certain Sheriff Jackson and Mustard had made their last run, they met at the McNemmish graveyard on Howard Street. Billy timidly pushed open the squeaky gate, while everyone tiptoed inside. Even without the help of flashlights, they quickly found the widow's plot. Billy and Daniel took their shovels and, as quietly as possible, scooped away the two feet of dirt that rested on top of the coffin.

"Hurry up," said Stefanie. "I'm getting nervous."

"Hey! This was your idea! If anyone should be nervous it should be the rest of us." A few more minutes had passed when Daniel heard a *thunk*. "That's it! I can feel the casket."

"Meow."

"What was that?" whispered Billy. He looked down, and there was a large Ocracoke cat seated by his foot. "Shoo. Go away," he implored the feline.

"Meow!" the cat cried louder.

"Shh!" shrieked Billy. He tried chasing the cat away with his foot, as three more cats climbed over the fence and into the graveyard. They each began to cry and mew as if they thought singing to the boys would be helpful.

"Get rid of them," exclaimed Daniel. Billy and Stefanie reached out to pick up the cats and put them back over the fence, but the cats were quicker. Since they could see in the dark, they either shot up a nearby tree or leaped to the other side of the fence. A moment later, two more cats entered the yard and ran in circles around the open plot.

"Okay, who's wearing fish cologne?" asked Billy.

"Very funny." The hissing and mewing sent an invitation to dozens of Ocracats. They came running from every direction, meowing at the tops of their lungs.

"What's all the commotion?" a raspy, high-pitched voice shouted from the house directly across the path.

"Criminee! Miss Dixie!" warned Daniel. "I thought you said she wouldn't hear us."

"She didn't hear us. She heard the cats."

"Shoot. We're going to get caught." Billy pointed to the chubby figure coming toward the graveyard with a broom in her hand. "Hide behind the gravestones!" He grabbed Mark by his coat sleeve, dragged him to one of the back gravestones, and plunked him onto the ground. "Don't move or make a sound." Then he leaped behind the gravestone to his side and huddled behind it, lost in the shadow. Daniel and Stefanie hid behind the two gravestones up front. Daniel peeked out and saw Miss Dixie walk toward the gate.

"What are all you kitties doing in here?" she rattled. "You're making a racket." She entered the graveyard and shooed them away with her broom. Some left, others went up the tree.

"She's going to see the open grave," Daniel moaned to himself. He looked around and saw a stone on the ground beside him. He threw it into the street. Miss Dixie turned quickly to walk back toward the street, but the mewing started all over again. Daniel and Billy were sweating bullets.

"What is the matter with you?" Dixie asked the kitties. She walked behind the gravestone where Billy was hiding and looked around. Her foot was plastered on his hand. Suddenly, one of the cats seated up in the tree jumped down and landed on her shoulder. Miss Dixie let out a blood-curdling scream and jumped backward.

Her husband called from their front porch, "Dixie. Get back here and forget the dagburn cats!"

Miss Dixie straightened her back and pushed her mussed hair into place. "Quiet down or you'll wake everyone!" she shouted back to her husband.

As she turned to leave, she walked directly behind Stefanie. Stefanie squeezed her eyes shut and held her breath. "Go home," she whispered under her breath.

A cat rubbed against Miss Dixie's leg and she bent down and picked it up, missing Stefanie's back by an inch.

Stefanie gasped at the same time the cat mewed. Miss Dixie paused for a moment, then addressed the cat. "Let's go kitty. The same for the lot of you." She opened the gate and several of the cats followed her out. A moment later, she walked back across the path and up onto her porch. No one moved. The kids sat huddled behind their gravestones and waited for Miss Dixie's bedroom light to go out.

"Finally!" Daniel lifted his head to see if any other house lights had turned on. Luckily, they had not. He swallowed hard. "My heart's pounding in my mouth."

"I think she broke my hand," said Billy, wriggling his fingers. Another cat jumped out of the tree and landed on his shoulder, scaring him to death. He reached up to grab it, but it jumped down and ran away.

"This is a nightmare," said Daniel.

Stefanie cast her eyes over to Miss Dixie's house. "She's probably asleep by now. Help me find the ring."

In order to expedite things, Daniel turned on one flashlight. Together the four youngsters bent over the casket and pushed the top open. Stefanie took the flashlight and hung over the side of the coffin. She swept the light back and forth over the contents. "I don't see the box."

"It probably slipped to the bottom of the casket because it's so small," said Daniel.

"Quick. Empty it," said Stefanie. She reached in and started tossing things out of the coffin and onto the ground. Billy and Daniel reached over and helped, examining each thing first to make sure they didn't accidentally throw away the ring box. Daniel had a flashback to the day they had the funeral and filled the casket with all of the widow's favorite things. This was the second casket belonging to the widow they were messing around with.

Mark was handed the flashlight and was instructed to aim the beam into the bottom of the casket, while Daniel got inside of it and searched the last remaining items. It took only a few more minutes to have everything out of the coffin and on the ground.

"It's not here," fretted Stefanie. "It's gone."

"It can't be gone," said Daniel. He took the light and beamed it into each corner of the casket. Then piece by piece, he went over the items on the ground.

"She's right," said Billy, "it's gone. Zeek Beacon got here before we did."

"Zeek!" bristled Daniel. He was disgusted. "Come on. Let's get everything back into the coffin."

Everyone worked quickly and silently while Mark stood aiming the light. Within minutes, the casket was covered and the dirt was packed down. Dejected, Billy and Daniel led Stefanie and Mark out of the graveyard.

"Shh!" said Mark.

"What's the matter?" whispered Daniel.

Mark pointed to Theodora's grave.

At first, no one heard or saw anything. Then there was an eerie, scratching noise coming from Mrs. McNemmish's casket. Stefanie whitened.

"She's in there," shrieked the girl.

"She is not," snapped Daniel. "We were just in there and she wasn't in there."

"Well, she's in there now. Listen." Again they all listened, and again they all heard the spooky scratching.

"What do we do?" asked Billy. He clung to Mark's arm more for comfort than assistance.

"We better do something fast," said Daniel. "The cats are coming back, and Miss Dixie's going to come back over."

As if in one thought, Billy and Daniel grabbed their shovels and scooped the dirt off the top of the coffin. The scratching got louder. No one wanted to lift the lid.

Daniel grimaced. "Everybody put your hand on the lid, and when I count to three, open it. One . . .two . . .three!"

Stefanie let out a scream when a cat came charging out of the coffin and leaped out of the graveyard. Three other hearts were beating so hard they could feel the fronts of their coats move. "Quick, cover it up," said Billy. He grabbed his shovel and quickly dumped heaps of dirt back onto the gravesite, then patted it down with his shoe. "It's Miss Dixie!" he croaked.

"Climb over the fence and go through the O'Neal's graveyard," whispered Daniel. "Hurry!"

Billy and Daniel tossed their shovels over the fence, then sent Stefanie up and over to the other side. Together, the older boys led Mark to the fence and climbed beside him. But when Mark got to the top, he refused to jump into the next graveyard.

"You have to jump. Miss Dixie is coming," Daniel warned him.

"Hey! Who's there?" called Miss Dixie. As she walked toward the gate, she thought she saw a moving silhouette on the back fence. "Darn cats!"

Billy and Daniel jumped to the ground, grabbed Mark's coat and swung him off the fence. Mark landed in a heap on the other side. "Quick, get up," said Billy. He looked at Stefanie. "Run!" he told her. Then he and Daniel picked up their shovels, grabbed each of Mark's elbows, and pulled him across the O'Neal's graveyard and out the gate.

"Come back here!" yelled Miss Dixie.

Stefanie ran ahead of the boys and didn't stop running until she raced up the front steps of her house, down the hall, and into her bedroom. She threw off her clothes and climbed into bed, gasping for breath. "He took it," she said, slamming her hands over her face. "I'll kill him!"

The boys hustled Mark home, deposited him on his front porch, then flew toward their own houses. None of the boys thought about the ring again until they were safe in their rooms. "Zeek," fumed Daniel.

"We have to get that ring back," thought Mark.

"We'll get it back, Miss Theo. I swear," pledged Billy.

Jump upon the bowsprit.

Feel the wind blow through your hair.

Taste the salt upon your lips.

Smell the sea mist air.

Follow where the stars will lead.

Trace the hourly sun.

Come with me across the sea

And share ye spectral fun.

CHAPTER XXV

Todd trotted to the breakfast table with a secret behind his smile .

"What are you so happy about?" grinned Elizabeth. Daniel and Lena looked at each other and shrugged. Their father wasn't usually so cheerful in the morning.

"Well?" Elizabeth urged him.

The ranger took a sip of coffee. "Dr. Hardison called last Wednesday."

"And?"

Todd could barely contain his laughter, which set off Lena giggling.

"Come on, Dad! What did he say?" asked Daniel.

"It seems that the silver trowel was actually the private property of the stonemason who helped build one of the newer sections of Westminster Abbey. I believe he said it was used sometime in the 17th century."

Elizabeth still couldn't understand why her husband was behaving so oddly. "Why is that amusing?"

Todd grinned until his cheeks hurt. "It seems the stonemason's name was Horatio Longsworth Scarborough."

"Scarborough," said Elizabeth, "as in the Ocracoke Scarboroughs? And that's funny?"

Daniel was beginning to wonder if his father had fallen out of bed and banged his head.

"Well, I wasn't sure if he was related to the Ocracoke Scarboroughs, so I wrote an email to Mr. Warrant in England and asked about the stonemason. He wrote back that Scarborough's grandson came to America and lived in Bath, North Carolina, so I had a friend of mine go over to the old church in Bath and check the record books for the name Scarborough. Apparently the family was originally from Liverpool, England, and split when they got to North Carolina. Some stayed in Bath and others went north.

"The name of the grandson who stayed in Bath was Richard Horatio Scarborough. It was his son, Henry, who brought the family to Ocracoke. So I went to our county records and looked up Henry Scarborough and followed his direct descendants all the way to today. I double-checked it with the baptismal records on the Internet's ancestry web page and found an Earl Longsworth Scarborough."

"Earl Scarborough," pondered Elizabeth. "We don't know anybody by that name."

"We know Earl O'Neal," said Daniel.

"Oh, you know Earl Scarborough all right," chuckled Todd. "Any guesses?"

Elizabeth and Daniel shrugged. "No."

"Well, the direct descendant of the stonemason is none other than Birdie."

"Birdie!" shrieked mother and son.

Ranger Garrish howled. "Can you believe it? The silver trowel actually belongs to Birdie. And the Abbey wants to know if he'll donate it back to them."

"Birdie!" laughed Elizabeth. "Are you sure?"

"Yup."

"Good night!" exclaimed Daniel. "How weird is that?"

"Well, you never know what you never know," said the ranger.

"This is unbelievable," chuckled Elizabeth.

"Wait. There's more. The Abbey has invited the four children and Birdie to come to England and present the stolen items to the curators in person. They're very grateful to the kids and want to reward them with a visit."

"What!" shouted Daniel.

"Hold on, Daniel. We can't afford that," Elizabeth told her husband.

"We don't have to. World Cruise Line heard the story and offered the four children, Birdie, and two adults tickets to sail over to England."

"Are you kidding?" screamed Daniel. "No fooling?"

"Whoa! I don't know about this," said Elizabeth. "Taking four kids and Birdie on a boat to England. Doesn't that seem a bit extreme?"

"I don't know. Could be fun," said Todd. "We've never taken a cruise." He grabbed Elizabeth around the waist and pretended to dance with her. "I think it's a great idea."

Daniel was ecstatic. "This is unreal! Wait until the others find out about this!"

"We'll need to talk to Birdie," said Todd.

Elizabeth chuckled. "Good luck with that."

Daniel called the others, and they met in front of the Community Store, where Birdie was working for Miss May Belle. They greeted each other, jumping up and down and jabbering about their invitation to England and their upcoming cruise.

"My mom won't let me go unless she goes with me," said Stefanie. "You think they'll let my mom go with us? I can't believe we're going to England! It was so worth climbing through that tunnel to get the tickets. I don't even care about the skeletons and the smell. This is the greatest thing that's ever happened to me. Do you think they'll let my mom go?"

"I don't know," said Daniel hurriedly. "We'll figure that out later."

"So Birdie is a Scarborough and he's related to the guy who used the trowel when they rebuilt Westminster Abbey," said Billy. "That is so bizarre."

"Not half as bizarre as the fact that they want him to go with us," said Daniel.

Mark saw Birdie inside the store and pointed.

"Well, here goes," said Daniel. The four of them walked into the store and walked toward Zeek Beacon's sweet, oversized, half-baked shipmate.

"Hey, Daniel. Hey, Stefanie. Hey, Mark. Hey, Billy," called out Birdie.

"Hey, Birdie," they all called back. Mark waved.

"Birdie, can you come outside? We need to talk to you," Daniel told him.

"I'm working for Miss May Belle," said Birdie, "and I don't just sweep up anymore. I stock shelves now, too. I learned where everything goes." His mismatched eyes lit up, and he swept them over the children. "Go ahead. Ask me where something is."

"We really need to talk to you," said Daniel.

"I know, I know. But I know where the stock is now. Go ahead, Billy. Ask me where something is. I can show you."

"Okay," said Billy. "Where's the cereal?"

Birdie clapped his big, clumsy hands, then took off down two aisles. "Come on," he told the kids. The four kids followed him to the shelf stacked with cereals. "We have dry cereal, and cooked cereal, and cereal bars," said Birdie. "Go ahead. Ask me something else. Ask me something, Stefanie. I'll find it for you. Go ahead. Ask me something."

Stefanie rolled her eyes. "Good grief. All right. Where's the peanut butter?"

Birdie took off down the back side of the aisles and stopped just before the produce. "Here it is. We have three different kinds of peanut butter. And some of it's smooth. And some of it's crunchy. I like the crunchy. I like it on bread with bananas and potato chips. Would y'all like me to make you a sandwich? I know how to make sandwiches. Mr. Buck showed me how to make sandwiches that other people will eat. He says not everybody likes chocolate syrup on their sandwiches, especially their meat sandwiches."

Billy wrinkled his nose. "Thanks anyway," he told Birdie, "but I think we'll have to come back for a sandwich. Right now, we really have to talk to you."

"Okay. I'll ask Miss May Belle if I can go outside."

The kids went outside into the parking lot and waited

for Birdie to come out. He joined them a few minutes later.
"What's up? Is something up?"

"You have no idea," said Daniel. He led Birdie and the
others over to the dock, where they could talk privately.
"Do you remember the tickets we found in the tunnel?"
Daniel asked him.

"Sure," said Birdie. "That's where the seeds came
from. Not the seeds the widow gave me, but the rest of the
seeds. And Mark showed me the slave quilt. And Stefanie
said she can't eat chicken anymore because of all the skeletons she saw and the finger bone that was stuck in the
wall. And Zeek wanted me to go back down there and
steal the rest of the stuff and hide it, but I didn't want to
do that because the stuff really belongs to y'all."

"Yeah, well, the tickets were for two candlesticks and
a silver trowel. Do you know what a trowel is?" Daniel
asked Birdie.

"Sure," said Birdie. "It's for building a brick house. I
helped build a house once near my granny's house on the
mainland. The builders had a trowel. I worked on the
roof. They explained that if I was the one to fall off, it
wouldn't make much of a difference."

Stefanie snickered. "Well, the trowel on the ticket
belonged to your great-great-great-grandfather from
England, and now it belongs to you. But the people at
Westminster Abbey in England want you to donate it to
their museum. They've invited you to go to England on a
ship with us so you can return it to the Abbey in person."

"They want me to come?" said Birdie, sounding quite
astonished. "Why do they want me to come? They can
have the trowel. I'm not using it."

"They figure since it once belonged to your relative, you'd like to go in person and give it back to them."

"Okay," said Birdie. "I'll ask Miss May Belle if I can go. I'm still doing community service for helping Zeek on the boat."

"I think she'll say it's okay," said Billy. "Todd will talk to her."

Todd did talk with her, and it was arranged that Birdie would accompany the four kids, Todd, Elizabeth, and Stefanie's mother, Marylee. They would leave for England sometime in early March. Dr. Hardison made arrangements for the newly packed crate to be shipped to England on the same ship. The sterling silver trowel was mailed to Birdie, so he could personally carry it with him to England and present it as a gift to the Abbey museum.

The Hatteras Breeze and the *Williamsburg Gazette* did a story on the kids and their upcoming trip to Westminster Abbey, but left out details about the artifacts. This pleased Todd immensely.

It did not please James Leonard, however. He rolled up the copy of the *Williamsburg Gazette* and slammed it onto his desk.

"Those little . . ."

"Shut up!" screamed Harold. "Let me think." He sank back into his oversized chair and ran a hand through his oily hair. He bit a fingernail and spit it out, letting it fly across his desk. "We have to find out the contents of that crate." He slammed down a fist, shaking the half-filled mug of coffee on his desk. "Twenty-five years of research and they march in, open the crate, and get free passage in order to return the stuff in person!"

Harold had a trick up his sleeve just in case this happened. "I'm going to book passage on the same ship. The kids don't know me, so it will be easy to shadow them. You get a porter's pass and we'll intercept the goods on the other side, now that we know where they're going. We'll need to work things out with our guys over there. If we can get the artifacts off the boat and out of customs, we can hide the loot in England until we've contacted our buyers." A slow grin swept across Harold's face. "So, it was the Abbey robbery. Thank you, children."

"I'll take care of my end of it," snarled James. "You get on that ship and watch those kids like a hawk. We can't let them take anything off that ship. We'll have to block their way somehow. You might need to take some men onto the ship with you," he suggested.

"I can handle the kids," said Harold. "You just make sure you come up with the appropriate paperwork and a truck to meet us."

James Leonard stared out of his office window. "I really want to hurt them."

That afternoon, after the excitement died down, Todd presented more information. "The minister said that a reporter called him and asked if you kids had stumbled onto a ring called the Blood of Moritangia. Dr. Hardison said he had never heard of it and didn't think it had anything to do with your research project, so he let it go. But when he described the ring to me, it sounded a little like old Mrs. McNemmish's ring. I think, just to be on the safe side, we should take the ring out of the coffin and store it in a bank vault."

Daniel gagged on his ice water.

"Are you all right?" asked Elizabeth.

Daniel nodded. "I don't think that's a very good idea," he croaked and coughed. He looked up at his father with tearing eyes. "It's the widow's ring. I think it should stay where it is."

"Well, I don't. Neither does your mother or the other parents. We'd all feel a whole lot better if we knew the ring was in a bank vault. We're meeting over at the graveyard now. Are you coming with me, or not?"

Daniel felt sick. "I guess," he mumbled. He and his father drove over to Howard Street, where they met Drum, Billy, Jeffrey, Mark, and Captain Austin. Stefanie arrived on her bike a few minutes later. The children stayed at a safe distance and watched the adults enter the McNemmish graveyard.

Todd stood over the widow's gravesite and stared down at it disappointedly. "It looks like someone's been messing around in here. I hate it when people disrespect the graveyards."

The kids stood stone still and silent, barely looking at each other. When they shoveled the dirt back over the widow's coffin, it had been pitch black outside, and they hadn't been able to see what a sloppy job they had done. The top layer of dirt looked like it had the mumps. The four men picked up their shovels and began scooping the soil off the coffin. When they reached the top of the casket, they dusted it off with a cloth, opened it, and peered inside. "Oh, man! What a mess! There's dirt everywhere in there."

"That means someone else opened the casket before we did," fretted Drum.

"I don't remember everything looking so jumbled," added Jeffrey.

"I think I'm going to hurl," whispered Daniel.

Todd and Jackson took everything out of the coffin, one piece at a time, and handed the contents over to Drum and Jeffrey, who dusted them and laid them out on a clean sheet. By the time they reached the bottom of the coffin, they realized the ring was missing.

Todd covered his face with his hand. "I don't believe this. This is horrible."

Jackson glanced over at his daughter. "Do you know anything about this?"

"Uh-oh," panicked Daniel.

Stefanie's eyes shifted right and left. "About what?" she asked without exhaling. She thought if her throat got any tighter, she'd keel over dead.

"About the ring being gone. Do you know anything about the ring being taken out of the coffin?" persisted her father.

Stefanie pulled the glove off her hand with her teeth, then shoved a bitten, blue fingernail into her mouth. "Where did it go?" she asked with a quivering voice. She felt the blood in her face drop to her kneecaps.

"We don't know where it went. That's why I asked you if you knew anything."

"Is the ring really gone?" asked Billy, attempting to sound utterly surprised. A single drop of sweat slowly rained down the side of his face and into his coat collar, making him shiver. "Do you think someone took it?"

Drum glared at his son. "Of course we think someone took it. It didn't just evaporate."

"Mrs. McNemmish did."

"Not funny," said Drum.

"What about you, son?" asked Jeffrey.

Mark snapped to attention. He shook his head so vehemently, his eyeglasses flew off his face.

Daniel retrieved Mark's glasses and pretended to be completely taken aback. "Why would y'all think we would know anything about the ring being gone? We sure didn't take it." For once, he was telling the truth.

"Well, this is just appalling," grieved Todd. "Drum, why don't you go get Teddy." Todd and Jeffrey searched through every item a second time before returning everything to the casket. "It's really gone."

Once again, Todd turned to the children. "Are you sure you don't know anything about this?"

"We're sure," said Daniel.

"We haven't been anywhere near here," Billy added for good measure.

"I bet Zeek's friend took it," offered Stefanie. "Zeek really wanted that ring. Remember how mad he was when he found out it was going to be put in Miss Theo's coffin? You should ask Zeek about it. I'm sure it was one of his goons who stole it."

"Stefanie's right. Zeek said he wanted that ring back," recalled Jackson.

"Maybe it was Zeek," reckoned Jeffrey. "It makes sense."

Todd let out a deep, frustrated sigh. "It does sound like him. He has absolutely no respect for anyone or anything.

And Miss Dixie said she thought she saw someone hanging around the fence the other night. I can't believe anyone else from the island would break into that poor old woman's coffin and steal her ring."

"It'll be hard proving anything," said Jackson. "Zeek will never own up to it. And everyone on the island knew the ring was in the casket. Everyone attended the burial. Poor Theodora. First her real coffin is stolen, then this one is broken into. It's like nothing is sacred around here anymore."

The four men covered the coffin in silence and neatly patted down the dirt on top. "When we get back from England, we'll have Rudy and Teddy shake down Zeek," said Todd. "Maybe they can get some information out of him."

"It might not have been Zeek," Jeffrey reminded Todd. "Like Jackson said, everyone on the island had access to it."

After the adults left the graveyard, the kids took their first relieved breath.

"Now we're going to be blamed for everything we didn't do," predicted Daniel.

Mark looked at Stefanie and shrugged.

"I'm with Mark," said Billy. He turned to Stefanie and appealed to her sympathetic side. "Can't you dance around a fire and sing to the moon or something to get Simple to help us find the ring?"

Stefanie was still in shock. "Are you kidding?" she asked her friends. "If I could do stuff like that, I would have turned my brother into a red herring."

DO YOU WANT
TO KNOW?

* Who has the ruby ring? How is it connected to the strange sandstone?

* What IS the sandstone? What makes it so dangerous that Blackbeard has never divulged its true nature?

* Who, living or dead, follows the teens onto the ship bound for England?

You'll find the answers to these questions and a whole new adventure in *Blackbeard and the Gift of Silence*. Coming in September 2007 from Tanglewood.

ACKNOWLEDGMENTS

The more I write, the more I realize how little I can accomplish without the support and help of a multitude of other people. There is no way to put into words how giving and caring my friends on Ocracoke Island have been throughout the years of research, trial, and error. History lives when people remember and you have been so gracious with your history and family stories. And I'd like to thank the plethora of island ghosts. You always pop up at just the right time.

To Joel, Jayme, and Stefanie. Thank you for eating microwave and take-out dinners. And sorry about the light going on at three a.m. when inspiration hits. But mostly, thank you for your love and support and pride.

Thank you, Peggy, for allowing me the privilege of continuing my ride on the *Queen Anne's Revenge*. Your excitement is the wind in the sails.

And Pierre. The finder of missing pieces. Thank you for finding my missteps and allowing me to make your suggestions appear like my flawless do-overs. You have the ability to find every four-leaf clover in a novel full of threes. No matter what my talent, my health would never allow me the privilege of writing, researching, speaking, or traveling without your help and guidance. I am forever grateful to you, as is my entire family. You are a wonder of wonders. Thank you all.

ABOUT THE AUTHOR

Blackbeard and the Sandstone Pillar: When Lightning Strikes is Audrey Penn's twelfth children's book. Best known for the *New York Times* bestselling children's title *The Kissing Hand*, she is also the author of *Mystery at Blackbeard's Cove, Sassafras, Feathers and Fur, A.D.D. not B.A.D., The Whistling Tree,* and *Pocket Full of Kisses,* among others. Ms. Penn takes her educational program, the Writing Penn, into schools, libraries, and children's hospitals, where she often shapes and refines her story ideas in partnership with kids. She is a sought-after conference speaker for groups of teachers and other professionals who work with children.

Mystery at Blackbeard's Cove, the first book in the Blackbeard quartet, was the culmination of a twenty-year project. Ms. Penn spent the better part of that time getting to know the history of Blackbeard and other pirates who frequented the Outer Banks of North Carolina and living descendants who still reside on Ocracoke Island. She researched the letters, journals, and diaries passed down through family and friends. Much of that knowledge and research has served as the foundation for the Blackbeard books.

Ms. Penn lives with her husband in Olney, Maryland, near Washington, DC. She has three children, all of whom excel at writing.

ABOUT THE ILLUSTRATORS

Philip Howard is the great-great-great-great-great-grandson of William Howard, Blackbeard's quartermaster. He lives on Ocracoke Island, where Blackbeard was killed on November 22, 1718. Luckily for Philip, the young William was not serving with Blackbeard at the time of the famous pirate's final battle. Philip owns and operates a quality craft shop on Ocracoke. In his spare time he collects island stories and tales.

Joshua Miller graduated from Ohio University with a Bachelor of Fine Arts degree in Graphic Design and Illustration. He has worked for 9 years as a computer animator and lives in McLean, Virginia.